*Lucky Stiff*

# Lucky Stiff

A Lillian Byrd Crime Story

# ELIZABETH SIMS

alyson books
los angeles

© 2004 BY ELIZABETH SIMS. ALL RIGHTS RESERVED.

MANUFACTURED IN THE UNITED STATES OF AMERICA.

THIS TRADE PAPERBACK ORIGINAL IS PUBLISHED BY ALYSON PUBLICATIONS,
P.O. BOX 4371, LOS ANGELES, CALIFORNIA 90078-4371.
DISTRIBUTION IN THE UNITED KINGDOM BY TURNAROUND PUBLISHER SERVICES LTD.,
UNIT 3, OLYMPIA TRADING ESTATE, COBURG ROAD, WOOD GREEN,
LONDON N22 6TZ ENGLAND.

FIRST EDITION: SEPTEMBER 2004

04 05 06 07 08 a 10 9 8 7 6 5 4 3 2 1

ISBN 1-55583-858-8

**LIBRARY OF CONGRESS CATALOGING-IN-PUBLICATION DATA**
SIMS, ELIZABETH, 1957–
    LUCKY STIFF : A LILLIAN BYRD CRIME STORY / ELIZABETH SIMS.—1ST ED.
    ISBN 1-55583-858-8 (PBK.)
    1. BYRD, LILLIAN (FICTITIOUS CHARACTER)—FICTION.  2. WOMEN
JOURNALISTS—FICTION.  3. LESBIANS—FICTION.  I. TITLE.
PS3619.I564L83 2004
813'.6—DC22                                             2004048573

**CREDITS**
COVER PHOTOGRAPHY BY PAUL TAYLOR/IMAGE BANK.
COVER DESIGN BY MATT SAMS.

# Acknowledgments

To my family and friends I offer up, as always, my deepest gratitude for their love and belief. Thousands of thanks go to my thousands of readers, whose pleasure means everything to me as a writer. Someday I hope you number in the millions. And to the booksellers great and small: I'm obliged to you.

For special help given to me in writing this book I'm indebted to Sherry Viola, MD; the Wayne County Medical Examiner's Office; and the Detroit Fire Department, especially Wanda Jenkins. Thanks also to Randall and Patricia Lamb for two handy details.

If Shirley Ososkie were alive, I would thank her for expressing herself so memorably.

I received, as usual, sensible and intelligent advice from Angela Brown.

Most of all I thank my beloved Marcia for her support and inspiration.

# ONE

I wouldn't have thought "Happy Birthday" could lend itself to the blues, but Blind Lonnie could pull the blues out of anything. He sat on his box like an old soft statue and *moaned* it. His fingers, the only moving parts of him, slowly plucked and squeezed his guitar, making the song unrecognizable unless you stopped and stood and listened, unrecognizable unless you knew the thing Lonnie liked to do best was make blues out of cheerful songs. I'd heard him blues up "Oh, Susanna," "Getting to Know You," "Camelot," "Jingle Bells," assorted circus marches, and the national anthem of Canada.

Blind Lonnie and I got to know each other about a year ago when I brought my mandolin down to Greektown and took up busking for money. Greektown was a decent place for buskers. I walked up and down Monroe Street, the main drag, looking for a spot to set up and gathering my nerve. I'd seen Lonnie there before—everybody knew Blind Lonnie; he'd grown old playing the blues on that street. He wore iridescent polyester shirts, wraparound dark glasses, and kept his silver hair in a conservative natural.

Musicians have the reputation of being a friendly lot, but when it comes to freelance commerce, established musicians don't always look kindly on newcomers. That is, they're happy to help novices except when they represent competition. Once a musician has established a habit of playing in a certain location, he considers that territory his. No matter that it's a free country, the sidewalks are public property, and that everybody else has to put potatoes on their table too.

I decided Blind Lonnie and I should make acquaintance. I stood nearby and clapped after his Brubeck-style tag on "Take the A Train."

"Thank you," he said.

"You bet."

He played another—"Button Up Your Overcoat." I stood and listened as the last note died away.

"Didn't you like that one?" he asked.

"Well, sure."

"How come you didn't clap, then?" I'd expected his speaking voice to be profoundly dark, like his sing-moaning, but it was a buttery baritone.

"I was just about to," I said. "How'd you know I was still here?" Sounds overlapped on the street—cars growling, people yakking, shoe leather clopping up and down.

"Blind Lonnie didn't hear you leave."

"But I'm wearing sneakers."

"Makes no difference. Blind Lonnie knows all."

I laughed. "You ever play anything but the blues?"

"Like what?"

"Oh...Chinese stuff."

Lonnie's mouth cracked wide and a laugh rolled out from his considerable gut. "*Chinese* stuff, hey? Lessee—" He tipped up his chin Stevie Wonder style. His left hand flew from its resting place on his thigh and settled on the fretboard of his jumbo Guild cutaway. With his right hand he stroked five smart notes. Pure Beijing, they rang out from the instrument's honey-lacquered wood.

He said, "My rice bowl, please."

I put in a fistful of change.

"Loud money's OK, quiet money's better," he said.

"It sure is. Hey listen, Lonnie, my name is Lillian Byrd. I play a little too, and—"

"What you play?"

"Mandolin. Irish, bluegrass, old-time. I'm not much into blues or jazz."

"Bluegrass ain't nothing but jazz in a major key."

I hadn't thought about it that way. "I guess it is," I said. "Anyway, I'm looking to do some playing down here. I don't want to get in your way. I intend to set up on weeknights when you're not usually here. I need to make a little money, see. And I just wanted to... I was just hoping... Like, do you have any problem with that?"

He shook his broad head. "Naw, I don't have any problem with that. What'll you do if I start to come around on weeknights?"

"I'll move on."

"That's right. Can you see good?"

"Yeah, I can see."

"Can you play good?"

"That's not for me to say."

"Open up your case and let me hear you."

"How come?"

"I'll tell you if you got a future in it."

"All right."

With trembling fingers I did as told and minutes later found myself playing the streets of Greektown with Lonnie's blessing. More important, he invited me to play behind him sometimes.

As I began to grasp the rudiments of improvisation, I played backup for Lonnie, essentially using my mandolin as percussion, backing his lead with chop chords or sometimes just single-note rhythm.

My progress was slow. Lonnie gave me no praise. One night, after I'd played what I thought was a nearly hotsy-totsy walking line beneath his "Stay as Sweet as You Are," I prompted, "Not bad for a girl, huh?"

He corrected, "Not bad for a white girl."

"What makes you think I'm white?"

"Oh, please. Please, Lily."

I wailed, "Is no one in this world color-blind?"

"Sing!" he commanded. He blasted out an A-minor chord. I fastened my voice to it and made up tragic lyrics.

*Oh, they call me Lily white girl,*
*My skin's so pale and drab,*
*I'm hot milk without the cocoa,*
*I'm the whale without Ahab.*

A few people stopped to listen. Blind Lonnie was laughing hard, but I gave it everything I had. It felt good to let my voice out. I'm no singer, actually, but here's a little-known secret: Anybody can sing mediocre blues. Great blues, no. Only a few can do that. But if you can hold a pitch and you've got decent backup, most people can't tell the difference. I sang on:

*They call me Lily white girl,*
*I don't know why they do.*
*I get so sad and lonesome.*
*Do you feel that way too?*

Lonnie stopped and said, "Why didn't you end on 'blue'? Like, 'I feel so down and blue' or something?"

"That'd be too cheap. In the blues you're not supposed to *say* you're blue. People are supposed to judge for themselves."

"Well, that's enough now anyway. Billie Holiday you ain't."
"Yeah, well, I'm twice the woman you'll ever be."
"Quiet now while I'm playing. Let's do 'String of Pearls.'"

Generations of Greek families strolled by, scrunch-faced grampas and gorgeous young teenagers with smooth black hair and that terrific Greek nose-mouth combination where if you took the nose and mouth separately, they'd look too big, but in combination their proportions are perfect, especially beneath those strong eyes and brows.

Greektown: A few crammed blocks was all it was, an old Hellenic neighborhood. An Orthodox church, home-style bakeries featuring honey-drenched baklava, a mob of restaurants serving lamb grilled, roasted, stewed, and braised, with or without every vegetable in the market. Greek seafarers settled here during Detroit's early boom as an inland port. The neighborhood somehow remained cohesive and was now a civilized island in the midst of ghetto blight. A Reno-sized casino had gotten in and resurrected a block gone to seed, and now more people came through Greektown, for better or worse. It was the kind of place you went on dates, once or twice per relationship. It's interesting as far as it goes, and it would be a nice addition to a city like New York or London, which are pastiches of neighborhoods. In such a city, Greektown would be a beautiful gem-like patch in the quilt, but it can't carry Detroit alone: One patch cannot a quilt make.

Because of all that, I admired the spirit of the neighborhood. Those old restaurateurs had seen everything.

In addition to establishing a relationship with Blind Lonnie, I got to know the other people on the street. Panhandlers hung out in Greektown, also around Hart Plaza on the waterfront. They picked odd places too: the median on Eight Mile east of the Southfield expressway, certain right-turn curbsides on

Woodward uptown. They were typical panhandlers: drunks, crazies, druggies. Most of them got government checks, most disappeared at night to their rooms in the welfare hotels scattered through the ghettos. They tended toward self-medication—cigarettes, alcohol, pot.

I knew the downtown ones by sight. There was Highland Appliance Guy, who towed a child's red wagon everywhere he went by means of a harness made of salvaged seat belts. He piled the wagon with ruined electronics: a stack of VCRs, about a dozen cordless phones; two or three boom boxes; thousands of knobs, wires, and circuit boards. He fastened the harness around his waist and pulled that wagon all over downtown. Why? Nobody knew. His pitch was, "A penny. Just a penny. Everybody can afford a penny."

There was Brown Blanket Lady, who hunched on the sidewalk wrapped in a filthy afghan, rocking. She held out her scrawny trembling hand in silence. I never saw her make eye contact with anyone, and I never heard her say anything. When someone dropped a coin or bill into her hand, she retracted it into her blanket like a spring-loaded bank.

There were Young Brenda and Drooly Rick, a couple who spoke, when coherent, of getting married and having kids in Montana.

At first I tried to befriend these people. You know, get to know them, because hey, the least of them speaks the truth, right? I'd learned long ago from my college professors that the poor are better people than the rich or the middle class, that prophets are commonly cast out of polite society, that the least prepossessing individuals are usually the wisest and worthiest.

These lessons were reinforced by literature. Quasimodo was insecure. Caliban was misunderstood. Boo Radley only wanted to make friends. Huck Finn had dirty feet but a heart of gold.

*Lucky Stiff*

So I shared small amounts of my busking earnings with them, listened to their philosophies of life. I bought candy bars in bulk and gave them away.

But when I really got to know and interact with these people, I found way less life wisdom in them than in the guy who fixed my car or the lass working the pizza counter or my landlord. I don't know whether that's an insult, but I guess it isn't a glowing testament either. One day I was playing, getting into it, my eyes closed. I played a long series of variations on an Appalachian tune called "Forked Deer," and when I opened my eyes I saw that the money I'd accumulated in my case was gone and Drooly Rick was running away down the street dropping coins. I kept my eyes open after that.

I realized that the mandolin gave me a leg up on the other buskers in terms of authenticity—perceived authenticity, anyway. If I used tremolo, I could play almost any basic folk tune and people perceived it as Greek music. Most people's dim impression of Greek music is that it's played on an unfamiliar, plaintive stringed instrument. The Greek instrument is the bouzouki, similar to the mandolin but not the same. It's bigger, with a different fret pattern and overall sound. But the bouzouki is also a short-sustain instrument, meaning that when you want a note to linger, you must use tremolo. So most visitors to Greektown light up when they hear a tremolo folk tune, even if the tune is an American Civil War ballad played on a mandolin.

I backed up Blind Lonnie on "Happy Birthday," listening carefully as I played. It was nobody's birthday that I knew of. Then we launched into some variations on a Mexican melody he'd learned off the radio. Earningswise, we were doing better than we had for a couple of weeks.

It was a Friday night, we were at his traditional spot at the corner of Monroe and Beaubien, and I was working through some chord progressions he'd assigned me for the song, just forming the chords with my left hand and then letting my right wander around the strings. I was enjoying the night. People were hustling by on their way to dinner or the casino. The air was heavy with the smells of food: lamb, spices, lemon, and the bitter air-taste of thick Greek coffee. Cars chugged along looking for parking places. A reggae band on a distant corner clanged out a song. The shadows of the buildings had been creeping across the street, and now the streetlights were coming on. This June Detroit night was turning cool. A woman wearing an open-midriff top and tiny come-fuck-me shoes shivered into the arm of her proud date as they hurried along. People stopped to drop money into Blind Lonnie's case.

Probably because I was concentrating so hard on my chords, it took me awhile to notice a man watching me from across the street. He walked past once, then he walked the other way, slowly. I glanced over. He stood at the curb not directly opposite us but off to the side. He leaned against a fat post and watched, then got behind the post and hugged it, his head poking out to one side, watching. From the angle of his gaze it was clear he was watching me as I stood behind Lonnie, who was seated as usual on his battered wooden box.

A really fierce Detroit lady cop had once told me all I needed to do to avoid getting jumped was to look around all the time and make bold eye contact with anybody who didn't look right. She demonstrated: "You give him a look that says *I see you.*" Her inflection deepened and her eyes slashed across my face. "*And I'm not scared of you.*"

I'd employed that direct look many times since, and, in spite of having been alone in some fairly dicey places, and in spite of minding business not entirely my own, I'd been all right. I gave this guy that look, but he kept right on watching me. So I watched him back.

He looked out of place in Greektown, out of place in Detroit as a whole, frankly. He could have been a European fashion model: the unmuscular, haunted type, only weirder. He wore a dark suit cut from what appeared to be raw silk, a glowing white shirt and a deep pink ascot. Perched at an angle over his floppy hair was a beret, for God's sake, and he was smoking a cigarette.

I tried to read his expression. His eyes, half hidden by the hair, were aggressive, but his lips were parted as if in a question.

He watched me and I watched him, and recognition dawned.

I knew this man.

He swung his arm off the pole and threw away his cigarette.

# TWO

I stopped playing. Lonnie lifted his head toward the man's footsteps as he dodged traffic across the street. A car honked.

The man stood before me.

"Lillian!" he said.

"Duane!" I said.

Simultaneously we said, "Oh. My. God."

I put down my instrument and threw my arms around him. He hugged me tight.

"Duane, Duane, Duane!" I laughed. "My God! I can't believe it's you!" Clichés poured out of me. "It's so good to see you. My old buddy! After all these years! I can't believe it!"

"Oh, Lillian," he said, burying his face in my shoulder, "I never thought I'd see you again." I felt moisture on my collarbone.

"Duane, it's all right." I stroked his beret. He sobbed a little. I held him out from me. "Hey, buddy," I smiled, "get ahold of yourself. Are you OK?"

"I—I'm all right," he said, sniffing hard and smiling too. With a brave flourish he produced a silk pocket square and blotted his eyes. "I'm overwhelmed."

Lonnie said, "Hey?"

I said, "Lonnie, this is Duane Sechrist, my old friend."

"Lonnie Williams." He held out his hand and Duane shook it.

"Pleased to meet you," said Duane.

I said, "My God, I haven't seen you since—"

*Lucky Stiff*

"That summer."
"That summer day."
"We were twelve, remember?"
*Oh, yes, I remembered everything.*

When I was born, my father and mother owned a bar on Detroit's southwest side called the Polka Dot, and the three of us lived in an apartment upstairs. The Polka Dot was a shot-and-a-beer type place, a neighborhood hangout not as rough as those around the nearby Ford Rouge plant, but none too cute either.

I grew up in the bar, and while I picked up bad language and a working knowledge of entry-level racketeering, I witnessed few actual fistfights. Somehow I feel this is significant. My father, who tended bar, didn't tolerate fighting, and he was good at heading off trouble. I like to think he tried to keep the place peaceful on my account.

Duane lived two blocks away and was in my grade. We were special and we knew it. We set ourselves apart because we viewed the world differently from other kids; we appreciated things other kids didn't. Other kids chewed Dubble Bubble; we chewed Clark's Teaberry. Other kids watched *Lost in Space*; we watched *The Dick Cavett Show*. Other kids liked The Monkees or the Supremes (depending); we liked the Weavers and Mel Tormé. Total childhood soul mates. I was different because my parents ran a saloon; he was different because his mother was a recluse and his dad wore military insignia on his everyday clothes. But those were just the surface elements.

On a deeper level, we recognized in each other a kinship. It was the unutterable galvanization of opposite-sex queers realizing that we could be intense friends through our queerness, and by being friends deflect our own confusion. It was a kinship that brought us closer year by year.

When not hanging out with Duane, I spent time in the Polka Dot. I'd come in after school and the place would be pretty dead, maybe just one or two guys hunched at the bar, muttering to my dad about their sorry luck. Al and Hiram were two of the regulars I remember—both of them in Ford jackets and dirty fingernails. Al was thin and Hiram was tremendously fat, and they worked midnights at the Rouge plant. My nickname at the bar was "the little bitch," which somehow my parents never objected to, so neither did I. I liked to sit at the smallest table, next to the jukebox, and do my homework. My dad or the barmaid would serve me a frosty eight-ounce Coke and I'd sip slowly as I worked on my story problems and vocabulary words.

I learned a great many things in the bar that no kid learns in school. I learned to listen in the bar. I learned what commanded the attention of adults, I learned what they liked to talk about. The children in my world were obsessed with candy, roller coasters, and scary movies. The adults in my world were obsessed with money, sex, and death.

One day I looked up from my science book, open to the chapter on monsoons, to tune in to a debate between Al and Hiram.

"OK, that much you do know," Al told Hiram. "But when a guy dies, what happens?"

Hiram said, "What do you mean what happens? He's dead!"

"I mean what happens to his penis? Do you know? Does it get hard or what? I bet you don't know."

A famous race car driver had just fatally crashed at the Michigan International Speedway, and this was the topic of the day.

Fat Hiram looked at skinny Al.

"When a guy dies," said Al, "he gets a hard-on right at the

moment of death, but only if it's sudden. And violent. Or painful."

Hiram buried his mustache in his beer glass, then came up for air. "That's bullshit." The depth of his jowls gave the word a special fullness. You could almost smell it as it came out of him.

Al demanded, "Why is it bullshit?" His voice was shorter and sharper.

"Because you don't know what the hell you're talking about."

The glasses on the bar jumped as Al slammed his fist. "Bullshit I *don't*! I say Cookie Callahan died with a hard-on. They even have religions about it."

I, in my braids and plaid skirts, had become a piece of furniture in the bar, as neutral as the coat tree or the shuffleboard table.

Hiram said, "So, likewise when a woman dies, do her nipples get hard? Or do they stay soft?"

Al responded, "Now, that one I don't know." He paused, then mused, "What if you commit suicide? I think—"

"So *you're* saying," Hiram demanded, "that you get a *reward* for dying fast and painful? What about the guys that die slow, like cancer?"

"They don't get hard when they die, they just slip away, you know what I mean."

"So you get to say goodbye to your family, but you get no final erection."

"Right." Al wiped his mouth with his sleeve and addressed my father. "How 'bout another here, boss?"

"Coming up," said my dad.

Hiram said, "Well, what good's an erection if you don't at least shoot before you go?"

Al said, "Well, you'll always be ready, you know."

My dad said, "Forever ready."

"That's my motto," said Hiram.

I paged through my science book knowing I wouldn't find the answer to Al and Hiram's sexual koan, but it was interesting to think about it. I didn't exactly know what a hard-on was, but before that afternoon I had believed it to be something nasty and surreal. Now I felt it must be something desirable yet banal.

While my dad drew beers and poured shots, my mother kept the books and looked after me, more or less. She made extra money sewing custom bridal gowns for an exclusive boutique downtown. Since she could always work on a gown, and I had the bar and school to hang out in as well as my friends in the neighborhood, she'd essentially wind me up and let me go every morning.

I did have something of a second mother. Her name was Trix Hawley. Trix was my parents' employee who, she told me, had been born into a family of barmaids and barmen. She worked part-time at the Polka Dot and part-time at Tommy's Char-Grilled in Wyandotte. When she worked at the Polka Dot she'd come in around 4 in the afternoon and stay until closing, mopping the place out before retrieving her purse from the lockbox and going home. Trix was an exceptionally mouthy redhead, and I liked her and she liked me. I liked listening to her mix it up with Hiram and Al. Whenever they blew hard about their inevitable futures as millionaires or kept studs, her favorite thing to tell them was "You couldn't pour piss out of a boot." She liked to tell stories on herself, all of which included the climactic line "I didn't know whether to shit green or go blind!" There was nobody like her.

When I'd snap my pencil in frustration over some hellish problem in long division, she'd come to my little table and go over it with me.

*Lucky Stiff*

"Lessee, five can go into two how many times? None, right? So you leave that space blank and go onto the next one. Now you've got five going into twenty-two. That's what you gotta figure out. See? That's how she works." Then she'd get up and sneak me a bag of Fritos or another Coke.

Trix was married but had no kids of her own, and she never spoke of her husband. Just as I couldn't imagine my schoolteachers trying on bathing suits at Hudson's or getting drunk, I couldn't imagine Trix kissing some guy I'd never seen, or going to a carnival with him, going to church.

She talked a lot about getting out of Detroit. She'd flip her coppery bangs and say, "I'll strike it big one day and then—p'chew! Outta here! Sitting by a pool with an umbrella in my drink."

Everybody in the bar talked about striking it big one day. Once I asked her how she thought it might happen for her.

"Kid," she said, "I'm a very lucky person. Good fortune finds me wherever I go. It's a matter of timing. Pure timing."

"Like how?"

"Like you gotta be patient. You wait for good fortune, then you jump on it and drive the son of a bitch for all it's worth. Most people just sit there. You gotta *work* with luck when it finds you."

I found that philosophy very impressive. Every time I walked into the bar I expected my dad to introduce me to a new barmaid, saying, "Trix's shoved off. She struck it big."

I asked my mom to buy me Trix cereal for breakfast. The television ads for it were nauseating, but I liked having the box in the cupboard: *Trix are for kids!* I imagined trading in my real mom for Trix Hawley. I wondered, if I suddenly became Trix's daughter, would my hair turn red like hers? My hair was ordinary brown, like my parents'. I understood that hair color ran in families.

15

A few times Trix baby-sat for me, and those were very good times. No homework, just popcorn and the eleven-thirty scary movie, plus she'd let me sip her highball. Seven Crown and Canada Dry, boy, you couldn't beat it. I first saw *Psycho* while tucked under Trix's arm on the couch in our apartment. Her commentary was enormously valuable.

"See, he likes her but she doesn't even know he exists, except as a motel guy... Now, see who's doing the knifing? You can't see their face. That's an important clue. See how they—are you looking? You can look. Don't be a baby. I swear. It's just a movie."

In the bar I learned:

That there is a system for picking winning horses, but nobody's perfected it yet.

That it's better to take a punch in the face than in the gut because your liver can bleed to death without you even knowing it, whereas your face bones and nose cartilage will act as cushions, absorbing shock as they crack. Then you've got a busted face but you're not dead.

That if you only commit one big crime and do it right, the cops will never catch you.

That Marilyn Monroe was a very nice but lonely person.

Al's and Hiram's arguments haunted my dreams:

"All I'm saying is, if you're playing one-deck blackjack and the rules say the dealer has to deal to the end of the deck and you know for a fact that the only cards left are three tens, and the dealer has a five showing, you should go out and remortgage your house and put all the money you can get on that hand because even if you don't take a card, the dealer's gonna bust. That's why card counting works."

"Yeah, but you've already bet on the hand before the deal. You can't re-bet in the middle of a hand."

"What's the difference? For Christ's sake, that dealer's gonna bust!"

I remembered all those things, and I remembered the last time I saw Duane Sechrist. That summer. That day. In the morning I said goodbye to him, my bestest buddy, whose parents were about to drive him up to some tough-guy summer camp his dad had picked out after finding Duane and me applying makeup to each other's lips and lids. Duane's appearance was unusual even then. While most pale-skinned children are also more or less fair-haired, his hair was a startling, thorough black. The makeup really accented that interesting hair and his soft eyes.

Although his mother didn't like to leave the house, she would go for rides in the car if she didn't have to get out and do anything. Duane and I clung to each other and cried, and he promised to write me every day. We were facing puberty, and both of us were unhinged at the prospect.

I tucked a five-stick pack of Teaberry into his pocket and hugged him once more, then he trudged toward his dad's idling car. I waved through my tears.

That night I awoke to a horrible crackling roar and thick smoke in my throat, and half an hour later my childhood was over. I remembered every second of it.

Duane said, "What are you doing here? Are you *begging*, Lillian?"

I straightened my spine. "I am not begging. I am busking. I'm playing a musical instrument in a public area for any money the citizens might wish to give. This is not a begging experience. This is a value-added street life experience for music lovers."

"Why are you doing it?"

"I like to play music. You know I was always musical."

Lonnie made a little sound.

Duane said, "Why are you doing this really, Lillian?"

"I'm broke, goddamn it, why else?"

"I see."

"What are *you* doing here?"

"Looking for my mother."

"What?"

"Lillian, we need to talk somewhere." When I last saw him, his voice was a squeaky altar boy's. Now it was smooth and pleasant, a sophisticated city man's voice. "We've got some heavy catching-up to do."

"Where do you live?"

"I moved back here last year from Fort Lauderdale, I've got a place in Indian Village."

"And you came here to find your mother? Where is she? I mean, are you literally looking for her on the streets of Greektown, or is this some kind of theoretical quest, or what?"

"I'm literally looking for her on the streets of Greektown. I have a very weird feeling, Lillian. Like I was meant to bump into you. You've stayed in Detroit the whole time."

"Yes. Why did you disappear after summer camp?"

"It has to do with my mother. My mother and father."

"Did you ever come back to the old neighborhood after camp?"

"Why...don't you know?" Duane's eyes cut right and left and he dropped his voice. "About my mom going crazy and disappearing? While I was at camp?"

"My God. No!"

"Then three years later my dad took off, and I haven't seen *him* since."

"No!"

"Not that I give that much of a shit about him, frankly. But

*Lucky Stiff*

it occurs to me that I ought to talk to your mom and dad about my mom and dad. I remember my mom gabbing on the phone to your mom and the two of them—"

"Duane, don't you know…about my mom and dad?"

His face settled into a mask of dread.

I said, "They died that night. The night you went to camp."

For the second time, we looked at each other and said, "Oh. My. God."

# THREE

Duane's spanking-new Thunderbird, in Oxydol white, was parked in the structure at Monroe and St. Antoine; I'd squeezed my nearly derelict Chevrolet Caprice into a street spot a few blocks away. He drove me to my car and I followed him to his house in Indian Village. Indian Village, on the east side, was one of the gorgeous old neighborhoods of Detroit. It had gone to urban blight, then been resuscitated by gentle yuppies, and now the big houses, whole blocks of them, were back to their original elegance and then some.

Duane's place was a duplex; he'd restored half and was living in it while redoing the other half, to rent out, he told me. He'd used lavish materials—curved copper panels in the entryway, bronze and marble insets in the floors, sleek hardwood trim and bold paints. The air conditioning was running and the place smelled fresh.

We had so much to talk about, so much pent up. We went to the kitchen and, while Duane brewed a pot of coffee, made small talk in a daze, saving up the big stuff for when our attention would be undivided.

"Are you seeing anyone?" I asked, glancing around for signs of cohabitation.

"No," he murmured. "I've made some friends up here, but not...no. You?"

"To make a long story short, no."

Our eyes met. I said, "So...you like guys, right?"

He smiled. "Always cutting to the chase. Yes, Lillian, I like guys. And you?"

"I like guys too. But not in the same way. You might say I like girls."

"I knew it. I knew it."

I smiled too. "We both knew it. For a long time."

I watched him prepare the coffee, seeing a mature man's face and body superimposed over the weedy lad I'd bombed around the neighborhood with. His face looked good. As a boy, his full upper lip and especially his ears had overpowered his face, but now the rest of it had caught up. His face was lean, the skin taut and clear, but it stopped short of being bony. His smile stretched bright and wide.

He'd grown into his body too. The current gay-guy fashion was big muscles, low fat, tight clothes, but Duane had gone retro, in more of a Cole Porter direction. His tailored suit was elegantly roomy, and he wore it with languor. Yes, that was it: His was a languorous body: not slack, but not quite ready for fast action either.

He was evaluating me too. As he drew water from a chrome gooseneck tap he said over his shoulder, "You look great, by the way. How do you stay so thin? Well, you were always a skinny kid. Of course, so was I, but now as a grown-up I can only eat about three ounces of food a day or I get as big as a *house*."

At first there was a weird tension that we talked hurriedly around, but then I began to feel easy with him, like in the old days.

"Sweetheart, do me a favor and look in the pantry." Duane pulsed the coffee beans in the grinder. "Do you see a package of madeleines? I'm assuming you've had dinner."

"I'm not terribly hungry. What are madeleines? These cookies?"

"Oh dear, oh dear. *Yes.* Those are madeleines." He flipped

his fingers through his lanky black hair, exposing, to my horror, streaks of gray. *Are we that old?*

I shut out that reality and said, "You know, you've really gone up in style, Cub Scout."

"Go ahead and say it: I've become effete."

"Don't know as I'd go quite—"

"Effete! Effete! Effete! I know I am. Effete and proud!"

"Whatever. How did you pay for all this? Granite countertops and all?"

"Oh, you *are* Midwestern. Taking for granted that it's paid for."

"You're from here too."

He pulled a pack of Marlboros and a box of matches from his side pocket and lit one. He blew the match out and pointed the charred end at me. "I'm *from* here, but not *of* here. Oh, I'm sorry. Cigarette?"

"Not right now, thanks," I said. "Come to think of it, I've never thought of you as a true Detroiter. No, I guess you never were."

"You were, though." His eyes narrowed as they evaluated my well-worn summer blouse, blue jeans, and sneakers. "And over time you've become *more* of here, I think."

"Maybe so."

"Sit down. Here, darling, try this. Shade-grown in Java. It's terribly politically correct, plus it tastes almost as good as the stuff that promotes oppression in the Third World. Cream? Sugar?" He handed me an ink-blue Fiestaware mug.

"Just black, thank you."

We sat at his kitchen table with the plate of madeleines between us. The table was a gorgeous slab of maple, the chairs carefully mismatched. Mine was quite comfortable. The seat seemed to mold to my butt.

I looked at him, suddenly emotional. "I can't believe we're together again."

*Lucky Stiff*

"You go first."

I swallowed some coffee. "I don't know if I can."

He took a hit from his cigarette and heaved a smoky sigh. "I probably won't survive my own monologue, but knowing that you'll talk next might just get me through it." He smiled sadly. "What did we do in those summers? I've thought so much about the fun we had."

"We rode our bikes all over."

"Yeah."

"What a neighborhood," I remarked.

"The river on one side, the tracks on the other, the Rouge down at the bottom—and the ghetto just around the corner."

"It's all ghetto now," I said.

"You know why my parents sent me to camp, don't you?"

"To make a man out of you."

"Right. Oh, God. My dad had such a hemorrhage when he caught us with that eye shadow."

"Yeah. I remember him yelling, *Why couldn't you kids play doctor instead? What's wrong with playing doctor?*"

"It was the primal cry of a father who suspected the worst. A Korean War veteran whose kid was a pussy. If he'd caught me raping you instead, I'm sure he'd have bought me that cello after all."

He broke a madeleine in two and nibbled. I tried one and liked it. It went with the coffee: a light, soft sweetness against the coffee's bitter strength.

"So I went," said Duane. "I had no choice. I knew it'd be terrible."

"And was it?"

"Yes and no. I was terrified of having to shower with the other guys, being a basic runt. However, I had a big ding-dong. That and that alone got me the respect of all the other runty guys, and the everlasting enmity of the bigger ones. They were like, *A pygmy like him doesn't deserve a big prick.* The age-old story. They pushed me around until one day at mess I went berserk and slammed the biggest bastard over the head with my tray. I had no idea I was about to do it. Don't laugh. The trays were steel. I actually cocked him cold in front of everybody, and after that I was extremely popular."

He smoked and sipped his coffee. "The day they took me to Camp Kalkaska was the last time I ever saw her."

"How long was camp?"

"Six weeks."

"Oh, yeah, I remember us whining, *Six weeks apart?*"

"So my dad picks me up after camp is over, and he's got a funny look. And I say, 'Where's Mom?' We're riding along in that shitty car—remember that diseased-looking Dodge we had?"

"Yeah, with the yellow quarter panels and all that rust. Lyndon Johnson rust."

"Right. Lyndon Johnson rust."

Duane and I had agreed that the rust field on the trunk lid looked like the silhouette of our thirty-sixth president.

Duane continued, "And I asked him again, 'Where's Mom?' I hadn't heard from them in six weeks. I'd at least expected her to send me some lousy cookies or something. I hate to admit it, but that camp did toughen me up. So I felt I was past crying over anything. But when he kept not answering me, I started to cry a little. I got a horrible feeling. I was sitting in the front passenger seat, in *her* seat, and I just got this clear, very clear feeling that she was in the worst kind of danger.

"My dad said, 'Son, I don't know where your mother is. She ran off.'" He reached for another cigarette. "Now, I knew there was no way my mother would have *run off,* especially while I was at camp."

"You and your mom were close."

"Yeah. But I was old enough to know that bizarre things happen to normal, ordinary people such as my mom and myself and my dad."

The kitchen windows shone black, beyond them the urban night. Duane and I gazed at our reflection in them, two people sitting at a table with mugs of coffee, smoke swirling above our heads, our expressions yearning. He got up and lowered a series of matchstick blinds. They were done in an understated natural stain, which complemented the mahogany of the window frames. It really was a lovely home.

My friend resumed his seat. "I'm hoping you can help me, Lillian. In fact I'm practically praying it. You can help me look for her." He pulled at his Adam's apple. "So my dad says she ran off, and I start asking all these questions. And he says to me, 'Didn't you notice how strange she'd been acting?' And I was like, 'I don't know…' "

"But she hadn't been acting strange, as far as you could tell?"

"Well, actually she had been, I mean, you know. Even kids know it's unusual for your mom not to want to leave the house. She was fairly afraid of the world. I guess she was a strange woman in general."

"But you loved her."

"I loved her so much. I'd have done anything to please her. I probably would've gotten *married* to please her, if it'd come to that."

"We could have married each other and then lived double lives of hot homosexual love."

Duane said, "I would have wanted a divorce eventually."

"I was *kidding*."

"I admit, having a marriage under our belts would've given us 'straight cred' when we needed it."

"Yeah," I agreed. "I remember your mom. She was really nice. She was a cookie baker."

"She was, yep."

"And she gave us cookies and ice cream at the same time, both things together. At my house you could have one or the other, but not both at the same time. Unless Trix was baby-sitting. Remember Trix?"

"No."

"She was the barmaid at the Polka Dot. She was great."

"I never set foot in the Polka Dot, you know."

"Really? I thought… I remember… I remember your dad coming in all the time…and…didn't you…"

"No, my dad made me afraid to ever go in. I mean, little kids didn't just walk into taverns anyway, for Jesus's sake. *You* felt normal walking in there because it was your home."

"But you came over—I remember playing Stratego in my bedroom."

"Yeah, but that was you guys' apartment. I'd come up the outside stairs in the back and knock. The bar was this fearful mystery to me. It made you an exciting playmate—you had access to this adult world, this dangerous adult world. Dear God, the stories you used to tell me."

"Al and Hiram."

"Yeah, Al and Hiram."

Duane ashed his cigarette with a sharp movement. The ashtray was a shallow opalescent thing. He broke the coal off the end of the butt and stubbed it out. We watched the coal smolder and go out.

I said, "So you're riding home from camp and your dad—does he try to tell you *why* your mother ran off?"

He tapped out another Marlboro and lit it.

"My dad launches into this lame explanation of how my

*Lucky Stiff*

mom just got weirder and weirder, and one day while I was at Camp Kalkaska she walked out, wandered off, never to return. And I was like, 'Well, we gotta go look for her!' And he says he had looked for her, and he had a feeling she didn't want to be found. He says, 'To be honest, kid, I think she's crazy.' And he tells me we're making a fresh start, and Lillian, we were on I-75, and before I knew it we'd blown right through Detroit, and I ask, 'Where are we going?' and he says Florida! We stopped at a party store in Toledo, and he started drinking beer and getting festive. He bought me all the junk food I wanted and said I'd have a new bike and my own room, which was strange, because I'd always had my own room. Being an only and all. You know how it is."

"I always gave thanks for that."

"I go, 'Well, what about our house?' and he goes, 'It's sold, gone, that's it,' and I say, 'Well, what about my stuff,' and he says, 'We'll buy you new stuff.' 'What about my bottle cap collection?' 'We'll buy new bottle caps.' 'What about my Superior Potato Chip Space Coins collection?' 'We'll buy new.' But I soon found they didn't have Superior Potato Chips in Florida, so that was lie number one."

"Lie *number one*?" I said.

"Well," Duane said, and fell silent.

I waited, and after a while he said, "I feel really horrible about myself. About the way I was then."

"What do you mean?"

"I was very into myself right at that time. Because it was at camp that I had my first—that I first messed around with another guy. And let another guy mess around with me. I was distracted."

"Well..."

"My father takes me, uproots me, we move to *Florida,* he

tells me my mom abandoned us, and I bought it. I mean, I let him convince me. I was so busy thinking about myself, and I guess I was sort of in shock, that I just let my mom go." His eyes welled up.

I took his hand. "Duane, you were twelve years old. What happened when you got to Florida?"

He blinked back his tears. "There was no new bike, no room of my own, no house, no nothing. My dad rented us a room in this roachy motel in Miami, and he went out every day. I guess he got work somewhere. We ate junk food. I went out too. I walked down to the Greyhound station every afternoon and hung around." He looked at me steadily. "I discovered I could make money too."

"Oh my God, Duane."

"It was as if something gave way inside me, spiritually."

I couldn't help asking, "Didn't you miss me? You went to camp and I never heard from you again."

Softly, he said, "I don't know how to explain it." He looked miserable.

I stroked his hand. "It's all right." I looked into his face. His eyes were dark and faraway. "Tell me more," I urged.

"I went to school, a toilet of a slum school. I can't even think about it. After a while my dad started to bring this woman around named Lynette. She was a waitress. They got married. We moved into a shitbox house. Lynette started out all right, nice and everything. She had no interest in disciplining me, which I appreciated. But I couldn't really like her, let alone love her. My dad wanted me to call her Mom. I'm sure she sucked his brains out through his weenie. He thought she was fantastic. And on that vulgar note, I have to go to the bathroom."

I got up too, and looked around, admiring the house. Duane had taste, all right.

*Lucky Stiff*

The original interiors of the houses in Indian Village were nicely finished in plaster and hardwood. Their architects had crammed them with terrific built-ins like nooks and shelves and window seats. Duane had added some very hip touches, like the metals in the foyer. He'd kept the place fairly minimalist—he hadn't gone and junked it up with a collection of kitsch or that lowbrow gay-guy art of winged penises and leather-masked cherubs. The fireplace surround looked new and grand—Pewabic tile, I guessed, in a muted mix of golds, oranges, and browns.

I gravitated toward a collection of photographs on the wall opposite the fireplace. There, illuminated by soft spotlights, were studio pictures of baby Duane, his mother and his father; grown-up Duane and three guys bare-chested with arms over shoulders in front of some beach club. I laughed out loud: There was a snapshot of Duane and me, posing on our bikes, holding the sharp sticks I insisted we carry against the threat of rattlesnakes and criminals. There was a picture of Duane at about age fourteen at a cookout, pretending to swallow a shish kebab. I noticed the photo had a ragged edge, as if part had been torn off.

Duane appeared at my side.

I asked, "Is this you in Florida?"

"Yeah."

"The picture got torn."

"My stepmother was in it."

"Oh. You really hated her, huh?"

"I just—it wasn't that she was all that bad."

"It was just that she wasn't your mom."

"Yeah. Sometimes I almost liked her. But after it was all over... I just can't stand to see her face."

My morbid curiosity was aroused. "What was she like?"

"Well, she had the coarsest vocabulary you ever heard. From a woman."

"I've heard some coarse ones."

"Like she'd say, 'I gotta take a leak.'"

I laughed. Duane said, "Only guys are supposed to say that. And she'd say, 'I didn't know whether to shit green or go blind.'"

I laughed harder. "Boy, I haven't heard somebody say that since—since—" I stopped abruptly.

Duane continued, "And when my dad would get on her case, telling her to do this, do that, she'd yell, 'Jesus Christ, what else do you want me to do—stick a broom up my ass and sweep the floor with it?'"

My mouth dropped open. I asked, "Did she ever tell your dad, 'You couldn't pour piss out of a boot'?"

He looked at me. "How'd you know?"

"What did she look like?"

"Well, she was…just regular, I guess, she was about five foot seven, my dad thought she was pretty—"

"Did she have blue eyes?"

"Yes."

"Fair skin? A few freckles?"

"Yes."

"Red hair?"

"No."

I let out my breath.

His eyes widened. "Wait. *Oh, my God.* Yes. She dyed it. *Yes!* I always wondered why she dyed her hair brown, a mousy, ordinary brown, when her roots were this rich red that I thought would have looked great."

"Her roots were red."

"Her roots were red, and I thought, Man, if I had a head of hair like that I'd—".

*Lucky Stiff*

Suddenly I felt weak, and I understood what people meant when they said "My head swam." I put a hand out to the wall, but it fell away from me and I sank to my knees.

My old friend took my arm and eased me to a sitting position on the carpet. "Lillian, what is it?" His voice was steady but tight. "What's going on? Do you want to lie down?"

"Oh, Duane." He crouched over me anxiously. I said, "Where is Lynette now?"

"I don't know. Like I told you before, my dad took off after we'd been in Florida for three years. I hit the streets, and I don't know what happened to Lynette. Lillian, you're scaring the hell out of me. I think she went to Las Vegas. She was always talking about going there, always talking about how lucky she was. I don't care about her. Tell me. What is this?"

I looked up at him. "Duane, I could be wrong. But I don't think I am. Lynette used to work at the Polka Dot, and she used to be called Trix, and she used to be dead."

# FOUR

We staggered back to the kitchen. Duane splashed water on his face at the sink and groped for a clean towel. He scrubbed his face. "I need a drink," he muttered into the towel. "You?"

"Hell yes."

He brought a bottle of brandy and two glasses to the table. He poured out generous shots. We raised our glasses.

"To, uh..." I said.

"Yeah," he said.

We drank. The brandy was smooth and pleasantly warm in my throat. I appreciated the brandy. It had a French label.

I said, "All right, Duane. We've obviously been connected in a deeper way, all this while, than we ever thought."

"It was fate," he said. "Talk, Lillian."

I recounted for him my memories of Trix.

"It sounds like her," he said. "It sounds just like how Lynette talked and acted."

I told him about the night that unfolded after we said goodbye on going-to-camp day.

"It was the first hot night of the summer, and we had the windows open upstairs. My mom was teaching me to play cribbage, and—"

"What's cribbage?"

"It's a game, a card game that has a little wooden board with pegs that you move based on the points you score. It's an old-timer's game. Anyway, we were sitting in the kitchen playing cribbage and drinking Vernor's on the rocks, and my dad and Trix were running the bar. My dad had just bought the deep fryer. He thought he could bring in more business if he could serve fried fish and stuff. My mom thought the smell would get on our nerves, but she wanted the bar to bring in more money too. I got to stay up late in the summers. My mom and I had a good time playing cribbage that night. We talked about stuff. It was good. When I went to bed she was putting on a pot of coffee for when my dad came up after closing.

"I went to sleep. I woke up. There was this big loud noise in my ears, like the worst nightmare, like an explosion that goes on and on. It was pitch-black in my room, which wasn't right, because the light from the alley always shone in. I couldn't breathe, and I realized the place was on fire. My mom was screaming somewhere. I heard her screaming my name."

Duane covered his mouth with both hands.

"I got up, breathed in, and fell down from the smoke. It was like breathing fur. I lay there for a minute. There was air near the floor and I gulped it in. Then I felt the floor get hot. I crawled to the window and started to climb out. I thought I'd have to jump into the alley. But a fireman grabbed me, he was right there on a ladder, ready to come in."

I sipped, swallowed, and closed my eyes. The scene outside the bar came back to me vividly: the flames stampeding through the place, the windows glowing orange, the fire trucks shooting water that disappeared into the flames like nothing.

I opened my eyes. "They brought my dad out, and then they found my mom. They gave them mouth-to-mouth, but they were dead. It didn't look like they were burned. Their faces looked normal, just slack and empty. My mother was naked. I couldn't believe it when the guy unfolded the sheet and put it over her, covering her face too. Then he did the same with my dad. It was like this slow-motion show that wasn't real. A cop took hold of me and wouldn't let me touch them, and the guy who lived across the alley came and took me to his place until my Uncle Guff and Aunt Rosalie got there."

"Oh, what a horror," Duane whispered. "What a night of hell. I am so very sorry, Lillian."

"Thank you," I said. "I'm all right."

"How can you be?"

"It's been a long time... The next day they found Trix. She was burned up, beyond recognition. They identified her by her wedding band." I took another sip of brandy. The fumes rose from my throat into my nose. I breathed them in. "So three people were killed in that fire."

Duane said, "I guess we both grew up all of a sudden that summer."

"Yeah." I reached for his pack of Marlboros, shook one out, and lit it. I had the urge to hold fire in my hand, to control it. I watched the match burn down to my fingers, then blew it out.

Duane lit up too. "Did they know how the fire started?"

I exhaled. "It was the deep fryer, a short circuit or something. That's what Uncle Guff said. They took me to live with them, he and Aunt Rosalie. They lived in Ecorse."

We sat smoking. I felt the effects of the smoke ease into my arms and legs, that distinct feeling of peace you get when you haven't had one in a while.

"Remember when you swiped those cigars?" Duane said.

"Do I ever." One afternoon I'd quietly removed two cigars from the box behind the bar. They were Muriel Panetela Extras, and I'd been fascinated long enough by the aroma of them, by the big deal Al and Hiram made of smoking them on paydays. Duane and I smoked them in a far-off alley, each of us quickly sick but undaunted in our determination to master the mystery of smoking.

"You should switch to Camel Filters, you know," I said. "I give you points for not smoking Marlboro Lights, but you really would enjoy your smoke more if you switched to Camels."

"Aren't they really harsh?"

"Marlboros are harsher. Take my word for it."

"Hmm." Duane watched the smoke curl toward the ceiling. He said, "How did you... How have you dealt with it?"

"You know, like you said, bizarre things happen. Strange, terrible things happen to people every day in this world. I accepted it. I mean, I was sad and horrified, and I cried for my parents and Trix, you know. But my uncle and aunt were there for me. They did everything they could to give me a life. A...a teenager-hood. I saw that nothing could be changed, and I guess I was a pretty self-sufficient kid to begin with. Guff and Rosalie were regular people; good, factory-tough people. I gave them hell, of course, being a teenager and all. But deep down I understood. Fires start, buildings burn down, people die. Everybody dies. Guff and Rosalie seemed to get over it fairly quickly themselves. They discouraged me from talking about it, from brooding on it. I think they thought that talking about something like that can be bad for you. They tried to protect me from reliving it. I never even saw the newspapers afterward. I missed you."

For a while, Duane and I sat in silence. There was so much to try to get my mind around.

"Duane," I said, "what did you mean when you said you hoped I could help you find your mother?"

His glass was empty. He picked up the brandy bottle, then changed his mind and put it down. He dropped his hands into his lap. "It's like I forgot her for a long time. I guess I felt a little like you must have felt: You go into shock, sort of, and you shut down. I was on and off the streets for a few years, then I snapped out of it. A very good guy helped me. He became my sugar daddy and he helped me get my GED, then he sent me to college. Imagine that! Well, he sent me for a year, anyway, then we broke up. I got a job and managed to stick with school. Now I'm an architect, do you believe it?"

Glancing around, I said, "Yeah, I believe it."

"I worked for a couple of firms—in Miami, Fort Lauderdale—until last fall. About every five years I'd get the urge to come back here and look for my mom. I had this fantasy that I'd find her wandering the streets, a bag lady, all dirty. And I'd rescue her, and she'd be," his voice spiked upward, "my mom again."

"Oh, Duane."

"And…I guess I still have that fantasy, because last September I moved up here, bought this place, joined a firm in Grosse Pointe, and launched a serious search for Juanita Sechrist. I feel now that my dad… Well, the she-went-nuts-and-ran-off story was always bullshit, but I feel he might have worked on her, you know, to drive her crazy. Or at least drive her away. I feel that."

He told me about checking all the public records he could get his hands on—phone books, death certificates, there wasn't much. He managed to look into the records of the hospitals and mental institutions, but found nothing about his mother. "I know, of course, she could be in some other state," he said. "I know that, logically. But in my heart I feel she's here. I *know* she's in Detroit somewhere. Last month I even talked to a private detective. 'That's a pretty cold trail, pal,' he said to me. He talked just like that. His attitude was very poor. I fired him before I'd even hired him." Duane shook his head.

"Did he venture any opinion as to what happened to your mom?"

"He said, 'Your pop probably killed her.' " Duane snorted sadly. "The cynicism."

"Duane, I—"

"When I told you I thought you could help me, I meant... Well, you knew my mom. I saw you on the street. At first I thought you were homeless. You're not, you said that."

"Right!"

"And..." he paused. "Well, what *do* you do, anyway?"

"I'm a hack writer."

"Oh, yeah?" He brightened up. "You mean like pulp fiction?"

"No, I write articles for magazines. Sometimes magazines even pay for them. I do some technical writing. I freelance here and there."

"Oh."

"I'm an ink-stained wretch. And it's not going well, OK? I try to pick up a few bucks with my music."

He brightened again. "OK, OK, but you know the street people, don't you? I guess I thought maybe you've seen her without knowing it. Or maybe you could sort of organize the street people to help us find her."

"Oh, God," I interjected, "Listen—"

"Maybe—maybe—I don't know. I just thought you'd, you know, *want* to help me. Being my friend and all. Being a Detroiter and all. Maybe you'd have an idea I haven't thought of. You always were the brains on the block."

"Duane, look at me." I took his hand and held it tight. He lifted his eyes to mine. The kitchen was so quiet I could hear his shirt rustle with his breathing. "The detective was right," I said. "Your pop probably killed your mom. He fell in love with Trix Hawley at the bar, and he cooked up a plot. He killed your mother. Trix didn't die in the fire, your mother did. It wasn't Trix's corpse they pulled out of the ashes of the Polka Dot, it was your mother's. Trix left town that night and became Lynette and dyed her hair, and your dad reported your mother missing a few weeks later. And he went down to Florida, you in tow, to meet up with Trix-Lynette again."

My friend pulled his hand away. "No."

"Yes. Did your dad ever slip and call her Trix instead of Lynette?"

"No!" He chewed his lips. "My mother cannot be dead. She is not dead. I know it. She's here."

"Duane, you have to think here, you have to reason. Trix Hawley did not die in that fire. She became your stepmother. A corpse was planted in that bar that night. The corpse had on Trix's wedding ring. They handed it to her husband, and he read the inscription and said, 'Yes, that would be my wife, then.'"

"Stop!" he screamed. He clapped his hands over his ears in the classic gesture of denial. "You have no idea what you're talking about!"

I stopped. I took a deep breath and forced myself to back off. But the blood was hammering in my veins.

If Trix Hawley were alive, that would prove that somebody else wearing Trix's ring was pulled out of that pile of ashes. That somebody else would have been a murder victim, Duane's mother or not. And the murderer set the fire in order to burn the body beyond recognition. There was no DNA testing in those days, and anyway, who would have questioned?

Hovering in the air above me, looming over my head, was the next implication, which evidently had not occurred to Duane. If the fire in the Polka Dot had been set to cover up a murder—most likely the murder of Duane's mother—then my parents had been murdered too. Most likely by Duane's father.

"Duane," I said, "this night has changed everything, whether you want to face it or not."

He couldn't do it. The evening had begun with the two of us rushing into each other's arms, but it was ending with a stand-off. He simply didn't want to deal with the fact that his mother *might* be dead and that his father might be a murderer. He grew more and more argumentative, challenging me to convince him of the logic that appeared plain to me.

Finally, sometime after 1 o'clock, I helped myself to a drink of water and picked up my keys. He saw me to the door. I stood there wanting to hug him but fearful of the emotional storm the night had unleashed in him.

Suddenly he put his hand out. "Lillian."

"Yes?"

"Promise me…promise me…"

"Duane, what?"

His eyes were so sad. "Just say you'll help me."

I pulled him in for a hug then. "I'll help you, Duane. I'll do everything I can to help you find your mom. I might need you to help me too, you know. We'll work together. OK?"

"OK."

"I'm going to think all this over, and I'll talk to you soon. I— I hope my ideas are wrong."

But all the while the feeling grew inside me, stronger and stronger, that they weren't.

# FIVE

Todd was waiting up for me, good friend. He bumped over to me, as was his habit, sniffed my shoes, then rubbed his chin on the uppers. I squatted to pet his fur and say hello. He was a rabbit who had seen a lot, and who now was inching onto his downslope, so to speak. His movements weren't as quick as they used to be, but he was still the same old Todd: inquisitive, calm, faithful. He was better than a tranquilizer to me. He watched as I checked his food and water dishes, then he nibbled a timothy nugget from my hand and hopped behind me into the bedroom. We had switched to timothy from alfalfa when the vet told me timothy had a higher ratio of cellulose. Rabbits need their fiber.

Rather than get to brooding, I stuck to my standard bedtime routine of reading for an hour before turning out the light. I'd picked up a used copy of the latest Calico Jones adventure at John King Books, and gratefully turned to its exciting pulp pages to crank my mind into neutral.

In this one, *The Ransom of Angeline Carey*, the gorgeous and accomplished private sleuth Calico Jones is called to San Francisco to locate and rescue an incredibly attractive beef jerky heiress who's been kidnapped by a PETA-like organization. I resumed reading where Calico Jones is exploring a cargo barge that's being towed out to sea beneath the Golden Gate Bridge. She's got reason to believe that clues as to Angeline Carey's whereabouts might be found on that barge, so she's

*Lucky Stiff*

investigating when suddenly she realizes that the tow cable has been released and she's now adrift alone on this barge full of hazardous medical waste, and strong tidal currents are moving it out to sea, and the fog is rolling in, and all Calico's got in her pockets are a ballpoint pen, four dimes, a small box of Milk Duds, and a sturdy barrette. Of course, she's got her .45-caliber semiautomatic strapped to her hip, but as you can imagine, it wouldn't be much help in a situation like that. I won't spoil it for you, but I'll just say that Calico Jones summons her phenomenal ingenuity, courage, and physical strength, and makes it out alive to continue her search for the kidnapped heiress.

Todd made himself comfy in his box of cedar chips, and I went to sleep comforted by the fact that at least in books everything usually works out for the best.

A sunny Saturday morning crept in around the blinds. I made coffee and toast and got out my notebook and my blue Pentel mechanical pencil. I shook the pencil and heard the wispy rattle of spare leads inside. Spare leads give me confidence.

My little flat in Eagle, two blocks north of Eight Mile, was a comfortable and cheap home for Todd and me. My landlord and his wife were more interested in having a stable tenant than squeezing rent dollars out of some well-off but nasty careless person who wouldn't take as much of an interest in them as I did.

For once I was glad to have neither a pending freelance assignment nor some brilliant idea for one that I would have to doggedly pitch to editors. I set my mind, such as it was, to working on last night's events.

I wrote "Facts I Know" at the top of a page, then I scribbled:

TRIX HAWLEY IS ALIVE.
SHE CHANGED HER NAME (LYNETTE) AND HAIR COLOR.
BILL SECHRIST MARRIED THIS LYNETTE AFTER A MOVE TO FLA.

THIRD BODY IN THE POLKA DOT FIRE WAS NOT TRIX.
THE BODY WORE TRIX'S RING.
JUANITA SECHRIST DISAPPEARED SAME TIME.
BILL SECHRIST DISAPPEARED (?) 3 YEARS LATER.
TRIX-LYNETTE WENT OUT OF DUANE'S LIFE.

Reviewing that list, I saw that everything depended on the first fact, that Trix Hawley was alive. How could I be sure of that? Well, I was sure, but I forced myself to admit she could in fact have died in the fire and Bill Sechrist had told the truth to his son: that Juanita Sechrist really did run off, crazily or not. I forced myself to admit that Bill Sechrist would have just naturally found himself attracted to a supernaturally Trix-like person.

KEY #1," I wrote, "FIND TRIX.

I drank my coffee and munched my toast and thought about the rest of it. If Bill Sechrist and Trix Hawley wanted to run away together, why not just run away together? Why kill Juanita Sechrist first? Maybe the body in the bar wasn't Juanita's. If not, whose and why? Why fake Trix's death? And why do it all at the Polka Dot? Were my parents and I supposed to be killed too, or did something go wrong? If we were supposed to die, why? Did Bill Sechrist and Trix have something against us?

I thought about the Sechrists, remembering everything I could about them.

Bill Sechrist and my father, Martin Byrd, had been navy buddies in the Korean War. They were as close as buddies could get: Bill Sechrist had saved my dad's life when a torpedo hit their ship.

"We were belowdecks scrubbing pans in the galley," my dad told me, "when there was this *WHAM!* and the next thing I knew I was up to my neck in seawater. Bill yelled *Come on!* and I knew we'd be sealed off any second, all the galleys were flooding, the

*Lucky Stiff*

torpedo had hit just aft of them. I couldn't move. My belt had caught on something. Bill swam over to me, cussing the whole way, and he took hold of me and *ripped* me loose. My belt just broke. We got out of there just in time. I had a bruise halfway around my waist for a month."

The story, which I asked to hear over and over, never failed to stir me. As I grew older, questions occurred to me.

"Were any other sailors killed?"

"A few guys." My dad would answer patiently and vaguely.

"How many?"

"Three, I think."

"How did they die?"

"I don't know."

"Did they drown or get killed from the torpedo?"

"I don't know."

"Did they find their bodies?"

"I don't remember."

"How did your belt get stuck?"

"I don't know. The ship lurched when the torpedo hit, we all got knocked off our feet into the shelves and everything. That's when I got stuck."

"Did you ever save his life back?"

"Never had the chance. Next time you get to crying about something or other, you just remember Bill Sechrist. And be glad. Because without him, you wouldn't be here, because *I* wouldn't be here."

"Would Mommy have married somebody else?"

"I don't know. Probably not."

"But if she did, they would've had me."

"Nah, you'd be half you and half some other kid. See? Because half of you's from your mom and half of you's from your dad."

That was unsettling, and I didn't like to think about it.

It was a coincidence that Daddy and Bill Sechrist were both from Detroit. After the war they returned to their wives and got jobs in factories.

Evidently the work didn't suit my father, because a year before I came along my parents decided to try the tavern business, and the Polka Dot was born. In a way I was their second child.

Even though we lived just two streets over from the Sechrists, my mom and dad and Bill and Juanita Sechrist didn't socialize as couples. Juanita Sechrist was a nice mom, plump and pretty, but you know she rarely left the house. It was just this thing everybody took for granted, this oddity. She didn't drive, didn't go to the grocery store. Once in a while she would force herself out to church, for confession and Mass. I once saw her exit the confessional just before I went in and wondered what she'd had to confess. I couldn't imagine. Did she, like me, fabricate sins to satisfy the requirement of confession?

Bill Sechrist came around to the Polka Dot often, after work. He was a foreman at Dodge Main in Hamtramck, day shift. So I remember him coming in as I was doing my homework and listening to Peggy Lee on the jukebox.

Sechrist was fanatically proud of having served in the U.S. Navy. Even though you're not supposed to, he pinned his most important campaign ribbons on the breast of his ordinary poplin jacket, and he wore his dog tags on a chain under his shirt. He left the top buttons of his shirts undone so that the tags could be seen and remarked upon. When he leaned over the bar or a table, the tags spilled out and dangled there interestingly.

"I want dog tags," I told my father once.

"No, you don't," he said.

How long had Sechrist and Trix known each other? I remembered them always being around the bar. They talked and laughed with my dad. I never noticed them acting like lovers, holding hands or kissing. Sometimes Sechrist would sing along to a stupid song on the jukebox: "The Hokey Pokey," "Too Fat Polka." And sometimes he'd sing slow songs with fake pain in his voice, "Goodnight, darling, I'll love you till you die…" His voice actually wasn't bad.

So Sechrist had a recluse for a wife and a pert girlfriend in the neighborhood gin mill.

I wrote "Insurance money?" then crossed it out, because he killed his wife secretly; he didn't want her death to be known. There couldn't have been any financial gain in it for him, because as Duane described it, life in Florida was far from deluxe.

And then, three years after going to all that trouble of liquidating his wife and life in Detroit and settling down in Florida with his sharp-tongued inamorata, Sechrist disappears. He takes off, or walks in front of a bus without identification on him, or gets abducted by spacemen. He dissolves. And Duane becomes a de facto orphan.

After the fire, as I've said, Uncle Guff and Aunt Rosalie protected me from the news coverage. Suddenly I found that strange. They'd made sure I didn't see any newspapers or listen to the radio or television in the week or so after the fire. At the time it didn't even occur to me that there would be news coverage of the fire. Later I wondered about it, but my characteristically morbid curiosity stopped there. My parents were dead, nothing could bring them back, I had been there, and I didn't care to know how the world had heard it. Then, having worked as a newspaper reporter for a while, I learned what a miserable muddle most reporters make of news. After that, I *really* didn't care.

But now I did. I picked up the phone.

"Uncle Guff, hi. Lillian here. How are you?"

"Fine, you?"

"Good, real good. How's Aunt Rosalie?"

"Good." His voice always sounded as if its edges had been softly scoured. "Gonna take her to the eye doctor in a few minutes."

"On Saturday? Anything wrong?"

"Just a checkup. They got weekend hours over there."

"OK, I'll take just a sec. Listen, I'm going to ask you about a long time ago." With older people it's best if you get them started shifting mental gears early in the conversation.

"Yeah?"

"It's about Mom and Dad. OK? Do you have any clippings from when they died? Did you keep any stuff like that?"

I heard him clear his throat. "No."

Generally, he was a man of few words.

"Oh. Well, then, do you have anything from the fire department?"

I heard him inhale through his nose, then exhale. "Why would I have anything from the fire department?" It was clear I had absolutely freaked him out. We had never, ever talked directly about these things.

"Well," I said, "I mean, like, they investigated the fire, right? They figured out what caused it. They always have to do that." I waited. "Right?"

Pause. "Right."

"Well, I mean, maybe there was a report of some kind, and I don't know, I thought maybe you'd have a copy of it."

"It was the fryer."

"The deep-fryer overheated or something, right?"

"Yeah."

"Well, I guess it's the 'or something' part that I'm interested in. You're probably wondering what I'm—"

*Lucky Stiff*

"I have to take your aunt to the eye doctor."

"OK, well, it's just that I bumped into Duane Sechrist, this kid I used to know in the neighborhood, and we were talking about old times, good and bad, you know, and I realized that I hadn't ever seen anything about the fire, never read Mom's and Dad's death notices, you know, and I thought I'd like to take a look at all that stuff. Now that it's been over for so long."

He said nothing.

I plunged on, "And I'm wondering about Daddy and Duane's dad, remember Bill Sechrist?—who was Dad's navy buddy? The guy that saved his life in the navy?"

"No."

"Uh," I said, "you never knew the Sechrists, never met them?"

"No."

"I thought maybe you would've met them. Bill Sechrist, anyway. His wife stayed home a lot. I thought you might've met him around the bar, you know. But you knew about Bill Sechrist saving Daddy's life, right?"

"I never knew that guy."

"Gee, I'm surprised."

Silence.

"Well, OK, Uncle Guff, I gotta run along too. Want to do early-bird bowling again Tuesday?"

"Yeah."

"OK, I'll call you."

"OK."

The mighty Detroit Public Library had helped me out many times in the past. I went over there with my notebook.

Detroit was a two-newspaper town in those days, two real newspapers, the evening *Detroit News* and the morning *Detroit*

*Free Press.* Then times got tough and somebody invented joint operating agreements and everybody felt cheated.

I requested the microfilm reels from both papers for two weeks starting from the day after the fire. At the viewer I ran up the headline in the *News*:

FIRE GUTS BAR, THREE DEAD

The story was on the front page, and there was a photo alongside.

*Fire swept through the Polka Dot Bar at the corner of Casimir and Mulhouse Sts. in the city's Delray neighborhood last night, killing husband-and-wife owners Martin James Byrd and Sophie Marie Byrd. A third victim is presumed to be a female employee.*

*"It was a triple tragedy," said Capt. Dennis Purtzer of the DFD. The blaze began on the ground floor of the 2-story building, according to Capt. Purtzer. Investigators were working to determine the cause, he added.*

*The Byrds' 12-year-old daughter, Lillian Woodruff Byrd, asleep in the family's apartment above the bar, was rescued by firemen. Her parents' bodies were found near the door to her bedroom.*

*"It looked like they were trying to reach her when they were overcome by smoke," said Capt. Purtzer.*

My heart flipped and clenched. Tears flooded my eyes. I took out a handkerchief and bawled quietly. (Now you know my middle name, which is Uncle Guff's real name. His baby brother couldn't pronounce Woodruff, so he was stuck with Guff forever. At least they didn't name me Lillian Guff Byrd.) After a few minutes I read some more.

*Lucky Stiff*

*A third body recovered by firemen was burned beyond recognition. Bystanders suggested the third victim was a barmaid who had worked at the Polka Dot for years. Efforts to identify the victim were to continue today.*

*"It went up just like that," said Hiram Bowers, an eyewitness. "I looked out my living room window and I saw a flicker over there. By the time I realized the place was on fire, it was too late."*

*He attempted to enter the building, he said, but was pushed back by the heat. "It's a real shame," he said. "They were the nicest people you could know. They're in God's hands now."*

The photograph showed the building in flames, a dramatic night-fire photo. I studied it. It had been taken from the viewpoint of the rear alley. The windows of the bar glowed white, and flames shot upward from them into the black sky. The flames lit up the back alley. There was smoke, but it didn't really show up in the picture except as black spaces above the flames.

There was nothing in the photo to suggest the fire department had gotten there yet. The first truck would have pulled up to the front of the building. If the DFD hadn't arrived, this photo had been taken very soon after the fire got going. I recognized our garbage cans. It gave me a peculiar twinge to look at the photo, knowing my parents and I were still inside at that point.

There was a car parked down the alley, its rear end just visible in the fire's glow. It was a light-colored Dodge and it had a large dark spot on the trunk. The credit line read, *"Photo by Earl C. Raymer. Special to the News."*

"Oh, no way," I muttered. I strained to see the photo better. Did the dark spot on the trunk resemble Lyndon Johnson? The image was unclear. My magnifying glass didn't help.

When you think about it, it's amazing that the microfilmed photographs were legible at all. First the negative was exposed and developed, then a print was made from it. Then the print was shot through a screen so that it could be reproduced by a million tiny dots on the newsprint. A plate was made of the whole newspaper page, then the newspaper was printed. Then a copy of it was photographed in miniature in the microfilm process, and I was viewing an enlarged projection of the copy on a ground-glass screen. When I thought about all that, I marveled that I could make out anything.

If that was Bill Sechrist's car, that placed him at the scene of the crime. Trix or no Trix.

There was nothing in the *Free Press* that day, the paper having gone to press before the time of the fire. But the next day there was a story, also on the front page. It confirmed Trix Hawley as the third victim and featured two photographs. One was of the front of the bar with streams of water gushing; the other was taken from the alley, about the same vantage point as the photo in the *News*. It showed a fireman hauling a narrow bundle over his shoulder, descending a ladder, and it revealed the darkness of the alley. The car was gone. The bundle over the fireman's shoulder, of course, was me.

I remembered the upside-down sensation of being carried. I remembered the roughness of the fireman's coat. I remembered trying to grab something. I remembered being set on the ground. The fireman's face was not visible in the picture.

"Thank you," I whispered.

# SIX

Suddenly I had a lot to do. I printed out the articles and death notices and jotted a few things into my notebook for handy reference. I noted Trix's full name, Patricia Lynn Hawley, as well as her husband's name, Robert N. Hawley, as well as the name of the photographer who took the shot of the Dodge in the alley. I wrote down a couple of questions for Duane and some more for Uncle Guff.

I wanted to get into some archives that wouldn't be open until Monday, so I fired up the old Caprice for a ride. I drove all the way downtown, then drifted through the streets on a southerly course.

It's funny how a car will either fit into a neighborhood or stick out in a neighborhood. My 1985 Caprice, in conservative evergreen, used to be a police car, an unmarked car for plainclothes detectives. I kept it clean and running, but barely. It continually needed spare parts; rust was encroaching into the body panels from the wheel wells. Although I'd never made use of the shotgun brackets in the trunk, the car's history made me feel tough and proud. Many a cop butt had beaten down the upholstery, many a cigarette had been squashed in the ashtray, many a pizza crust had been tossed out the windows. Many a sigh had been heaved in that backseat.

For a few years after I drove my car away from the auction block, it looked like the vehicle of an old person who liked it and was too cheap or broke to buy a new one. After a few more years, with the Caprice model changing drastically in appearance, my car looked older still—verging on vintage, owned perhaps by an enthusiast. It looked like an aficionado's car—a Chevy buff who was hanging tight onto this one, with a plan to customize it into a lowrider and then drive it to Los Angeles and sell it for a fortune to some gang dude.

Now, I had to admit, it looked like a ghetto car. The car of an impoverished person trying to keep up appearances. The rust was not fixed, the body not Bondoed and repainted. But I hadn't let things totally go. The backseat was not piled with trash, the roof never played host to bird droppings for long, the wipers and taillights worked.

If my pride in the Caprice were to diminish, however, it would descend to the last rung of used cars—the outcasts, the hulks condemned by neglect to the category of true eyesore. Rust and bad dirt—tree sap, bug guts, tar—would engulf it. It would stop running of its own accord, humiliated into flatlining.

Well, I was talking about cars belonging in neighborhoods or not. The Caprice had long been a misfit in Detroit's swanky northern suburbs, and had recently experienced snubbing in my humble zone of Eagle. But in the neighborhood of the Polka Dot, the car would have fit in when new, and it fit in now.

I cruised slowly down Casimir Street. I hadn't been down it in years. No need; it wasn't on the way anywhere. As a grown-up I'd driven by the site of the Polka Dot once or twice during periods of depression, topped off by a trip to the cemetery.

I pulled over and got out about a block away from our old corner. I locked the Caprice and walked. The day was bright and warm, the air still. Such weather in, for example, a forest, makes the forest especially lovely, but no weather could make that neighborhood lovely. The sunlight fell on the scene like a harsh wash. In the absence of a breeze the air smelled stale.

*Lucky Stiff*

The concrete was egg-carton gray, the buildings worn and morose. A few peeling wood-frame houses sagged behind weeds and broken fences. Sparrows scratched listlessly among the weeds. The masonry facades of the commercial buildings were eroded, their windows filthy or painted over or broken out. The stench of urine wafted from a doorway. I glanced in and saw a pile of liquor bottles and trash. Illegible, joyless graffiti marred the door itself.

A scraggly old dude perched on a thin metal window edge, arms folded, head bowed. The former baby clothes store was now a liquor store. A turbaned Sikh smoked a cigarette in the dimness of that doorway.

I haven't mentioned that the Polka Dot was razed after the fire. The building next to it, an apartment low-rise, had been saved. For a long time the small footprint of the Polka Dot's lot was unoccupied; it had been junk-strewn and vacant the last time I visited.

Today, though, I saw that some advantage was being taken of that plot: a taco truck was parked there, broadside to the street, awning out, freehand sign propped. TACOS GOOD FOOD. A tempting smell came from it.

"Hi there," I said to the proprietor.

He tipped his chin toward me in a friendly way. He wore a Detroit Red Wings cap and an oversize Western shirt with snaps.

"Two tacos, please," I said, reaching into my pocket.

"For drink?" His hands were large and already busy making the food.

"Oh. Coke. You got Coke?"

He nodded. "Coke."

I handed him the money and he handed me the food and a paper napkin.

53

I sat at a folding table beneath the awning and ate. Looking up, I noticed something I hadn't ever before. It was something about the sycamore tree that had shaded the Polka Dot's front windows. A soft black scar ran up the trunk and disappeared into the summer branches. I realized that it was a scorch mark, an old mark. That fire had burned hot.

I pictured myself telling the taco man, "I used to live here." Since I had just bought something, he would give me a polite look.

With more intensity, I would say, "Here, right here on this spot."

He would nod and say, perhaps, "Yeah."

Then I would look at the dirt and weeds and feel lonelier than I already did.

On Monday morning I drove over to *The Detroit News* offices, went in through the main lobby, and asked to see someone in the research department. A pleasant manchild with a flurry of purple hair came down and escorted me up to his domain. As the elevator compressed our spines, he assured me the archives would cough up what I wanted. His name was Burt.

"Yeah," I said, "but the credit line says 'So-and-so, special to the *News*.' It wasn't a staff photographer."

"Mm, in that case we probably don't have the negative. We might, but probably not. We'll have the print, one print, I bet. Let's see."

In a few minutes I was holding a black-and-white 8-by-10 of the shot down the alley. The picture was good and sharp. Even without my magnifier I could tell the car was the Sechrist-mobile. There was the gangrenous patch of rust on the trunk lid, shaped exactly like LBJ's profile: the high wrinkled forehead, the long mournful nose, the knoblike chin.

I let out a long sigh. "That's the car," I said aloud. "I can't believe it."

Burt stood by, attracted by my intensity. "What's it all about?" he said.

"Oh, just... I was involved in a... Oh, Christ. In a long story that's getting longer by the minute." I studied the picture some more. To my dismay, the license plate was obscured by the top of one of the garbage cans in the foreground. There was no way to know whether the depth of field would've allowed the plate to be legible anyway. The car was in focus, but not perfectly. The photographer had focused on the middle of the flaming building; the oblique angle of the shot permitted most of the scene to be in focus. It was a good news picture.

"Do you have the negatives?" I asked.

Burt shook his purple pelt. "Just that shot."

"How 'bout a contact sheet?"

"Let me check for sure."

He returned with a wide file envelope and shook out its contents on a table: the other photography for that day's issue. We sorted through it.

"Nope," he said.

"I see." I drummed my fingers. "So if I want to see this guy's other shots from that night, I have to find him, right?"

"Right."

"Burt, do you recognize the name? Earl C. Raymer? Like, did he do a lot of photography for the paper back then?"

"You know, that name does sound familiar. He probably did some other work for us."

Freelance photographers, like news stringers, crawl around the city, looking and listening. When they come across breaking news, they're on it like black on coal. Earl C. Raymer was probably the first journalist to the scene, having noticed flames leaping into the sky over the treetops as he drove along the nearby artery of Fort Street. He spun his car down side streets, slammed on his brakes, ran around to the trunk, and grabbed his camera.

He would have quickly moved all around the scene—all around the building—shooting a few rolls of Tri-X, working for the most dramatic angle he could get. He would have used a tripod because he would have wanted to make long exposures in the dark night: a half second, maybe even a whole second or two. He would have made the same shot with different exposures. He might have added a flash to fill in some detail. Very possibly he snapped a shot that showed the Dodge's license plate. Did he hear my mother screaming?

That night was good luck for him: The fire produced fatalities, so the story and photos ran prominently.

I went home and called Duane.

"I'm working on this, buddy," I told him. "Listen, I'm trying to remember something about our conversation the other night. Didn't you tell me that your mom and dad were supposed to go on a vacation for a week in the U.P. after they dropped you off at camp?"

"Yeah, they did. I've been thinking about that too—like, maybe my dad used that time away from home in his plot against my mom somehow."

"Do you know exactly where they were supposed to go?"

"My dad said they were going up to see the Soo Locks. I do remember my mom looking uncomfortable at the thought of being so far from home for that long."

"Did they have luggage in the car?"

"I guess so. I guess they must have...*yeah*. I remember this brown suitcase of my mom's. Yeah."

*Lucky Stiff*

"OK, now Duane, I want you to think about your mom. Her habits. Did she like downers? Did she take them sometimes?"

He blew out his breath.

"Duane, are you with me?"

"Yeah. I'm thinking. She did take pills."

"It strikes me that she was exactly the kind of woman with exactly the kind of problems doctors used to give tranks to."

"I know she took Librium. I remember her saying it by name."

"Her doctor, her gynecologist, probably—did he prescribe it to her?"

"Yeah, he must've. I remember her pill bottles."

"Yeah," I said. "Yeah. How much did she drink?"

"Where are you going with this, Lillian?"

"Come on, Duane. Your mom was taken advantage of somehow. I know some cops, you know. I'm friends with some cops, and I'm doing what they'd be doing: asking every question I can think of."

I waited.

At length he said, "Well, she did drink during the day a little bit. Sometimes. Not every day, though."

"Did she drink with your dad at night? Did they used to get drunk together?"

"I guess... I guess they did. I hauled out empties with the trash most weeks."

"OK, thanks, Duane. I've got a lot more to find out, so—"

"She wasn't an alcoholic, though."

"Oh, for—" I caught myself and said, "No, probably not."

"She took good care of me."

"She sure did. She was a good mom."

"She was the *best*."

I hung up and started to dial Uncle Guff's number, then

decided I'd talk to him at bowling tomorrow night. I thought about Earl C. Raymer.

Detroit is the kind of town where people tend to stay put, for the sake of familiarity, comfort, or economics. I got out my Detroit white pages. Earl C. Raymer was listed. I made a note of the number and address, and took off again. The address was on a pretty block on the north side of town, Stratford Street. Tall shade trees arched their boughs over the pavement. The house was a half-brick Tudor with peeling trim and a shaggy front yard.

I rang and stepped back hopefully. An elderly white woman came to the door and allowed me to speak to her through the chain latch.

"Good afternoon, is this the Raymer residence?"

She gave me a lovely smile. "Yes, it is!"

I introduced myself and explained what was on my mind. She let me in and showed me to a seat in the living room.

Mrs. Raymer was built like my landlady Mrs. McVittie, straight up in one column from the ground. "Can't be too careful these days," she said.

"You said it."

"Honey, would you like a glass of milk?"

"No, but thank you very much."

She lowered herself into a vinyl recliner. "Earl's not here," she said.

"Oh."

The walls were packed solid with framed blowups of photographs by Earl C. Raymer. There was an enormous shot of the Polish-American mayor Roman Gribbs with his arm around TV anchorman Bill Bonds at a swanky party. There was a picture of a pissed-off-looking Frank Sinatra emerging from the Roma Cafe. There was a shot of Al Kaline signing baseballs for a bunch of kids in wheelchairs. There was a picture of a burning building, not the Polka Dot, the foreground strewn with rocks and bottles, a looter lugging an armload of clothes past the flames. Twelfth Street, 1969.

I said, "These are marvelous pictures. Is Mr. Raymer... Did he go out or something?"

His wife smiled brightly. "I'm really not sure. I think so. Yes!"

"Does Mr. Raymer have his old negatives, do you think? From his photography?"

"Oh, yes. He keeps everything!" She laughed. "For years and years now, oh, he's got heaps of stuff."

"Well, I wonder if I might, uh, do you think I could take a look through the stuff? Is it well-organized?"

"Oh, it's all in boxes and boxes, everything's marked, he's been doing this for *years,* you know! Years and years! It's all down there."

"Down the basement?"

"Mm-hmm."

"I know it's asking a lot, but it's very important to me that I try to find film he shot the night my parents died in a fire."

"Oh, I'm sorry! I'm so sorry to hear that. Oh, my."

I waited.

Mrs. Raymer smiled and said, "Honey, would you like a glass of milk?"

"Ah, no, thank you, Mrs. Raymer."

She folded her hands and smiled at me so pleasantly.

I noticed stacks of mail layered on a buffet along the wall. Casually I got up and looked them over. I saw an envelope from a hospice affiliated with Henry Ford Hospital, an envelope from Medicare, and another one from the hospice, among junk mail.

"Is Mr. Raymer in a hospice?" I asked, turning to her.

Her chin quivered. "I don't think so. I'm not really sure. No."

"Do you have children, Mrs. Raymer?"

Her eyes brightened, then dimmed. "No, definitely not. I don't think so."

"Mrs. Raymer, I'll be right back, OK?"

I walked through the kitchen, found the door to the basement, flipped the light switch, and went down to confront the archives of Earl C. Raymer.

The smell was very musty. Old mold, that constrictive smell. I was surprised to find only a ping-pong table and two metal shelving units filled with canned goods. My sneakers squeaked on the concrete floor. I saw a crap-colored water line on the cinder-block walls, an ugly boundary about a foot from the floor.

I returned to Mrs. Raymer, who was watching two robins perched in shrubbery outside the living room window.

I said, "Was there a flood? Did your basement get flooded?"

She smiled, glad to see me. "I don't think so. No, no. We never had a flood—so far, anyway. Knock on wood!" She reached out to rap the coffee table.

"All right, well, thank you very much, Mrs. Raymer. I'm going now."

She followed me to the door. As I closed it behind me I said, "Lock the door now, Mrs. Raymer. OK?" I heard the chain latch slide into place.

One of the next-door houses had a car in the driveway. I rang there and spoke with a young Hispanic man holding a baby on his hip. He told me the Raymers' daughter stops by twice a week. "I try to look in on her the other days," he said. "Is she all right?"

He confirmed that Earl was in the hospice, with terminal cancer.

"This is a funny question," I said, "but have you all had some basement flooding? From heavy rains, maybe those storms last year?"

"Yeah, that's when it was," he said. "Six houses on this block had raw sewage come up knee-high."

"Next door?"

"Yeah. Earl had to hire a truck to haul away all his stuff that got ruined. I felt awful for him. His photography materials. Tons of stuff—pictures and film and everything. He stood there and cried."

# SEVEN

The next day's dawn was a gray one. Drinking my coffee, I stood at the window and watched a soft drizzle fall into the grass of the McVitties' backyard. My windows were open, and I breathed in that gradual freshness such a rain brings. Hardly a breeze stirred it. It was a soothing rain. I smiled and called Uncle Guff.

From him I learned that Aunt Rosalie's eye doctor had pronounced her cataracts to be somewhat worse. She would probably need surgery in a few years.

"Oh, that's too bad," I said. "Well, I guess they've got that surgery down to a science these days."

Uncle Guff agreed. "It's like an assembly line, those places. Easier'n getting a tooth out."

I heard Aunt Rosalie yell, "Yeah, but it's still my *eyes!*"

"So, Uncle Guff, you still want to do early-bird bowling?"

"Well…." he said in his tone of equivocation, which was as if he were about to sing.

I prompted, "If this weather keeps up…"

"Yeah," he said. "Yeah…"

"We could go fishing instead."

"Maybe we better."

"I think we better."

Uncle Guff loved to fish in the rain. Not *rain* rain, not a downpour, but drizzle, soft lukewarm summer drizzle just like this. It was his belief that the fish bit better in such weather, although neither of us had ever conducted a controlled study on it. It didn't matter to me; I liked to fish, and I liked to fish in the company of Uncle Guff. The good part was, Aunt Rosalie would never come along in the rain. She warned that we'd be struck and killed by lightning. For years I'd argued with her, pointing out the difference between a thunderstorm—a real storm that produced lightning—and gentle, long-term, soaking, nourishing drizzle, to no avail. Finally I took a cue from my uncle, who merely ignored her and took off in his hat and slicker. It wasn't that he didn't want her to come; he enjoyed his wife, he just didn't want to spend that much energy combating her notions.

Besides, we played it safe: only shore fishing in the rain. Uncle Guff had a sixteen-foot Grumman open boat with a twenty-five-horse Johnson outboard on it, and we went all over the river in it. But we never took it out in really bad weather.

I picked him up in the Caprice and we swung over to Pap's Bait & Tackle for worms, potato chips, and Cokes. Then we went over to the old chemical works, a sprawling abandoned factory in one of the great riverside brownfields. I parked next to the rotting guard shack and we carried our stuff—tackle boxes, poles, folding stools, buckets, food bag—through a gap in the fence. Nobody was around, nobody cared.

The factory had a burly freighter dock that jutted fifty feet out into the river. It was the best fishing pier around, we felt, and we had it all to ourselves.

We got ourselves set up in a few minutes. Our standard bait-casting rigs comprised a sinker and a long leader with two short leaders coming off of it horizontally, on swivels. The hooks, when the rig was settled in the river, were positioned one and two feet off the bottom. This rig worked great for us.

I pinched a fat nightcrawler in two and threaded the halves

onto my hooks. Uncle Guff lowered a bucket on a rope the twelve feet or so to the water, let it fill, and hauled it up. This was our hand-washing water. Setting my rig down, I rinsed the worm guts from my fingers. Then I rared back with my pole and cast out my rig. It whistled out and splashed in. I gave the sinker time to touch bottom, then reeled the of slack. We used Japanese rods and reels from Kmart and five-pound-test monofilament.

The corroding walls of the factory loomed behind us. This setting was not a bucolic one. Belle Isle, for instance, was bucolic. Bishop Park in Wyandotte was a bucolic place to fish from. Sometimes we fished those places. But there was something about the chemical works dock that gave us special pleasure. Maybe there was a bit of perverseness in us, or maybe it was the feeling we got moving around on the thick weathered planks. The worn wood, the creosote, the gargantuan pilings beneath us: the architecture of industry now serving a sporting purpose.

Our view swept from the fuzzy green line of the Canadian waterfront to the other factories, mills, docks, and marinas up and down both shorelines. The big boats and the little boats of the Great Lakes, they all had to pass through the Detroit River, which is essentially a strait between lakes Erie and St. Clair. It's a mighty, wide waterway. All of Henry Ford's iron ore floated on the Detroit River. All the latex from those rubber plantations. All the coal for the furnaces of Detroit. The drizzle dissolving into the surface of the water created an even, delicate carpet. Our lines disappeared in a blur. I thought about the fish swimming below and licked my lips at the prospect of a fried perch or walleye dinner. An American freighter from Duluth slipped slowly past us, going downstream. There were no small boats out today.

*Lucky Stiff*

Uncle Guff resembled my father but not uncannily so. Their physiques were wiry and agile, but my father's face was rounder, Uncle Guff's squarer, especially in the mouth and jaw. Their noses were the same—slightly beaked, narrowing at the tip, like their father's, whose likeness I had studied often in an ancestral album. Although Uncle Guff hadn't been a serviceman in wartime (punctured eardrum from childhood), and although his demeanor was quiet, I thought he was the fiercer of the two. It was the eyes, his blue eyes there behind the lenses of his bifocals. Someone who knew him less well might describe his gaze as hard. But that wasn't it. Uncle Guff was not pitiless; his temper was long. He was, perhaps, more willing to see the world for what it was. My father, in creating the Polka Dot, built a place where people could pretend that the world was more comfortable than it was. My father had served in a war, but aside from the torpedo attack, he hadn't seen combat. Uncle Guff worked in a steel mill all his life, among fire and heat and dirt and danger, among brutish machines and tough workers. He turned crumbly elements into hard, useful stuff.

The older I get, the more I understand that if you're going to view the world honestly, you must adopt a measure of fierceness.

I handed him a can of Coke and opened one for myself. I was wearing my commando-green poncho and my Vietnam hat, shorts, and my Chuck Taylor basketball sneakers. My sneakers would get wet through, but it didn't matter. Uncle Guff sighed and settled his thighs into his camp stool. Water dripped from his broad-brimmed oilcloth hat onto his yellow slicker.

"Boy, I wonder how many times we've gone fishing together."
"Hmm," he said.
"Hundreds, I guess."
"Yep."

" 'Member when you used to tell me what was in the ships? *That one's full of coal. That one's full of postholes.* 'Member?"

"Yep."

If you knew what to look for, you really could tell what the ships were carrying. Low in the water with heaps on deck, it was coal. Low in the water with no heaps, iron ore. High in the water, empty. Postholes.

I sipped my Coke and set it on a plank. "Um, Uncle Guff..."

He wasn't the type to say a prompting "Yeah?" He just waited, his forefinger curled beneath his line just ahead of his reel.

I began again, "So, you know, I was sort of asking you about Dad and Mom? I was thinking about the old days. And I was wondering, you know, about the...the aftermath of everything. Well, I guess, first of all—did Mom and Daddy have life insurance?"

"They did," answered my uncle. "They had Mutual of Omaha."

Instantly my mind's eye beheld the shield of the Mutual of Omaha company, my mind's ear heard Marlin Perkins's voice announcing, "Mutual of Omaha presents...*Wild Kingdom!*" Maybe you remember that program. It was a marvelous show, with senior naturalist Marlin Perkins and his hunky sidekick Jim Fowler venturing into the darkest jungles, the hottest deserts, the remotest islands, to discover and show us American kids the secrets of nature. Who could ever forget Jim's wrestling match with an anaconda? Or the way Marlin's voice would crack with tension as he described an encounter with a cranky beast on some isolated veldt?

"OK," I said, turning off my TV memory machine, "and that money would have paid for their funerals, and my upbringing, right?"

Pause. "Some, it did."

*Lucky Stiff*

"Of course, you and Aunt Rosalie covered the rest."

He said nothing.

I asked, "Was there an insurance policy on the bar itself? The business and the building?"

Another pause, a long one. "Yeah."

"Did Daddy and Mom own the building, then?"

"Well, there was a mortgage on it."

"Oh. Like, did they have a lot of equity in it by that time? A significant amount?"

The tip of my rod quivered, and I felt the nervous, darting nibbling of a fish. I waited as the nibbling grew stronger, tuggier, then set the hook—or hooks, as the case may be—with a firm jerk. I cranked my reel. I brought up one yellow perch on my upper hook, keeper-size for that sweet species of panfish, about nine inches long. I grasped it, flattening the spines of its dorsal fin safely against my palm, and peered into its white mouth. I freed the hook and dropped the fish into the second bucket Uncle Guff had half filled with the cold river water. It swam around and around, its golden-green sides slipping along the bucket's wall. The bait on my other hook had been robbed off, possibly by the same fish.

I baited my hooks again, rinsed my hands, and cast out my rig. Just as I did so, Uncle Guff got a strike and pulled up two perch, one a keeper. The too-small one he removed from the hook with wet hands and threw back. The healthy, mulchy smell of the river saturated the air all around us.

After he'd rebaited and cast, he said, "The insurance didn't amount to much."

"How much was it for?"

"You know, Lillian, it was so long ago I don't remember."

"Hmm."

"There was no significance to it."

"Uncle Guff, I want to tell you about something. Remember I told you I bumped into this guy, Duane Sechrist? Who used to live in our neighborhood, and his dad knew Daddy, and saved his life in Korea?"

My uncle sighed.

I went on, "I know this is all in the past. It's a long time ago. It's finished. But can you understand that sometimes people need to—well, dig back? Especially if questions come up, things they didn't used to know about?"

He just waited silently, his eyes on the tip of his rod.

I told him all about Duane's story. I told him about Trix and how it seemed she turned up as Duane's new mom. "She was this barmaid. You've got to remember Trix. Supposedly she died, all burned up, they found her wedding band—do you remember all this? And then, I swear, Uncle Guff, she turned up in Florida as Bill Sechrist's new wife."

"Eh?" he said, the first reaction I'd gotten from him.

"Yeah, so I think there was foul play," I talked on, pouring out my suspicions and fears.

I told him about the Sechrists' Dodge with its Lyndon Johnson rust. I told him about *The Detroit News* archives, and Earl C. Raymer.

"...And I know you said the fire department thought the fryer caught fire by accident," I said. "I'm not saying it didn't. But I called over there and a clerk said she'd look for that arson report. I'm going to call back tomorrow. I just want to look all this stuff over, if only to settle my mind that it really happened the way...the way I always thought it did."

I got another fish on, this one a nasty ugly sheephead, which I threw back.

I went on, "And you and Aunt Rosalie are my only, my *last* links to the past. You know? Did you meet the barmaid's hus-

*Lucky Stiff*

band, this Robert Hawley? Did you and Aunt Rosalie go over to her funeral? I saw in the papers that it was a day after Daddy and Mom's. It seems to me the Sechrists would have gone to Daddy and Mom's funerals. Or come to the funeral home, anyway. I don't remember seeing them, though." I had not been taken to Trix Hawley's funeral. "I was wondering what Trix's husband might've been like."

Uncle Guff pulled up two walleye, which are good eating. This day was turning into rather lovely fishing. The drizzle kept up, easing just a bit as the afternoon commenced. I watched my uncle as closely as I dared. Other than the "Eh?" when I told him about Trix turning up in Florida, he hadn't reacted to anything I said. He was really a tin soldier when I suggested that foul play had been involved in the death of his brother.

Was he freaked into a stunned state, or was he on guard and coolly shutting down, having gone on the defensive as soon as I'd questioned him the other day? Or were his feelings just...not there?

He got up, rainwater cascading from the folds of his slicker, and approached the edge of the pier. There was no railing. We had set up our folding stools and our stuff a safe body-length-and-a-half from the edge. It looked as if he had decided to walk right off into the river. But he stopped, the toes of his battered work shoes even with the edge of the last plank. A sudden gust would have blown him in.

He spoke my name loudly, as if calling me from across the channel.

"Yes," I said from behind him.

He turned quickly and took a step away from the edge. He appeared to be gathering strength for a tremendous task. His hands at his sides were lightly curled as if ready to either grasp or punch.

He came over and sat down, scooting his stool a few inches closer to mine. He cleared his throat. "Umph," he said. He paused. "You know how you made friends with that golfer in California? And then somebody got killed?"

"Yeah, I remember that."

"You were trying to solve a mystery. A mystery to you."

"Yeah."

"And remember the first time when you pretended you were a detective, and you tried to help the police, but then you got shot? Remember that?"

"I do quite well."

"I think you're starting to see everything that way."

He got up again, restlessly. He stood over me and put his hand on my shoulder. I looked up into his strong blue eyes. I saw dread in them. "Lillian," he said, "you're starting to think that this thing is something you should investigate. Like a mystery. Listen to me. *It isn't.*"

# EIGHT

Before I climbed the steps to my flat, I knocked on the McVitties' door and offered them some fish. They owned the house and lived in the lower flat; I paid them rent for the upper. They were good people, although Mr. McVittie got crabby and emotional at times.

They accepted the fish enthusiastically. I'd put eight perch on a stringer for them, enough for a light meal.

"Oh, those look good!" said Mr. McVittie. "Not as big as the ones me and the boys get out of Lake Superior, you know, but—"

"Thank you, dear," Mrs. McVittie chimed. She was a sweet old thing.

"You're welcome."

The first time I'd given them perch, I'd cleaned and filleted them, small as they were. Mr. McVittie ridiculed that, so I gave them their fish whole from then on.

Todd watched me clean the fish I'd kept for myself and fry them with some sliced potatoes. I wrapped the fish guts in newspaper. "If you were a kitty, you'd be singing," I told him. I offered him some bunny chow and ate my dinner on the balcony with a can of Stroh's. These days I couldn't afford Scotch, my beverage of choice. The rain had stopped. It was warm and damp out.

I felt keenly lonely, because usually after fishing—whether we caught anything or not—Uncle Guff and I would go home to his place and eat with Aunt Rosalie.

But I'd felt rebuffed by Uncle Guff, scolded, and unfairly so. His tone had been distinctly edgy. I told him I had to cover a city meeting for a freelance job and took off after we unloaded his stuff.

Those dreadful events of yesteryear were utterly over for him. He'd been a grown-up and had experienced it from a grown-up's perspective, with a grown-up's life experience. I had not.

Obviously, he feared I would make trouble, possibly embarrass myself. Or perhaps he thought I'd make myself unhappy chasing after something that didn't exist. Trying to force a new version of events. Trying to alter the past.

I set aside my hurt feelings and decided I'd put his mind at ease when I saw him next. I had to make him understand I wasn't about to do anything stupid—not deliberately, anyway—and I wasn't about to go chasing after imaginary criminals.

"Only real ones," I muttered to Todd.

I took my newspaper-wrapped bundle of fish by-products out to my garbage can in the alley. The night was soft. Venus, bright and near, hovered above the treetops. I thought about a special friend of mine, and wondered whether I should call on her. I pulled a few raspberry leaves from a patch of canes in the McVitties' backyard and took them up to Todd, who had nosed at his bunny chow indifferently. He loved raspberry leaves.

In the morning I began with the Detroit Fire Department arson investigation office, where I had already inquired about the Polka Dot fire. The clerk told me she'd found the file. The DFD kept routine fire reports for only ten years, I learned, then they purged them. But arson investigations were kept for much longer. If a fire "has a fatal," as the clerk put it, the bodies go to the medical examiner's for autopsy and the fire is investigated for arson as a matter of routine. And those files stay around a long time.

I asked when I might come in and take a look at it.

"Oh," she said. "Please hold."

A Lt. Minetti came on the line. After ascertaining that I wasn't a law enforcement professional, he told me I couldn't just boogie in and look at the file.

"Isn't it public information?" I asked.

"Not exactly," he said.

"But isn't the case closed?"

"Oh, no. New information could come in anytime, on any case. No matter how old."

I tried to persuade him but quickly realized I wasn't going to get anywhere.

I hung up and called Lt. Tom Ciesla of the Eagle Police Department. He and I went back a long way, starting with my last steady job, at the *Eagle Eye* weekly newspaper. We'd lost track of who owed whom how many favors. To be honest, though, mostly I owed him. And it was time to shamelessly ask for one more.

Fortunately, he was in the mood to listen. "Well, it's been awhile, Lillian," he said. "What've you been up to?"

I sketched out the bones, sparing most details for the sake of a compact narrative. He had not before heard how my parents died.

"I'm sorry," he said, when I described it.

"Thanks, Tom. So you see, my quest is a personal one. I had a conversation with someone the other night that makes me think—well, that this case maybe should be made active again."

I practically heard his eyebrows rise. He started to ask a question, but I went on, "It's not even worth me explaining things totally right now, because I think the stuff in the arson report might make me realize, no, this is over, there's nothing to support my suspicions. So essentially, Tom, all I need is a look at that arson investigation file. They'll fax it over to you, you being a cop and all. You could tell them you need it for some, uh, reason, uh…I don't exactly know what you could trump up, but something. Then I could come in and take a look at it, and tell you a little bit more, and hopefully get your advice as to how to proceed."

"That's all, huh?"

"Yep."

He paused. "That's it."

"Right."

"OK."

An hour later I was seated next to him at his desk at the Eagle PD. The other cops had said hi to me nicely, remembering when I used to come in to look through the weekly bust summaries.

"Is Erma around?" I asked Ciesla.

"She's in court today."

Det. Erma Porrocks shared an office with Ciesla. I liked her too, and wondered how she was doing.

"Oh, you know Erma," Ciesla said. "Kicking ass with her size fives."

I laughed. Ciesla was looking spruce: nice sport coat, as always, good oxford cloth shirt, clean tie, polished shoes. He'd grown a black mustache since I saw him last. I looked for any ravels or missing buttons but didn't find any; catching a whiff of fragrant aftershave, I wondered if he'd gotten himself a steady girlfriend.

Before he let me look at the file he said, "The guy I talked to, Minetti, said this report was done by their top investigator in those days. Said he was legendary in figuring out how fires got going. He wondered why I wanted a look at this."

"What'd you tell him?"

"That I had somebody on my back about it, a family connection with a screw loose."

"Oh."

"I said if I tell her I've looked into it, she'll be pacified and will forget about it."

"Have you done much arson work?"

"As a matter of fact, I have. Remember the Smithy Machine Tool fire last year?"

"Yeah."

"Well, two guys owned that company, and they were in financial trouble. One night the place got torched, and the next day each guy accused the other. It was actually rather brilliant for them to do that. I worked with the fire department on it after they determined arson, and eventually we got them. They'd been sloppy with their taxes, so we got the IRS to put pressure on, and to save themselves they each tried to cut a deal whereby they said they witnessed the other one setting the fire. So they both went down for it."

"What a couple of assholes."

"Yeah. I took some courses too. Arson's pretty interesting."

He smoothed the stack of pages on the Polka Dot fire with his hands. "So you want to see this? I looked through it while you were driving over. I'll go over it with you."

"Can I take it with me?"

"No. Take notes."

I got out my notebook and pencil.

Ciesla said, "The report starts with the date and time, the dispatch time was oh three-thirty, arrival at the scene was oh four hundred—you see, it's military time, they got the call at 3:30 in the morning—"

"And they didn't get there until half an hour later?"

"That's the arson investigator, not the engine company. The engine company calls for the investigator."

"Oh. And there was an investigator up in the middle of Saturday night?"

"They work different shifts, you know. As you can see, it says that a preliminary inspection took place after the fire was out, at 5 A.M., then he came back at 7 A.M. for a better look. In full daylight."

Together we looked at the first paragraph, and Ciesla read it aloud. "I observed a two-story brick building, commercial use as a tavern on the first floor, a one-family residence on the second floor. Investigation revealed that fire originated at electric deep-fry unit (see diagram) on ground floor. I observed blackened oily residue in the cooking vat, indicating overheating. The appliance was not fully consumed. Capillary line to the temperature probe was broken. Corrosion on capillary line not observed."

"What's the significance of that?" I asked.

Ciesla made a sound of admiration as he looked sideways at me. "He put that in, that's a bit of inside knowledge, an inside observation. You see, he can't suggest *why* and *how* the capillary line got broken. Corrosion does it sometimes. Every arson investigator knows that. Here he's saying, whatever it was, it wasn't corrosion."

"What could have done it?"

"Those cookers—they're much better made now. They're safer. If you ever saw one of those old ones, you could easily see how overenergetic cleaning, for instance, could've broken that line. Or someone could have just reached in and broken it with their hand or a pliers. Not while it was filled with hot oil, though, of course—it would have to be done beforehand."

*Lucky Stiff*

"How do you know this stuff, Tom?"

"I told you. I worked a lot of arson cases in my early days on the force. Some restaurant fires. This is taking me back. Anyway, that's how that capillary line could've failed."

"And would that have made a short circuit?"

"It would've disabled the thermostat. The cooker would have just stayed on and never shut off, not knowing that the oil was hot enough, thereby heating the oil past its flash point. These days appliances like this are made to fail safe: to shut off if the thermostat breaks."

He handled the pages of the report firmly, grasping them between thumb and forefinger, careful to keep the pages in order. "Here he describes the burn pattern on the wall as being consistent with that point of origin. And here's the clincher: 'No accelerant found.'"

"Accelerant—meaning like gasoline?"

"Yeah. Ninety-nine arsonists out of a hundred use a flammable liquid to spread the fire. This inspector found none."

"Tom, forgive me, but I don't get it. Wouldn't the liquid get burned up? Can they tell stuff from residue? Could they tell so much from so little even back then?"

"An investigator looks for burn patterns consistent with an accelerant. You know how you spill something on the floor and it puddles and runs, and gathers in low places, if any? Arsonists pour their accelerant around to make pathways for the fire. Most people are amazed at how much evidence arsonists leave behind."

"I see."

"He wouldn't have run any lab test of materials from the building because he found nothing suspicious to test. Today's tests are better, of course—they've got quicker and cheaper ways to identify accelerants. OK, now, we see he found no other points of origin. That is consistent with the failure of this electrical appliance. And so here's the key word in his conclusion: '*accidental.*'"

Ciesla turned a page, then hesitated, his hand hovering over the pages. He looked at me closely. "Now, here's the summary of the autopsy reports. Want to go on?"

I nodded.

"OK. 'Postmortem examination concluded that cause of death for all three victims was asphyxiation due to smoke inhalation.' The medical examiner found soot in their windpipes, you see. And the diagrams here, showing where the bodies are found. Here's the fryer."

"One body was burned really badly," I said.

He sorted through the pages. "There are copies of the complete autopsy reports here too. No photos, though. They didn't fax those. Let's see, yes, it's this one… 'Extensive charring… mm…uh…Yeah, this one was on the ground floor. But the medical examiner says cause of death, asphyxiation. She succumbed to the smoke first, then her body burned after she was dead."

I saw from the diagram that the body identified as Trix's had been found draped, or collapsed, across the bar at the end nearest the fryer. "OK," I said, "so are there ever times when somebody is, like, knocked out or something, and their body is placed in a fire?"

"Well," said Ciesla, "they find people who've been shot and then the murderer tries to cover it up with a fire. But there you've got a bullet hole, of course. There have been cases of people being drugged and then burned, but then that would show up on the toxicology report. Which the medical examiner would do if there was anything suspicious about the fire. Otherwise, they more or less do it at their discretion. Let's see. Yes, here. This Patricia Hawley's blood alcohol was one eight.

That's drunk. What's her body weight? The body weighed 122 pounds. She didn't have to drink all that much to get drunk at that body weight."

"What's this?" I said, pointing.

"Other intoxicants...drugs. The ME said she'd ingested two things besides alcohol. He pronounced them carefully: "Propoxyphene hydrochloride—that's Darvon—"

"A painkiller, right?"

"Yes. And chlordiazepoxide. I'm not sure what that is, right off the bat. A CNS depressant, obviously. Uh, central nervous system depressant."

I copied down the word.

"So," I said, "she was strung out?"

"Looks like she was, to some extent. But not to a fatal extent. See, the ME noted the presence of these drugs, but he still says cause of death was asphyxiation."

I looked at him and he said, "Just because she had drugs in her system doesn't mean she'd been drugged by somebody."

"Right, I understand. Could she have been restrained in some way?"

"Well, the autopsy would've showed that—I take that back. *Could've* showed that. If she was tied up, you'd expect there to be marks or residue of the rope or tape."

"But the body was burned up."

"It was burned, but it wasn't anywhere near totally consumed. There were 122 pounds left of her. There might've been some evidence of restraints. Just like the arson investigators, you'd be surprised how much information the ME gets out of corpses."

Of course, I'd watched enough television and read enough Calico Jones books, among others, to know very well that medical examiners are wizards of death.

"And wait," said Ciesla, "let's look at the diagram again. OK, this is a rough sketch, but—look at how her limbs are drawn."

I saw a drawing of a sprawled body, arms flung out, legs apart.

Ciesla went on, "And let's look at the ME's sketches: Yes, here, see, she'd have been in rigor mortis, all stiff, you know. If she'd died with her hands and feet tied together, they'd have stayed that way, whether the rope or whatever burned up. See? But her hands are at her sides, her feet are slightly apart. The way they force them to put the body on a stretcher."

They were only sketches. But just beneath them in that folder, if Ciesla lifted a few pages, were my parents' autopsy reports, with sketches of their bodies, remarks on what their organs were like when they were cut open, and toxicology reports on them. Their blood, their urine. Their stomach contents.

"Excuse me," I muttered, and fled to the corridor. I rushed into the washroom, where I was good and sick, twice.

I washed my face and hands and rinsed my mouth with cold water, then returned to Ciesla's desk.

"I'm sorry," I told him. "I don't think I can look anymore."

"You got pretty green there all of a sudden," he said. "I appreciate that you made it to the bathroom."

"Will you tell me what the toxicology reports say on my parents?"

He sorted through the pages in his firm-handed way. "Um, let's see... Sophie Marie Byrd, negative, everything negative for her... Martin James Byrd, negative except for alcohol. Point oh three. He'd had one beer, maybe. Small amount of alcohol."

"Thank you." I blotted my upper lip with a hankie. "It's hot in here."

He took my wrist. "You feel clammy. Breathe."

"I'm all right. What if I could cast some doubt on these conclusions? What if I could show the fire to have been deliberately set?"

"How?"

"I don't know how yet."

"Well, if you did, we'd be looking at murder. Very old murder."

"What if I showed that Patricia Lynn Hawley was not this victim? That... I mean, that it's somebody else's body in Patricia Lynn Hawley's grave?"

"Can you do that?"

"You're such a cop, you know?" I told him about Trix and her distinctive vocabulary. Meeting up with Duane Sechrist. Duane's missing mother. Bill Sechrist's car's Lyndon Johnson rust. The car in the alley when it was supposed to be 300 miles away. "So, see," I said, "it's very clear that things aren't what they seem." I'd laid it out pretty well.

Ciesla paid careful attention to everything I said. Then he said, "OK, this Sechrist family lived where?"

"Two streets over. Same block, two streets over."

"And this Bill Sechrist hung out at the bar?"

"Yeah."

"So he could've left his car at the bar—parked in the alley, and walked home after drinking at the bar."

"Well, yeah, but see, the car was *moved* during the fire."

"So what?"

"So see, he was at the scene, Tom!"

"So were all your other near neighbors. For example, the guy you said that lived across the alley, well, he was there too, right? He was within fifteen yards of the scene the whole time, right?"

"Well, yeah, but—"

"The fact that any particular individual who habitually was around *was* around that night is not a significant fact."

"But Bill and Juanita Sechrist were supposed to be away, up north, that night. Their son said so. They were in Kalkaska that afternoon. They could've driven back by nighttime."

"Their son said they told him they were going to stay up north?"

"Yeah."

"So they changed their mind."

"OK, OK. But what if—what if we exhume Patricia Lynn Hawley's body and do DNA testing on it, which I guarantee will show that it's...well, not her. I can *almost* guarantee you that it's Duane Sechrist's mom, which could be determined by comparing the body's DNA to a blood sample from Duane."

Ciesla suppressed a smirk. I felt a sudden stab of hatred toward him for that.

He said, "To exhume a body, you need a good reason. Not suspicion. You need the consent of the family. You need a court order. You can't just go over to the cemetery and say 'Let's dig her up.'"

"I know that!"

"There's no way any judge is going to give an order based on evidence like this. Which, I mean, is none. You have no evidence of the existence of this Patricia Hawley. You have no evidence incriminating Bill Sechrist. You have hearsay and speculation. You have nothing. You have a car with a funny spot on it. Where are any of these people? Where is this Patricia Hawley, then? Where is this Bill Sechrist? Go find him and talk to him. Go find your friend's mother. That would end your suspicions, wouldn't it?"

"Oh, Tom."

"Lillian, one of the best arson investigators in Michigan history concluded that this fire was accidental. Three victims. Smoke inhalation. This incident was simply…" He stopped and looked at me with pity. "Very sad."

"Yes," I said softly, "it was."

# NINE

Back in my flat I faced the fact that I needed help. I needed the kind of help cops couldn't give. I sat on the carpet with my notebook and thought. As a journalist and busybody, I'd investigated suspicious things, crimes, gotten involved in police work—interfered in it, truth be told. My success had been spotty. I envied cops their resources. I envied them their authority.

Ciesla and Porrocks and the rest were busy with today's crimes. On TV and in books, you'll see cops who've gotten bitten by the bug of an old unsolved case—or who've carried that old unsolved case around in their heads and hearts from the beginning. They don't sleep well until they get the bad guys. Usually these cases are horrible brutal crimes against attractive, innocent women or children. The cop is haunted. He keeps going. He finds new ground to go over, he revisits old ground—anything to keep his hands on it. He talks to cops in other towns, other states about it. He looks for suspects and fugitives in prisons, on the streets, in slums.

Then something happens: a stroke of luck. He finds a piece of evidence that was overlooked or forgotten. He gets a tip that the bad guy is living in a motel on the outskirts of El Paso under the fake name Mike Stone. Somebody gets busted for selling drugs, and they cut a deal in which they tell where Joe Blow, a.k.a. Mike Stone, said he hid the murder weapon. Then the cops go dig it up, and there's the bloody chain saw with Joe

Blow's prints still on it, having been preserved, nay, *etched* into the metal by the strength of Joe Blow's guilty acidic sweat.

Then the cop gets a plaque, the newspapers go ape, the relatives weep and bake cakes for the cop, they write the cop's kids into their wills for good measure. It's great, just great: a happy ending, all thanks to a tenacious, tough cop who wouldn't quit.

I wished I were a supercop. Better still, I wished I were Calico Jones, with her worldwide network of contacts, her trust fund, her degree from MIT, her biceps and her glutes and her .45 pistol.

I was a spindly, sneaker-wearing dweeb with no money and a crappy car. I was nothing. But I could be tenacious, and I could choose whether to ever quit on this. I needed resources. I needed someone with a good mind, an incisive mind, someone who knew criminals, who knew law enforcement, who overcame tremendous problems every day, who could think up creative ways to attack an investigation, who was calm and cool. Who was rich. And sexy. Why not?

You can see where I'm going with this. I needed Minerva LeBlanc. Yes. You don't need an introduction to her, of course. You've probably seen the movie *Inside Johnny Florida*, based on her best-selling true-crime book, her first book. You've probably seen it more than once, it was so good, everybody's favorite crime movie. Or you've read the book. And you're doubtless aware of her dozen other books, all just as smashing and graceful and philosophically stunning as the first, some of them so awesome in their insights into the mysteries of the human mind that presidents, prime ministers, mobsters, and religious leaders quote from them.

Minerva LeBlanc doesn't just chronicle crimes, she *solves* the fuckers. Where the police stumble into a dry gulch, she steps around and makes rain. She's not supernatural, it must reluctantly be admitted. But…well…you know. I needn't go on and on.

Perhaps you're wondering how she managed to recover from the dreadful disabling attack she suffered during the course of her last research trip. Five years ago now. My God, time gets away.

I knew Minerva LeBlanc. She'd been unlucky enough to be in Detroit investigating the Midnight Five—remember the Midnight Five? Of course you do—when she met up with me for a one-night stand. I too had been drawn into that case. I'd danced and fallen half in love with the last victim—number six—and wanted more than life itself to bring her killers to heel. I wrote about it afterward: the insanity of the perps, the gullibility of their victims. It's common knowledge that the perps attempted to murder Minerva LeBlanc in Detroit. She was found half dead, her head smashed, her brain exposed, the victim of a horrible bludgeoning attack.

What was not widely known was the fact that she was found in my apartment. In my bed. The Detroit media got a piece of it, but her family—her patrician Eastern parents, that is—used their influence to keep much from being made of it. They were ashamed that their daughter had had sex with me before getting sent into the oblivion of a coma that lasted the better part of a year. I knew in my heart that Minerva and I were destined for more than just a one-nighter. But that's all we got.

I'd made contact with her parents after the attack; they'd put her in a special facility back East. I wanted to come and try to wake her up from her coma. But the parents didn't want anything to do with me; they wouldn't tell me where the facility was. I'd resigned myself to never seeing her again, when I saw an item in the paper that said she'd come out of the coma and was beginning to recover.

I journeyed immediately to the New York medical center

mentioned in the paper to find her working with the best doctors and therapists. Her mind and will were so powerful.

She remembered me and agreed to see me. I wept with happiness. She had no memory of the assault that almost killed her, though of course she'd been told about it. She'd read my piece in the *Motor City Journal*.

On that short visit I held her hand and felt the warmth of her, the aliveness of her. She was tentative. She was having bad trouble with her right arm and leg. The doctors hadn't expected the language center in her brain to be damaged, but somehow it had been. Her speech was slow and halting, but she was working on it. We didn't kiss.

I kept up with her, writing letters, sending little things, telephoning once in a while. She was so busy getting well, so busy coming back to life, that she wrote only short notes in response to my lengthy ramblings.

She went back to live in her Manhattan apartment and commenced to read up a storm. Reading would help her language processes, she believed, which she still wasn't satisfied with. Her short-term memory wasn't too good either, she said, although I observed that nobody's short-term memory is very good. She told me she thought she could work again soon, write books again. Over time her language skills improved tremendously. Her intelligence was undamaged. She hadn't the energy for romance. I didn't know whether she had the inclination for it either, and I didn't push it. I sent her books and articles I thought she'd like. I thought about her, fantasized about her, wrote ridiculous poems about her (which I read aloud only to Todd), and tried to fall in love with other people.

And that's where it was now, four years after she opened her eyes. I reached for the phone.

"Damn it," I said to Todd as her voice-mail picked up.

I left a message, then tried to take a nap on my couch. After an hour I got up and looked at the notes I'd made with Ciesla that morning. I put them down and played with Todd. We had a new game, Jump on Monty, which involved a rubber toy dog that squeaked like a rat. The way you play Jump on Monty is you hide the rubber dog behind your back, then you squeak it. Todd comes racing from wherever he is and stops short, looking for Monty. You squeak it once more, then flip it over your shoulder so that it lands in front of Todd. He quickly circles the toy then makes a precise vertical pounce, landing on it, causing it to squeak, of course, which sends him rocketing away in delight. He waits, behind the bathroom door or beneath the couch, aching to hear Monty squeak again.

Most rabbits would be frightened of an object tossed from above, but something about the rubber dog caused only taut ecstasy in Todd. We'd named the toy Monty after Todd's old nemesis, an ill-mannered neighborhood cur whom we hadn't seen around in a while.

After we tired of playing Jump on Monty, I cleaned the bathroom. The tile had grown a little mildew, what with the summer heat and humidity. I scoured it off and sloshed bleach water around. I took down the frosted globe over the lightbulb and washed it in hot water and soap. I cleaned the basins. I found a chip in the enamel of the sink and got out my liquid-fixer for that, put a dab on, and blew on it to dry it. I hung there on the rim of my sink, blowing into it.

The phone rang and I jumped for it.

Minerva's voice sounded thrillingly strong. "Lillian, my friend."

"How goes it, woman?"

"It goes fine. Better and better." I could hear a smile in her

*Lucky Stiff*

voice. She said, "Tell me about it." There was just a very slight hesitation in her speech, not really an impediment, just a little catch.

It seemed that all I'd been doing for days was telling my story to people. I launched into it again. She listened. It took awhile, especially with the addition of the fire investigation report. Every now and then I stopped and asked, "You still with me? You OK?"

She was. Once she answered, "I love to listen to you."

Her combining the words "I," "love," and "you" in one sentence made me gulp. I hoped she didn't hear it. I don't like to expose my hand quite that heedlessly.

"So," I concluded, "I need some advice here. That's what I'm asking you for. I need to prioritize. Should I work on the prove-it-was-arson angle, or the find-Trix angle? Acquiring hard evidence on either one would open up the case for the cops. Or rather, bring the cops into it in the first place. And then, whichever one I pick to concentrate on, what the hell do I do next? How do I go about it?"

I heard her breath coming softly and evenly over the phone line. "Lillian, I'd like you to step back for a minute here."

I waited.

"You need to think about something."

"Yeah?"

"You know that what happened is over, finished. And there's nobody from the past trying to reach into your life."

"Yeah, but—"

"Just listen to me." Her voice slowed a bit. She spoke deliberately. "This one feels pretty deep to me. You need to ask yourself whether you really, in your innermost heart, want to find the answers to your questions."

"Minerva, of course I do. I—"

"I wasn't finished."

"Sorry. I'm sorry."

"I want you to think about it, deep in your heart. You went through hell that night when you were twelve. The rest of your life has been a recovery from that."

I didn't agree, but kept my mouth shut.

She continued, "You might come across some devastating information. *I* find this case fascinating. I'd like to—well, never mind what I'd like, for now. Lillian, what if you find your parents were in fact murdered, or killed unintentionally in a murder cover-up, but you never find out who did it? Will you spend the rest of your life going after it? Will you tear yourself up over it? What if you find out who did it, but then you can't find them? What if the perp or perps are inaccessible to you, to the police, everybody? What if you never find out just *why* those murders were committed, if in fact they're murders? You're not going to get the perps to sit down with you and tell you exactly why. *Exactly why* is something in criminal cases that gets…it's the last thing you ever find out. Criminals go to their graves rationalizing their acts. You're not going to get an admission. You're not going to get an 'I'm sorry.' No matter what you find out, it's not going to be satisfying, because the rationalization for murder never makes sense to a normal, loving, dear, straight-up person like you."

Her speech was slowing down perceptibly. She was getting tired. I was hypnotized.

After a moment she went on, "You're a wonderful person who has worked hard to be healthy, mentally and emotionally. I know this about you, Lillian: You could live out your life putting this horror of the past in a box, *back* in its box, and never look at it again. Life goes on. Life goes forward. 'Though much is taken, much abides.'"

I exhaled in amazement. "You read that poem." Two years ago, about, I'd sent her a copy of Tennyson's "Ulysses."

"And I love it. Thank you again."

There were those three words again, "I," "love," and "you" from her lips, oh so close.

She was almost finished. "You could spare yourself what's to come. You *must* consider that, Lillian. Do you want to risk the pain that could be lying out there waiting for you? The pain that almost surely *is* lying out there waiting for you? How strong do you feel? You must understand that kind of pain destroys people. It does. It does. I've seen it happen. Trust me."

"I have been thinking about it," I said.

"And do you want to go forward?"

*"Hell, yes."*

# TEN

Minerva tried not to betray her excitement to me, but I could feel it. We talked for only a few more minutes that afternoon; she was tired. She wanted to think about the case overnight and talk again in the morning.

I went to bed early myself, my head and heart fiery with passion. What do I mean by that? Well, I didn't need Calico Jones to help me to sleep, I'll tell you that much.

I woke up with a song on my lips. "I can't give you anything but love," I crooned in the shower, massaging my belly to the song's easy beat.

As I brewed my coffee I pictured Minerva on the phone to the airline, "Yes, one first-class ticket to Detroit. When's the next flight? Oh, *good*."

I would go and pick her up, carry her bags, chauffeur her to the Ritz, help her out of the car. I'd give her a nice back rub with lavender oil, then get on the phone to room service for a yummy snack of Dom Perignon and pâté on party rye. We would make zestful love, Minerva's energy startlingly unflagging, mine hyper as always when in the sack. We would have to delicately scrape each other off the ceiling after our volcanic orgasms.

In the morning she would wake in my arms and murmur, "I've never felt better in my life. I love you, Lillian. Do you hear me? Listen to me carefully. *I love you.*"

"Ah," I sighed, pouring myself another cup of joe and

breathing in the freshness of the morning. Songbirds trilled in the trees. Todd's ears quivered.

The clock ticked to 9:30 and I could stand it no longer. I dialed Minerva's number.

A stranger answered.

"Uh, I'm calling for Minerva," I said, flustered.

Pause. "Just a minute, please."

Minerva came on the line sounding rested.

I asked, "Who was that?"

"Oh, that's Tillie."

"Who's Tillie?"

Minerva's voice was steady. "A friend."

"What kind of a friend?"

"Come on, Lillian."

"Oh. I see."

"Look. I met Tillie in rehab. She's an RN."

"And she's living with you?"

"Can we get on to business?"

*Oh*, I thought, *now it's all business. All right. All righty-dighty.*

Minerva began telling me her ideas, all the angles and ramifications she'd thought of since we'd hung up yesterday. "Of course Ciesla is going to discourage you," she said. "He's seen the results of your work...uh, of your style of investigation before. Even if his reaction was 'Holy cow, Lillian's on to something,' he's not going to say it. He'd feel he was being irresponsible to encourage you."

Blood bubbles popped behind my retinas as I took notes and snarled bitter silent recriminations.

*Yeah, well, you don't feel too goddamn irresponsible for encouraging me, now do you?*

"Right," I said.

Minerva went on, "What you've got here is a love story gone wrong."

*Do I ever.*

"And," she added, "it's probable that greed was involved. We have to figure out who betrayed whom."

*How come I didn't hear about this Tillie before? This wonderful goddamn Tillie?*

"Right," I said.

"Now," said Minerva, "Trix is the key."

*I bet Tillie has perfectly formed tits and a high round butt and—*

I said, "We find Trix and we're home free, then?"

"Oh, well, no, don't make any assumptions about that. It's too early to say that."

*—and a little snicky-smile and a closet full of those cutesy pajama uniforms nurses wear these days—and oh, NO! I won't make any fucking assumptions, far be it from me!*

"OK, you're right," I said.

"It'd be a good idea to make contact with Robert Hawley, her quote-unquote widower. We don't know how much he knows. Did Trix have life insurance? Does he know it was a setup? Was he involved? Or an innocent party here? Just somebody who got fucked over?"

*Fucked over! Yes! Fucked over!*

"I can start looking for him right away," I said.

"Lillian, do you know you're really biting off your words?"

"Oh! Am I?"

"Lillian. Dear. Please. You don't have the right to be angry with me."

"I'm not angry."

"You are too. You're furious."

I stopped, got ahold of myself, and let out a long sigh. "All right. You're right, Minerva. I—everything's fine. I'm fine."

"You need to focus on what's important right now. Lillian, I'm working with you on this."

*Lucky Stiff*

"Yes—God, I—thank you. *Thank you*, Minerva. Man. I really suck sometimes."

"You do not suck." She went on, "OK, this Robert Hawley, if he was involved, is obviously not going to tell you anything. But you can get a sense. If after you've talked to him you feel there's something there, I can get somebody to look into the insurance angle for us. That could be interesting."

"Yeah. What do you mean, you'd have somebody look into it? Couldn't I just—"

"I want a licensed PI to represent us in any contacts with an insurance company."

"Oh."

It was disconcerting to talk with someone with the vocal cadence Minerva LeBlanc now had. Her speech was just a shade slower than normal, so that I had to give her time to finish her sentences—extra time so as not to inadvertently interrupt. Yet she was free to interrupt me at will. This did not, however, bother me a damn compared to the idea of that little fucking Tillie hanging around Minerva's apartment. *Tillie.* I'd never heard a stupider name. *I bet she's a great cook too. And wait, let me guess, she's the greatest lay on the eastern seaboard. I bet she's won tongue-kissing contests in every back room from Key West to Provincetown. God! Damn! It!*

Minerva said, "I think this is a good start."

"Yeah. Uh…"

"Why don't you call me in a couple of days?"

"OK."

"Lillian?"

"Yeah?"

"One thing at a time, OK?"

"OK."

I began my search for Robert Hawley that day at the public

library. I scored a PC carrel and settled in. Actually, I had a PC at home, I composed my freelance work on it, but I'd been too broke to keep paying for connectivity. I had a love-hate relationship with the Internet anyway. I'd been way behind the American public's stampede toward its wonders, only dragging myself to it when I thought it would be a good resource—a reference desk right in my home. But after the first ten times my PC crashed for no apparent reason, I had to force myself not to hammer it to pieces.

I felt unenthusiastic about finding Robert Hawley. I wanted to get right going on the trail of Trix. Duane's guess that she went to Las Vegas was probably a good one. But was she still there, and if so, how the hell to find her?

"Trust me," Minerva had said when I spoke my doubts. "Just see what you can learn from this guy."

Giving thanks that I had a middle initial for him, N., from the death notice for Patricia Lynn Hawley, I did a people search and got two Robert N. Hawleys in Michigan. I knew, of course, that not everybody gets nabbed by these Web databases. But it was a better and quicker start than if I'd begun with a stack of phone books. Reporters and investigators hate unlisted phone numbers.

One of the Robert N. Hawleys lived in inner-city Detroit, an apartment number on Forest Ave. I knew the neighborhood, a scuzzy one, from my days at Wayne State. The other lived with a missus in Novi, one of the milk-run suburbs on the route from Detroit to Lansing. I mapped both addresses, noted the phone numbers, and went out to the public phone.

I punched up the Detroit number and got a recording of a very young dude trying to sound hip and ironic. "This is the number for Bob and the band. If you're a record producer, leave a detailed message. Otherwise, I don't give a shit."

I took a breath and gathered myself before ringing the Novi number, because I had a sudden feeling about it.

"Hello?" said a mature female voice.

"Hi," I said brightly, "is this the home of *the* Robert N. Hawley?"

"Uh...well..." A short laugh came over the line. "Which Robert N. Hawley do you mean?"

"The one who ran track for Mumford High School in Detroit, ma'am, class of '89?"

"Oh, no. No. My husband—ha-ha, my husband's much older than that, in fact I think he graduated from high school in 1964 or '65. I think. And he went to Chadsey, as a matter of fact."

"Oh."

"And he played football there. At least he *claimed* to be a football hero..."

"Oh."

"Well, I'm sorry I can't help you."

"Ma'am, thank you very much anyway. You have a good day now."

The name was right, the age was right, the Detroit background was consistent. My feeling was right. It was worth a jaunt out to Novi.

I fired up the Caprice and pointed the nose westward. The suburban landscape spooled by, then Northwestern Highway with its edge-cityscape of office high-rises and greenbelts. Its TGI Friday'ses, its Bennigan'ses, its Lexus dealershipses.

Then came the last clinging farmers' fields, the pint-size cowherds, and then came the shopping centers and condominiums of Novi.

Number six on the railroad's run between Lansing and Detroit, Novi had been named in the purest postwar utilitarian fashion, right off the sign at the railroad stop: "No.-vi." Novi. Rhymes with "go-high." Emphasis on neither syllable.

The Hawley home was shoebox-style tract house in one of the cheaper parts of town. It was built of that dismal blond brick that was considered sophisticated in the Ed Sullivan era. But the scrawny saplings that had been planted fifty years ago—ancient history—had grown into tall maturity, maples and catalpas and oaks, lovely in every season.

I drove past the house, parked beyond it, and walked back.

The current Mrs. Robert N. Hawley was a pretty woman in the pejorative sense of the phrase: tall fluffy hair, dyed to match the harvest-gold kitchen appliances and waist cinched tight into a pair of what I swear were Cheryl Tiegs jeans, nail job, swingy earrings, bangles, and a bit of eye shadow at 11 A.M. She was the same age I imagined Robert Hawley to be, late fifties. No, on second look somewhat younger, actually. She might have been just fifty.

I introduced myself, having backed off from my idea to impersonate a March of Dimes walkathon recruiter. Yes, I used my real name, wanting to play this one straight. I felt it was the right thing to do, and moreover, something told me I'd get further that way.

*Be careful*, I reminded myself. I felt concern for Robert Hawley, who had, in remarrying, put the ugly past of Trix's death (he thought) behind him. I knew the conspiracy involved Trix and Bill Sechrist. It was possible Hawley had been involved, as Minerva suggested, but how likely was that? Not too. Even *my* credulousness would be strained by that.

No, I had to be careful not to shock a regular family guy into an aneurysm. My focus was on Trix. Maybe he could tell me something that could help me find her.

I made Mrs. Hawley laugh at the door by confessing I had played a trick on her by telephone.

*Lucky Stiff*

"So what's up, then?" she asked. She wasn't the slightest bit suspicious or guarded, the way most people are these days when a stranger comes to the door. She reminded me of the neighborhood moms of my childhood: bored out of their skulls, eager to talk, interested in anything new.

"Well," I said, "I think your husband really is the Robert Hawley I'm looking for. I need his help. Not money," I hurried to say. "Not anything like that. It's his memory of someone I want to know about. Someone I used to know. It's that—I'd just like to sit down and do some remembering with him. I take it he's not home."

She shook her head, fascinated. "But oh, I'm sorry! Won't you come in? I can get your phone number or something…"

"Thank you, Mrs. Hawley."

"Oh! I didn't even tell you my name," she said. "It's Adele."

"Adele, thank you. In fact, it might be better if you talked to him about this first…" I followed her inside.

She showed me to the kitchen. "Won't you sit down? Like I say, Bob's not here, he's at work."

I noted that she spoke of her husband in a somewhat contemptuous tone. It wasn't pronounced, but it was there. I'd heard it first when on the telephone she'd said, "…at least he *claimed* to be a football hero…"

The furnishings were consistent with the exterior of the house, humble and tired. Too much of it, too: tables and stuffed chairs and side chairs and recliners and lamps, lamps, lamps. The kitchen was beat-up Early American and smelled greasy. The stove and refrigerator were Kenmore. The tabletop was clean, but there was a feeling of covered-up despair in the place. A definite patina of forlornness.

I sensed that Adele Hawley, though, was dealing with it pretty well. She had her routines. She had her customs. "Would you like some coffee?"

99

"I sure would, thank you. Just black. Adele, maybe you can help me decide how to bring this up with your husband." The coffee was supermarket roast, acidic and thin, plus the pot was three hours old if it was a minute. "Mm, good coffee," I said.

A happy smile. "Thank you! Thank you, uh, oh, I'm sorry?"

"Lillian," I reminded her.

"Lillian! That's such a nice name!"

"Well, thank you. Listen, Adele, I guess I'll just plunge in here."

Her eyes searched my face alertly.

"OK, well, first I need to know one thing. Was Bob married before you to a woman named Trix?"

Adele's face went suddenly blank. I watched her. I said a moment ago that she was pretty—that is, she worked at making the most of her looks, within the parameters of the working-class suburban culture of the American Midwest. Her features were softening with age. The chin line had gone long ago. Her nose appeared to have been violently flattened: the result of one or two breaks, I guessed.

It'd taken me time to notice the nose, to begin to wonder why it looked the way it did. It was the kind of nose you'd expect to see on a guy, or a really jocky woman. Or, I thought, looking again into the face of Adele Hawley, a battered wife.

# ELEVEN

I watched her eyes roaming, searching the middle distance. She closed them, tilted her chin toward the ceiling, and said, "Heh. A-heh. A-hah!" She rolled her lower lip in a pretend pout, then chomped on it. Her lipstick was a dark maroon that didn't go with her bronzy, fluffy hair. She opened her eyes and gave me a sharp little smile.

I realized that somehow I'd just turned her into a woman with a secret.

"Well," she said slowly, "Bob was married to a woman before me, but her name wasn't Trix. It was, I believe—" And here I beheld the classic second wife choking ever so slightly on the name of the first: "—Patricia."

"Ah," I said.

"Is this about—Patricia?" She rubbed her hands in an unconscious gesture of relish.

"Yes."

"Would Trix have been a nickname, then?"

"Yes."

"Well," said Adele, feigning casualness, "I myself don't know much about Patricia. She—I guess—I don't know whether to be grateful to her or furious at her. I've been both, actually."

"Yeah? How so?"

"May I ask you what your interest is? How come you want to ask Bob about this person?"

"Well," I said, "I used to know Patricia when I was a kid.

And—uh, do you know that Patricia—well, that Bob was a widower there for a while?"

"I did."

"OK, well, Patricia died in an incident that also took the lives of my parents. Like I say, I was a kid then. And—I know this sounds very strange, but, well—I'm looking into the possibility that it might not've been an accident."

Adele Hawley's small smile broadened.

I continued, "And I've never met Bob, and it occurred to me that he and I should talk. I'd like to tell him some information I've got, and ask him a few things in turn. I don't want to upset him, though, so I'm glad to be talking to you first… Maybe you can give me some idea of—"

"Well, well, well," interrupted my hostess. "Excuse me for a moment." She left the room, and I sat there surveying the decor. There's only one way to really give you the feel of what it was like sitting in that kitchen with the view to the living room beyond, and that is to summon the ghost of Joshua Doore.

If you spent time in Detroit in the 1970s you may remember an intense television advertising campaign for a chain of furniture stores called Joshua Doore. The jingle was sung with great playfulness and verve, and it went,

> *You've got an uncle in the furniture business: Joshua Doore.*
> *Joshua Doore!*
> *He's a remarkable guy with a remarkable way*
> *to give you bargains on your furniture every day!*
> *So pick it out in the showroom, pick it up at the warehouse—*
> *take it home in the crate!*
> *Yeah.*
> *You've got an uncle in the furniture business: Joshua Doore!*
> *Yeah!*

*Lucky Stiff*

If that tells you more than you needed to know about the Hawley home, I'm sorry. You may also feel that that tells you more than you need to know about my mind. What can I say? I would prefer not to be the kind of person who would remember such a carcinogenic jingle word for word. I am, though.

My hostess returned. She placed a few envelopes facedown on the table, near her place. They appeared to be saved letters.

Pointing to a grouping of photos in a wall nook, I asked, "Are those your kids?" The word *grouping* would have been used by a Joshua Doore sales associate.

"Yes, that's Bob Junior and Kelly." Her gaze lingered on them. "They got out," she sighed.

I made no comment.

Adele said, "Kelly's about to have our first grandbaby."

"Oh, how nice."

She reached into the refrigerator and pulled out a quart bottle of Budweiser. She twisted off the cap and took a slug. "Ah," she said. "Want one?"

"Gee, no thank you. I gotta drive. Otherwise, you know."

She pulled up her chair again and leaned over the table toward me. "I met Bob before Patricia died."

That was interesting.

Adele responded to my expression and continued, "When he was with Patricia he didn't have dime one. He was hot for me."

"Where did you know him from?"

"We both worked at BG."

"What's that?"

"BG Construction, you know."

"Was that a firm in Detroit or out here?"

"Oh, in Detroit. Redford, really, which was Detroit. We moved to Novi—well, I'll get to that. I got a summer job typing and filing, in the office. And Bob drove a truck. Dump truck."

"I see."

"Once he laid eyes on me, he made up every excuse under the sun to come into the office! Hah! All the guys did."

"You liked him."

"I thought he was King Kong and Paul Newman rolled into one."

"Yeah," I said, "Good-looking young guy?"

"You got it. And I was pretty. Oh, I was pretty-pretty-pretty. I'm not bragging, just trying to be honest. Huh, look at me now!" She glanced at me sideways, and I took my cue.

"Oh, you're a lovely lady still! Very charming."

"You think so, Lillian?" She sucked on her beer.

"I know so!"

She appreciated my enthusiasm. "We saw each other in secret. It was so thrilling! All that hot passion. I was stupid. I was just a kid myself, just eighteen. I wished Patricia dead so often, to myself. I never spoke it out loud. And then it happened."

"Wow," I said. "Must've been spooky."

"I was scared for a while, that's how dumb I was. I thought maybe I had special powers."

I smiled indulgently.

Adele went on, "After Patricia died, Bob had money all of a sudden. I wanted to go to cosmetology school. He offered to pay for it." She shook her head. " 'N' I did it, I married him. My parents were glad. They thought driving a dump truck was a good job!"

"Well," I said mildly, "any honest work is a good job in my book."

Adele paused. "If we were talking about a better man, driving a dump truck would be a good job."

I listened, catching on. *But what's with the envelopes?*

"Like I say," she went on, "I was a kid. I didn't know squat.

He told me he won the money in Las Vegas. Fifty thousand dollars, he got. I believed him then. I didn't care. I had goals. It wasn't like I wanted him to buy me diamonds, blow all his money on me. I had goals. Cosmetology school—the one *I* wanted to go to—cost $4,900. I married Bob, and he paid it, and I went. But by the time I graduated, the rest of the money was gone. I wanted to set up a salon, but no way at that point. No way."

"What happened to the money?"

"He pissed it away, one thing 'n' another. He did buy me some nice jewelry, all of which went too. I was too dumb to see where the money had come from, but later when I thought about it, it was obvious. Life insurance on Patricia."

"Well, what would be unusual about that?"

"Not unusual, Lillian, you're absolutely right. But he lied to me about it, said he'd won it. Why not tell the truth? He was always too cheap to gamble, I knew that."

"Hmm," I said. "Well, I could see a guy telling a lie like that. Not wanting you to perceive anything creepy about the money. You know, buying you gifts with the first wife's insurance money—that might creep out a young girl."

Adele checked her wristwatch. She said, "I don't usually have a drink in the middle of the day, you know?"

I nodded believingly.

She said, "We got married six weeks after Patricia died. One thing that did disturb me was living in her house, so we moved out here to Novi. It's peaceful here."

"Did part of the money go for a down payment on this house?"

"It did, 6,000 of it. The place is all ours now!" She glanced around sarcastically.

I asked, "Do you know what happened to Patricia?"

She smiled her secret, sharp smile again. "I do now."

I looked at the envelopes. "What are you smiling about?"

She turned the envelopes faceup. There were three, two pale pink, one pale blue. I paid careful attention. She fanned them out, and I saw they were all addressed to Robert Hawley at this house, in the same hand, a neat slanted script. The postage stamps told me the letters were not all recent.

The return address said "Trix Robertson," and the addresses differed. The postmarks were illegible. I focused on the return address of the most recent one—with today's postage rate—and tried to memorize it.

Quietly, Adele said, "Patricia wrote these." Her voice had gradually changed over the course of the past five minutes; it had become tighter and higher-pitched. I realized she was busting with pent-up excitement. I met her eye and cocked a brow conspiratorially.

Suddenly it poured out. She banged her beer bottle down. "I said Patricia wrote these!" She snatched them up and waved them in my face. "These letters came for Bob, and I didn't give 'em to him. There was another one, the first one. God, when was it—Kelly was a baby, Bob Junior wasn't born yet. I gave it to him and wanted to know who Trix Robertson was. He wouldn't tell me. He acted…he got so mad! He scared the hell out of me. I kept these, these ones that came later. Didn't give them to him."

I asked, "Did he *beat* the hell out of you too?"

She looked down in silence. After a minute she said, "Why?"

"It's just a feeling I have."

"I loved him."

"Course you did."

"But as of today, boy… As of today I think I'm a new Adele."

I smiled.

She said, "Trix Robertson. Get it? Very cute. She couldn't use Hawley anymore."

"Well, I believe she married another guy. What's in the letters?"

"A woman asking for money. A woman with—" A light dawned in her eyes. "—no leverage! No leverage! The letters are like blackmail! I mean, writing to a man at his wife's house! But no threats! Begging for money, asking for money. And now I know why! No leverage! Until today I thought this Trix was a girlfriend, a girlfriend who thought she might reveal herself to me, out of spite, to hurt our marriage. Or to hurt our children. I'm pretty smart, I'm nobody's fool, I'm no dummy."

"That's right," I agreed.

"But now I'm *pissed*. Now I see what happened. Hah! Bob Hawley. Hah!"

"When did the most recent letter come?"

"I guess a couple years ago. Yeah. A couple years ago. Oh, I'm pissed now. I am pissed. I could blow his head off while he's sleeping. I could cut his balls off and stuff them into his mouth and let him bleed to death. That's what I'd like to do."

"Now, Adele—"

"That's exactly what I'd like to do. Blow his head off. Stab him about fifty times in his goddamn gut."

"Adele—Mrs. Hawley—"

"One of these days I'm gonna do it, I swear to God. The next time he touches me. I swear." She sighed, her corona of rage subsiding. "You know, it's so hard to be an honest person."

"That's for sure."

"I've tried." She held the sweaty beer bottle to her temple and rolled it around to her forehead. "Patricia isn't dead," she murmured. "Well, how do you like that?"

"Listen, Adele, let me look at those letters, OK? I need to find

Patricia. If I can actually find her in person, prove she exists—"

"You can nail Bob's ass to the—"

"Well, yeah, but…" Questions spurted through my brain. Was Bob Hawley the mastermind of the plot after all, not Bill Sechrist? Were they partners in it, each disposing of his wife, in one way or another? Juanita Sechrist—really dead? Trix Hawley—fake dead?

I heard a thump and a bang from the front room.

"We're in here," called Adele sweetly.

Horrified, I said, "Did you call him home when you left the room?"

She just smiled that sharp smile again.

Bob Hawley strode into the kitchen. He was a massive son of a bitch, with thick shoulders, small hooded eyes, and a beer gut the size of a Shop-Vac. The gut was supported by a sagging belt with a brilliant silver Coors buckle.

"What's going on?" His voice was harsh and panicked. Anger and fear in equal parts. "Who are you?"

Forcing myself to remain seated, I said, "I'm the daughter of the Byrds, the couple that got killed in that bar fire with Patricia. Long time ago." Making my voice very calm, I went on, "Please take it easy, Mr. Hawley. I need you to help me."

He stood in the middle of the room, legs spread wide, feet planted in dusty boots. "What do you want?" I noticed that his small eyes were bloodshot. He was one unappealing bastard.

"I want to talk to you about Bill Sechrist."

He paused, mystified. *"Who?"*

"Bill Sechrist. Come on, man. You've got to help me find Patricia. Or Trix, or whatever she's calling herself these days."

"I don't know what the flying fuck you're talking about." He folded his arms in a visible effort to make his chest expand beyond the boundary of his gut.

Before I could speak again, he said coldly, "Hey, *she* sent you. Didn't she? To my fucking house! Yeah, she sent you all right! Well, you go back to Las Vegas and tell *Trix Fucking Robertson* she can go to hell and suck dick!" He unfurled his arms, cocked his fist, and stepped in my direction, but I was ready. I flung my coffee mug at him with one hand, and with the other grabbed and threw Adele's beer bottle. He had to duck once, twice, and I snatched the letters from Adele's hand and bolted for the door. I was running fast down the street to the Caprice before he'd made it to the doorstep.

# TWELVE

I wanted to talk to Blind Lonnie. More accurately, I wanted him to talk to me. No, more accurately still, I just wanted to be with him. It was Thursday night; sometimes he played Greektown on Thursday nights. I loaded my mandolin into the Caprice and drove down there. Muggy air gushed in through the windows.

He was sitting on his box at the corner, playing a blues medley of pop crap, a soft smile on his lips. The crap, specifically, was the kind of nauseating show tunes from the kind of nauseating hit musicals—Broadway, Disney, you name it—that people eventually request to be played at their weddings. The songs people begin to ask piano players at fern bars to play, and play them straight, too. In short, the brainless ditties that are destined to become tomorrow's sentimental favorites.

Lonnie was trashing them brilliantly. Sweat glistened on his fat, smooth face. He was humiliating those songs. I came up and set my mandolin case deliberately on the concrete sidewalk. Lonnie knew the sound of my case.

"Ah," said he. "Lillian."

I made a gagging sound and he laughed. He came to a stopping place and gave me his open A. I tuned to it and said, "Let's clear the air here some."

"OK," he said, " 'Come Rain or Come Shine.' "

"OK," I said, "F?"

*Lucky Stiff*

"Yeah."

We hit it, and I relaxed into the music. "Ah," I murmured. "Ah."

It's a fairly simple melody—you can go all over the place with your chords if you want to, and lots of players do. But I just floated along behind Lonnie's precise lead, sticking to F major, throwing in a few flatted fifths in the break. It had been not quite a week since Lonnie and I last played. I tried some fancier improvisation, but failed to get it going. My sound wasn't bold, it wasn't clean. Disappointed in myself, I went back to playing two-note chords. Improvisation takes practice.

A buxom teenager lagging behind her well-fed Greek parents stooped and, with an impulsive gesture, emptied her coin purse into Lonnie's case.

"Thank you, little lady," said Lonnie.

She stared at us intensely, longingly, then scurried after her parents.

I smiled at his acuity. Did he hear her necklace clicking as she bent over? Her clip-clop strappy sandals and short footsteps? Or did he hear her Lycra-blend skirt stretching over her butt as she stooped?

"Funny how flexible F natural can be," remarked Lonnie when we finished the tune. I didn't answer. He inclined his head toward me. "What's troubling Lily tonight?" He played some slow arpeggios in F.

"Oh, Lonnie."

"Problems?"

"Yeah. Everybody's got problems."

"That old boyfriend of yours got you shook up?"

I had to laugh. "Well, yeah, in a way."

"Tell Lonnie."

111

"Oh, it's just that I feel I'm losing my mind."

"Yeah."

"And it's a convoluted story, and I don't understand it. There's this thing that happened when I was a kid, and I thought I'd left it behind, thought I'd left a bunch of sad, sad shit behind. Y'know?"

"Mm-hmm." He switched to playing a slow five-note rock scale in B.

"And I was so glad to see Duane. But the past can't come back in just the pieces you want. In just the pieces you miss. You get pieces you wish you hadn't…" I trailed off, thinking.

"Mm," said Lonnie.

"There's business now that I have to take care of. Shit I need to know. I learned *some* shit this week, and now I see that once I know some shit, I need to know more. At first I was excited. Now I fell sick. No one but me knows what I know."

Lonnie laughed softly.

I added, "And suddenly it's going fast."

Lonnie said, "Because more people are in it now?"

"Yeah, how'd you know?"

"That's always the way."

"Lonnie, how'd you lose your eyesight?"

He switched over to A-flat. "Never had any to begin with."

"Oh."

"So I don't miss it. See?"

"I guess so."

"Lily, if somebody was to blindfold you now, you'd be surely scared, right?"

"I would."

"But if you was me, you wouldn't be. It wouldn't be nothing to you." When I didn't respond, he said, "You got more than you need."

I thought about that, and said, "I'm still scared."

"Of having to do something? Or of learning more truth? Never mind, you're gonna say 'both.' " His left hand moved up his fingerboard while his right drew notes from the strings. He changed keys again, then went back to A-flat. I began to discern a tune, a theme. I listened harder, not quite believing it.

I said, "Lonnie, is that Chopin?"

He smiled.

I said, " 'Polonaise in A-flat?' "

He was laughing, playing it: that stirring, dense piano piece from the military tradition of Eastern Europe. He was hitting the melody recognizably enough, supplementing the strong bass line with agile flourishes in the upper register. He was putting *wit* into it. I listened in amazement, suddenly joyful.

"You can play anything," I said.

"Not the point here," said Blind Lonnie.

"You're as good as the Cambridge Buskers. Better."

"Who?"

"Oh, they're a couple of guys, couple of Brits who do what you're doing right now. Flute and accordion. You should hear them play those warhorse overtures, 'Poet and Peasant,' '1812.' They do Elgar, Rachmaninoff, everybody."

"You got them?"

"Yeah, I got two of theirs on CD. I don't know if they're still recording."

"Lend 'em to me, will you?"

"Yeah! Sure."

"You go home now and listen to your Chopin and your Beethoven. Leave Mozart alone. Hit you some Brahms. Hit you some Grieg."

"How come?"

"Because something Little Memphis Jim tol' me one time."

"You knew Little Memphis Jim?"

"Yeah, I knew him. We played together around St. Louis before Jim met up with that deceitful white horse."

"Oh, yeah."

"Anyway, Little Memphis Jim told me this one time: When your chips are down, listen you to heroic music. You need to have your beats on one and three."

He meant emphasis on the first and third beats of the measure, as opposed to on the second and fourth, which is mostly what you get in jazz and blues. Rock as well.

I said, "One and three. But blues is heroic, in its way. It's about perseverance."

"Yeah. But I'm saying for *you*."

"How did you know I'm into classical too?"

"Blind Lonnie hears it in your playing."

I just had to shake my head.

He said, "Little Memphis Jim studied with Horowitz."

"Horowitz? Little Memphis Jim studied with Vladimir Horowitz? He did not!"

"That's a true fact."

I tried to picture the austere Horowitz, his thinning hair combed back on his delicate skull, sitting at a Steinway with Little Memphis Jim, a hunchbacked sharecropper's son who wouldn't, in those days, have been permitted to drink from the same water fountain. I pictured a bottle of bourbon and a couple of ashtrays. A New York skyline beyond the windows. I tried to picture them talking. I really couldn't. Then I pictured their four hands on the keyboard, speaking that way. Two legends on a piano bench.

"Wow," I said.

*Lucky Stiff*

"Remember," said Lonnie, "you got more than you need."
"Thanks, Lonnie."
"Don't make too much of this."

I went home and got out my boxed set of Beethoven's symphonies, Von Karajan's Berlin sessions. I lay on the floor and listened to number three (the Eroica) first, of course. I let the music move through me. Then I listened to numbers five and seven.

Todd snuggled up to my side and I stroked his fur, so soft and brown.

*The insistency of it*, I thought. That was one thing Beethoven had going, he was insistent. And fearless. He took risks, that son of a bitch did. He challenged destiny. You know he gradually lost his hearing when still at his peak as a composer. Yet his music is filled with triumph. *And death,* I thought. You can't have one without facing the other.

I put on Artur Rubinstein playing Chopin, all the polonaises. I let the music swell and wash over me. I felt the strength of it. I relaxed and went to sleep.

In the morning I phoned Duane.
"Want to go on a trip with me?"
He thought he did. When I got done talking, he really did. He offered to buy tickets and I let him.
He called back. "Is tomorrow too soon?"
"Nope," I said.
"OK, I'll pick you up at 6 in the morning. Our flight's at 7:50."
"Good. Duane?"
"Yeah?"
"Would you also please bring a fistful of hundred-dollar bills?"

"What for?"
"Use your imagination."
He paused. "OK."

I again got out the letters I'd grabbed from the Hawley's table. I'd read them all yesterday as soon as I'd gotten home from Novi. The letters bore the imprint of Trix all right.

This one was the first in the series, which would have been the second letter Trix sent, according to Adele.

*Dear Bob,*

*I could shit on your grave. Things have gotten worse. You don't know. I never expected the double cross from you. I didn't take steps I should have, and now I've got it up the ass about as far as it can go. I need the money.*

*Nothing has worked out for me.*

*You on the other hand have got a new house. New wifey. Cuntstruck again, that's you Bob. New kiddies too I bet.*

*I didn't deserve it and you know it. You might just as well stuck an icepick in my eye.*

*What can I do? If you have any feeling left, send me my God Damn money. Before you have to start paying for college ha ha. Imagine how happy St. Peter will be to see you then.*

*I need it Bob. Like I said before I've got in a little trouble.*
*—Trix*

The others were similar. I laughed sadly at myself. I'd thought Trix liked me, really liked me as a person. Therefore, how could she have been part of something that hurt me so terribly? And if it wasn't supposed to happen that way but went wrong, how could she have run away, not owned up to her part in it? But, I mused, the affections of children are taken for granted.

*Lucky Stiff*

In the letters Trix spoke of "the money." Not "money" but "the money," so it was clear there was a specific amount in question. She closed her last letter with the pathetic plea, "Even a few bucks. For God's sake Bob." It, like the other letters, was undated. I used my magnifier under my strong desk lamp and made out the postmark. Adele Hawley was about right: The letter was eighteen months old.

So Trix was desperate. The address wasn't fresh, but maybe I could work with it. I was ticked off enough at Minerva not to bother telling her what I was about to do. *Why would she even give a shit anyway?* I thought bitterly. *Bet she's got that little Tillie on the jump day and night. Bet it's a lot of fun.*

I'd taken Todd along on trips before, but lightweight was the way I needed to go this time. I could get away with just my gym bag with a change of clothes and extra underwear, plus my purse and notebook.

I called Billie, my animal friend. A waitress by night, she also shared her home with an assortment of neutered cats, dogs, rodents, and the occasional reptile. She agreed to look after Todd for a few days. "Don't tell me," she said. "You're off on a possibly dangerous adventure and you don't know exactly when you'll be back."

"Well, yeah," I admitted with some annoyance.

"Lillian—"

"Don't start with me."

"Fine. Fine."

"Thank you."

She said, "I still have your pet carrier. Sorry I haven't returned it yet." She'd borrowed it a few months ago to transport a baby raccoon she'd rescued from the jaws of a stray rottweiler in her neighborhood.

"Whatja do with the rottweiler?" I asked.

"It could take care of itself," she answered. "It was the raccoon that needed me." She nursed the raccoon back to health and into adulthood, but it hadn't grown to be terribly docile. She drove the animal out to her favorite nature preserve, where she released all the wild animals that came into her care.

"OK," I said, "I'll fix up a box and we'll be over later."

"Make it late, OK? I'm working closing."

"OK, after one?"

"Yeah, that'll be good."

*What the hell,* I thought, *who needs sleep anyway?*

I tried to nap through the afternoon, then gave up and listened to more music, some Vaughan Williams, a smattering of Grieg. I ate up some vegetables and bread that might go bad while I was away. At around eleven-thirty I got out my Cambridge Buskers CDs and put them in my purse. I found a cardboard carton in my closet, shredded a few brown paper bags into it, and added Todd.

"You're going to meet all your good friends again," I told him. " 'Member Billie? And Salome the cat and Nini the cat and Butch the friendly dog and Roscoe the mostly friendly dog and Pammy the rat and all her kinfolk?"

He looked at me balefully, I thought. We'd been having such a nice, quiet time at home. Who the hell wanted to go out at this hour? I put a few timothy nuggets in the box too.

"Sorry, Toddy, it's important," I explained. "If I can talk to a treacherous bitch in a faraway desert land where water flows like gold and pictures of cherries roll on thousands of little wheels going nowhere, I can get some answers."

He looked up at me with his shining black eyes as I folded the box flaps over him.

"Course," I added, "it'll all depend on what the questions are."

I slung my purse over my shoulder and carried the box downstairs to the Caprice.

# THIRTEEN

On the street, I inhaled the night-city air: the moisture from the tall old trees in the neighborhood, warm asphalt, cut grass, exhaust fumes from a passing motorcycle. I put Todd's box on the grass and unlocked the passenger door. As I was opening it I had a sudden uneasy feeling. I turned to look behind me, but no one was there. I glanced up and down the street.

"Just as well to get out of town for a few days," I muttered, loading Todd onto the front seat.

Riding in the car appeared to bore Todd; I'd noticed that news radio seemed to hold his attention, so I put on AM 950, the CBS affiliate, and together we listened to the drone of the announcers.

I drove down to Greektown and cruised the streets for a free parking space, not that I expected to find one. Busy time down there, lots of people out enjoying Friday night. Partaking of a little kebab action, a little gambling action. I saw Blind Lonnie playing to a semicircle of listeners.

With resignation I swung into the parking structure. No spaces on the lower floors, but when I got to the fourth it was practically vacant. The air was cooler in the concrete structure.

"Todd, be good, OK? I'll be right back."

I left the windows cranked down a little, grabbed my bag, and scooted out, cursing having to pay to park my car for ten goddamn minutes.

The stairwell smelled like urine.

*Lucky Stiff*

I hurried up Monroe Street to Lonnie. He was playing "Margie," bluesing it up like a ballad to a dead prom queen instead of the perky tune it'd been written as. The semicircle of people stood listening, hands on their hips or in their pockets. Lonnie hit his final chord in his signature way, an upstroke, except he hit this one with such force that he snapped his E string.

"Aw, sumbitch," he murmured as a small shower of money plopped into his case. He bent forward, reaching for the compartment where he kept his spare strings. The people moved off.

"Hey, man," I said.

"Lily, hi. Where's your axe?" He hadn't heard me set my case down.

"Didn't bring it. I just stopped by to give you these CDs I was telling you about, 'member, the Cambridge Buskers?"

"Oh, yeah!" He straightened up holding a string envelope. He reached out and I put the jewel boxes in his free hand. "Thank you! You need 'em back soon?"

"Naw, whenever."

"So how are you? Did you do some listenin'?"

"Yeah, I did."

"And?"

"I'm going to Las Vegas in the morning."

"Would that be a positive, bold step, then?"

"Yes. Yes, Lonnie, it would."

"Awright! When you comin' back?" He extracted the broken string and threaded in the new one.

"Few days, I guess."

"Well, stay away from the blackjack tables."

"I don't even know how to play blackjack."

"All the worse!" Lonnie let out a grand laugh. He cranked his string. "All the worse!"

121

In the parking garage I took the elevator, avoiding the pee-saturated stairwell. As I hurried toward my car near the end of a row, I noticed that that end of the garage was dark, much darker than it had been.

I walked over something crunchy. Broken glass. I stopped, looked up, and saw a light fixture overhead, busted out. The scattering of glass was fresh and more or less compact: hadn't been driven over, hadn't been trod around.

There was another splash of shards twenty feet along, then the suggestion of another in the deep darkness beyond. The garage was dead quiet.

"Shit," I whispered.

Cautiously, I advanced down the row. I saw no one. I slipped my keys out of my pocket. My scalp tightened. I took another step, then another. I stopped uncertainly. Everything felt wrong. My saliva went metallic. *Go back down*, I thought, *and find a security guy or somebody*. The very air of that parking garage felt poisonous.

The quiet was suddenly broken. It came from the darkness, a hollow scratchy sound, like something being shaken back and forth in a large container. It *was* something.

It was Todd in his box.

I heard the box hit the concrete floor and silence for a moment, then Todd scrabbling hard.

"Todd!" I shouted.

Someone had watched me. Someone had watched me carry a box to my car, followed me here, and jimmied or busted the car door, peeked inside the box, and got an idea.

In a swoop I understood the plan. Todd had become an impromptu decoy. I, being the sloppy-hearted animal lover, would risk coming to his rescue and be lured into the clutches of evil.

*Lucky Stiff*

I needed only a few frozen seconds to consider. Todd was a treasured friend, a faithful friend, and I was as fond of him as I was of Uncle Guff. Todd's life with me flashed through my mind. Our first meeting at the state fair so long ago—an old farmer, a crabby livestock judge, a bitten finger (mine); our battles with Mrs. Gagnon's dog, Monty; our games—Mad Scramble, Find Punkin', Jump on Monty, and all our nameless fun. Todd's alertness whenever danger came around had saved my bacon more than once. Ah, the naughty times, the good times. He was an exceptional rabbit, tractable and patient, yet inquisitive and plucky.

But he was, after all, a rabbit. In another lifetime I might have raised rabbits for slaughter, or hunted them. I ate meat. I caught and killed fish and ate them.

In the final analysis, whoever was there in the shadows had sadly overestimated me. While I would grieve if something bad happened to Todd, I'd be alive to do it. Perhaps I could support another bunny in memory of him.

All this, though not in the fully formed way it takes to tell it, rolled through my mind. I stood poised in the dimness. I guess half a minute had passed since the elevator doors slid closed behind me.

I turned and ran.

A rough voice in the shadows said, "Goddamn!"

I took off fast, but the elevators and stairs were a good thirty yards away. I heard the sickening sound of footsteps behind me.

I reached the metal stairwell door and grabbed the knob. I turned it this way, then that, but the door didn't give. I realized that in my haste I was pressing hard against the door, and my body weight was making the latch bind. I was too panicked even to swear. I backed off, tried the knob again, and swung the door open. I practically threw myself down the concrete staircase. I could move rapidly, but my little ballet with the doorknob cost me.

I was grabbed from behind, a hairy arm flung itself across my throat, and I was yanked backward into a solid, round belly. The man felt like a cow or a pig, some broad animal. Smelled like one too. I willed myself not to struggle, for the moment; I wanted a second or two to size up the situation.

The hairy arms spun me around, and I beheld my attacker wearing a black ski mask with a yellow pompon on top. I believe the rest of his ensemble comprised a dirty T-shirt, blue jeans, and sneakers.

We were on a landing between floors. He threw me up against the wall and hauled back with his fist to punch me. His eyes, small and bloodshot, were on my midsection.

I sidestepped. He checked his fist and grabbed for me again. I flung one hand skyward, which caught his eye, allowing me a split second to drive my knee into his crotch.

My knee hit something very hard. He bellowed, but to my astonishment he remained upright. The son of a bitch was wearing a cup!

Panting, he backhanded me in the face, then delivered the gut blow I'd avoided once.

I can't begin to describe the pain of that. I know this wasn't the kind of pain Minerva LeBlanc had warned me about, but it was pretty goddamn bad. It felt like an express bus plowing into my belly all the way through to my spine. My knees buckled and I went down on all fours. Gasping, I looked up. I saw the Coors belt buckle. *I knew it: Hawley.*

I had in fact hurt him a little, as he belatedly grabbed his groin with one hand and, bending down, cuffed me on the side of the head with the other.

This all happened in a few seconds. My mind struggled to keep up. I realized he wasn't trying to kill me, or he would've done it by now, either by strangling me when he first caught me, or hitting me hard in the face, then stomping my head when I went down.

The advice from a dozen self-defense minicourses, magazine articles, and angry-dyke bull sessions came to me in the form of voices shouting in my head.

*Gouge his eyes out!* hollered one.

But I have to get to my feet first.

*Use your keys as a weapon!* screamed another.

I need to get a breath first.

*Drive your fist into his throat!* insisted yet another.

"Help," I croaked. I rose to my knees.

Hawley slapped me across the mouth and treated me to another gut punch. He stood back.

I didn't hear any of the blows he laid on me.

My mind was slow now. I began the process of what I thought was getting up, in order to fight back or flee, but found myself sitting on my butt, my back against the concrete wall.

Satisfied that I didn't have the means to mount any more defense, he crouched down to my level.

Dimly, I saw his eyes studying me through the holes in his mask. Up close, I felt the man's viciousness, his menace. His contempt. It was there in his hate-bitten eyes: his belief in his own privilege, in the violent supremacy of his needs over those of anyone else.

Clearly and loudly, he said, "Drop it."

I slid all the way to the floor and watched his sneakers stride away. The sneakers pattered quickly down the stairs. I lifted my head, but didn't have the strength to hold it up, and it kunked down on the stinking concrete.

I was out for a few minutes, maybe ten, who knows. It couldn't have been long, because no one had found me. I roused and shifted my body on the concrete. With every move the muscles in my back and stomach cramped and clenched. I felt cold.

Opening my eyes required conscious effort. The first thing I saw was a giant Todd, wavering darkly there, out of focus, then in, then out again.

The stairwell door had stuck open somehow, and he had chewed out of his box and hopped around and down the stairs until he found me. He eyed me, then moved closer. He put his brown face right up to my nose. I crawled up a few steps, then had to stop. Todd bumped up at my side.

I had to work to remember what had happened.

"Hey!" a voice called out. "Ellert, zat choo?"

I crawled up another step as someone came up from below. "Hey, yurrat music lady." It was Drooly Rick, one of the street people. He smelled like a thousand bar rags, and his nose was running. But he helped me up the steps to the next landing.

I told him I'd slipped and fallen.

"Oh," he said. "Well, I just come inna take-a piss, you know how it is, 'n' I thought yurrur Ellert. But I guess he ant here." He bent closer. "Yur mouth's bleedin'. Here." He dug in his overcoat pocket and pulled out a wad of filthy tissues and pressed them to my lips.

I gagged and pushed his hand away. "Thank you, but I think I'm gonna be sick."

He backed off. I coughed but didn't throw up.

"I'm OK," I told him. "Thank you, Rick. Thanks a lot, OK?"

"Got 'ny cigs?"

"Ah, unnh." It hurt to take a deep breath. Man, did my gut hurt. "Not on me."

He exclaimed, "Where'd 'at rabbit come from?!"

"Never mind, Rick. It's my rabbit."

"Oh."

*Lucky Stiff*

"You run along now, OK?"

The only time I'd felt even a tenth this bad was after getting talked into joining a rugby game with some women who had been the kind of girls who scared the crap out of me in junior high school. They needed a substitute at the last minute and were desperate enough to ask me. Once the game started I realized it was a long-awaited grudge match between two bloodthirsty teams. I was clobbered around in the scrums like a rag doll. My ears rang for a week.

I sat and breathed for a while, feeling my face and head with my fingers. A couple of goose eggs were coming up on my head. My lip hurt but didn't feel badly torn. I pulled up my T-shirt and wiped blood off with the hem. I looked down at my belly. A couple of vast red marks spanning my midsection were starting to turn purple. I pressed on them and wondered if I was bleeding internally.

When it became clear I wasn't going to feel much better anytime soon, I grunted to my feet, palming the wall for support. My vision cleared after a minute. I scooped up Todd.

"I'm sorry, boy," I murmured.

He snugged his hind feet under my arm and looked up at me.

"God, I'm sorry, Todd. You would never desert me. Yet I abandoned you. Oh, Toddy."

His expression was calm.

I made him a promise. "I'll never let anybody hurt you."

His whiskers stirred. He understood.

Together we trudged up another flight to the Caprice.

I drove to Billie's and stood in the glare of her porch light. I rang the bell. When she opened the door I just handed Todd to her, saying, "Don't even ask."

Her eyes were huge and scared, scrutinizing my face.

"Jesus Christ, Lillian, come in."

"Can't, hon, gotta go. Everything's all right. I promise I'll fill you in later. 'K?

Cradling Todd, Billie ran her hand through her frizzy Lucy Ricardo hairdo and shifted her weight in her pink scuffs. She heaved a tree-bending sigh and said, " 'K."

# FOURTEEN

Morning came damn soon. I nursed myself with a shower and ice packs, longing for a beautiful loving girlfriend to croon over my injuries and feed me broth. Calico Jones always had a brand-new beautiful loving girlfriend to croon over her injuries and feed her broth. By the time I had to get up and dressed, I didn't look all that bad. Fat lip, bruise on one cheek—granted, but I got out the plastic baggie full of makeup I'd accumulated from one occasion and the other and used it to good effect. I applied a swath of scarlet lipstick, widening my lip line, which helped a lot.

However, I deliberately did not do the best job I could. I realized almost as soon as Bob Hawley had finished kicking the living shit out of me that I could put the beating to good use. I stood back from the mirror. You could tell, all right. And you could tell I'd tried to hide it.

I was waiting on the stoop when Duane pulled up in his knights-in-white-satin Thunderbird at 6 o'clock on the nose. He noticed first that I was moving slowly, then got a look at my face. As I dropped into the passenger seat he looked me over closely.

"Oh, no," he said.

"I'm all right. Really. Put 'er in gear." I related my evening to him as we made good time to Detroit Metropolitan. "So you see," I concluded cheerfully, "we're on the right track."

"I sure don't like it." He had come to accept the possibility that Trix-Lynette-Patricia was alive. But he hadn't yet managed to get his mind around the fact that his mother was almost certainly dead.

"That's irrelevant," I said. "Got the money?"

"I got the money, Lillian."

"You didn't shave, did you?" I reached over to feel his cheek.

"No. I feel like a thug."

"That's the idea. Got your shades too?"

"Yeah. I brought my leather baseball cap too."

"Oh, good. That sounds perfect."

The phrase *off-season* is much too mild a description for Las Vegas in June. *Off-season* suggests a merry-go-round that's been shuttered because the leaves have begun to fall. The Nevada desert in summer is so hideously harsh, so appallingly hot, so flat and dusty, that you fear your very eyeballs will shrivel in your head if you don't blink often enough. The heat feels like an enemy.

Plunked on a blazing plain between barren mountains, the extravagant buildings of the Strip and downtown look like mistakes. The whole town looks like a mistake, down to the last house—like temporary shelter for a wandering tribe. Our pilot informed us that the temperature this afternoon was 112 degrees.

Another thing about Las Vegas, a good thing, is that there appear to be no deeply stupid people living in that town. The dryness and heat motivate everybody, the dull as well as the smart, to keep their lips closed. There are no slack-jawed yokels in Las Vegas.

While Duane arranged for our rental car at the desk inside the terminal, I bought a detailed street map, borrowed a phone book, and made some notes.

"Who in God's name would live here by choice?" I said, as we struggled to breathe while waiting at the curb for the shuttle. "I don't care that it's a dry heat. Don't talk to me about dry heat. This is worse than Palm Springs."

"Nobody moves to Las Vegas expecting to live here on the cheap, and year-round to boot," answered Duane. "Everybody thinks they're going to make a big score, then they'll never have to leave their air-conditioned mansion... Or they'll do Switzerland in the summer. Or at least Lake George or someplace."

In the car lot I became acquainted with the sun's custom of turning every automobile into an individual heat bomb. It took the air-conditioning in our silver Mercedes ten minutes to cool the car to the temperature outside, then another five to cool down to something approaching life-sustaining. Having offered to drive, I got practically second-degree burns on my hands just dealing with the controls to try to get the air-conditioning going in the first place.

Thinking about it, I realized that those who don't make good in Las Vegas must feel they *have* to stay there year-round, and forever. Because leaving equals defeat. What better city is there in the whole world for opportunity? Not only does Las Vegas as a municipality keep having growth spurt after money boom, with all the chances spurts and booms offer, it's also the place where just pure luck could reach out any second and transform you. You go from school bus driver or wallpaper sales representative to person who gives away Cadillacs as room service tips and flies to Vienna in a jet-copter for dinner. It's really true, a streak of luck in Las Vegas can take you from shit to shine, just like that. No, once here, you *can't* leave.

And of course the tourists don't stop coming, they never stop coming.

Consulting my map and notes, I drove north away from the airport, then headed west across town on one of the commercial main drags that serve the many subdivisions. There I found a particular strip plaza and parked.

"Can't I come in?" Duane begged.

"No. I want you to get the full effect."

I headed into a shop while Duane lit a cigarette and walked into a cool mist from an apparatus that was set up beneath the awning of a coffee shop next door.

My errand didn't take long. I came out. Duane looked and said, "Dear God."

"Ya think?"

"Dear God. Did you do something to your chest too?"

"Very astute, Cub Scout."

"You look utterly…un-Lillian-like."

I turned and inspected my new look in the coffee shop's glass window.

My wig was eye-catching in hue, rather a cross between daffodil and aluminum foil, and it was short and spiky and really happenin'. Plus it was reasonable, only $22.95.

In the restroom of the shop I had artfully stuffed two handfuls of tissue into my bra, to give myself that slut-that's-got-it-all look. My chest now strained the fabric of my neon-blue leotard top, which I'd dug out of my dresser that morning. I'd hoped my tightest and rattiest jeans would work, and now, looking into the glass, I saw that they did.

My face felt all right. My stomach was awfully sore, but as I hadn't died yet, I concluded I'd been right to skip medical attention. What really bothered me was my knee where I'd hit it on Bob Hawley's crotch cup. The whole knee was black-and-blue, stiff too. The son of a bitch.

"I wish," I said, "that I had some very snappy red boots."

"Yeah," said Duane, "that'd be a good touch. Those penny loafers are incredibly lame."

I looked down at my tattered Bass Weejuns. "Oh, well."

"You're limping."

"No, I'm not."

"Think I need anything?" he said.

I had instructed him to ditch the Cole Porter gestalt in favor of a crasser look. He'd selected this day a pair of black jeans with leather insets over the pockets, a slipover rayon shirt with speedboats printed on it, and sharp-toed lizard-skin boots. No underwear.

"You're perfect. Did you bring a jacket, though?"

"No."

"No kind of a jacket? You need one. Because a guy in a jacket could be carrying a gun. A big-ass gun."

"Lillian, I'm not going to threaten anyb—"

"Goddamn it! Relax! I *told* you. We want to look tough, but all we're going to be is nice. I told you."

"All right, yeah."

"And I'm telling you, in that shirt and those disco pants, your shoulders and your ass look good, but you look too unarmed." I ducked back into the wig shop.

"My boyfriend needs a sport coat, know where we can get a good one for cheap?"

The proprietress, a chatty hillbilly with nails like scalpels, gestured down the street. "Next mall over, they got a House of ManWear."

"Great, thanks."

There Duane picked out a shiny black job, an Armani knockoff that fit him nicely. With his sunglasses and black leather cap pulled low, he looked thrillingly menacing when he remembered not to smile.

I got behind the wheel again. "OK, let's go." I liked driving a Mercedes. I liked the way the seat pressed against my lower back when I gave it the gas. The engine was amazingly quiet.

We found the return address Trix had used, no trouble. It was in a mobile-home court that once, long ago, had surely been photographed for a social studies chapter on the booming, affordable real estate projects in the American West. I pictured dads with pipes leaning on their push mowers, kids on nice bikes zooming around, moms leaning out from kitchen windows calling gaily to their loved ones.

Now, though, the place featured trashed cars and sagging awnings, busted foundations, and wary old people spitting into the gravel.

"Why did it have to be a trailer court?" Duane muttered. "This is *so* trite."

I sniffed one of the characteristic smells of suburban poverty: old motor oil, spilled, leaked, congealing and sending fumes up from every paved surface. You know that hot, fucked-up smell?

We parked in front of the number, got out, and knocked. This trailer was a venerable single-wide, its aluminum skin pitted and gouged. A kitchen chair with torn vinyl sat on the gravel next to the door. Surrounding the chair were hundreds of filter cigarette butts. A new VW Beetle was parked on the slab.

There was something surreal about the trailer court, something weird, something I couldn't put my finger on at first. Something beyond the look and feel and smell of the place, this hard inland sea of metal and concrete.

"Remember, don't talk," I said.

"Mmph," said Duane.

A female circus ringmaster came to the door; at least that's what she appeared to be. Little spangly tuxedo top, painted-on pants, full makeup job, big-top hair. I had resolved not to be unnerved by anything.

I let her get a good load of us.

"Hi," I said, trying to convey a respectful type of friendliness, like detectives do. "Trix Robertson?"

The ringmaster shook her head.

"She live here?"

"Not anymore. What do you guys want?"

"I'm Steffi Cordova. This is Chino. I'm actually lookin' for somebody else. I was told Trix might be able to help me."

"Yeah? Who?"

"Do you know where she lives now?"

The ringmaster hesitated. Her outfit baffled the hell out of me until I realized she was dressed for work in Las Vegas. The outfit, while ridiculous with its gold braid and satin trim, appeared to be of good quality. Such costumes would be worn by dealers or cocktail waitresses at one of the better hotels, I guessed. Or maybe she was in a show.

Subtly, I rubbed my finger and thumb near my ear. I said, "I'd be very appreciative."

"Well, is she in trouble?"

"Let me put it this way. By helping us, she could get out of some trouble she don't even know she's in."

"You guys bail enforcers?"

"We work for a guy."

"Yeah? Who?"

I pulled a fresh $100 bill from my back pocket. "The same guy you work for." I held up the portrait. "You know this guy, don't you?"

She was fascinated by my cryptic nonsense.

I said, "My other boss is named Chip."

She got that one. "Ha," she said. She looked at her watch. "I gotta go to work." She pressed her lips together.

"So you gonna help me?"

She plucked the money from my fingers. "Next door," she said, pushing past me. She turned and locked her front door, then headed for the VW Beetle. She stopped and turned back to me. In answer to my surprised expression she said, "We used to share this place until I threw her out. She can't keep a job. Can't keep straight either. I tried to help her. You know?"

"I see."

"When I threw her out, she didn't go far."

"She live there with somebody?"

"No. She was, but he left. She's runnin' a business outta there now."

"Yeah?"

"Get what I mean?"

"Oh. Yeah."

The ringmaster laughed bitterly. "She's actually found a way to pay the rent at last!"

As if on cue, the flimsy door of the next trailer popped open and a man stumped out, leaning heavily on an aluminum cane. He was a young guy: weathered face, stained T-shirt, straggly greasy hair—all of a sudden I guessed disability checks—and he was swinging his free arm and singing.

"...She made an angel out of me...I never knew I'd be so free—"

"Now that's what I call a walking advertisement," I murmured.

"H'h," said the ringmaster.

Right then I realized what was striking me as so surreal about the place, so strange and somehow ominous. It was the sound. A low hum pervaded this place, but with an annoying

*Lucky Stiff*

uneven high-pitched buzz over the top. As if the place were engulfed by invisible locusts.

It was the air conditioning. All those trailers so close together, all of them with air conditioners hanging on them like cubic tumors, every single air conditioner running for all it was worth, beating back the tremendous desert heat on behalf of their human masters.

The man gave us all a fishy look, then slung himself into a decaying Buick Riviera circa 1988 and pulled out. Gravel squirted from the tires.

The ringmaster took off too.

Looking over to Trix's trailer—down one more notch on the scale of decrepitude from her neighbor's—I saw a blind flick inside.

I ascended the metal steps to the door.

# FIFTEEN

I rapped on the door, which hadn't shut tight behind the last customer. It flipped back and forth on its hinges.

It was pulled open wide and Trix stood before me.

I don't know why—I'm just stupid sometimes, sadly stupid—but the instant I saw her I realized I was hoping for her to look good. I was hoping for her to appear to be in good health, and to be pretty—the way I'd remembered her from so long ago. I was hoping for her to *be young*. Isn't that ridiculous?

Time had not been good to Trix.

Of course, she was older by decades. The hair was thinner and was no longer dyed brown as Duane had described it; it was back to deep red—auburn, more accurately, and from a bottle now. Those roots would be gray. Graying, anyway. Prettily done, though; she'd spent some time on the hair. Her posture was just this side of stooped. That wouldn't be far away. Her face had held up relatively well. The flesh appeared firm, the jawline still there, still plenty defined, some of the usual creases—corners of the mouth, a few under the eyes—yet no deep seams.

The eyes themselves, though, were the disaster of Trix. It almost hurt to look into them. You know how some people carry around so much despair that no matter what type of expression they try to put on, you can still see it in their eyes? With Trix that despair was so there, so hard upon her, that her trying to pretend it didn't exist made it nothing but worse.

*Lucky Stiff*

She wore a crotch-length dress in dreadful stretch tigerprint, nylons, no shoes. One long dangling feather earring swung against her neck in the breeze of the outrushing conditioned air. She was way too skinny. She held a mixed drink and an unlighted cigarette in one hand.

"Hi, Trix," I said with a warm smile. "I'm Steffi Cordova, and this here's Chino. I'm looking for somebody, and I think you might be able to help me."

She looked keenly at us, and I swallowed and tried to maintain pleasant eye contact.

"In return," I said, "I'd like to help you."

I saw her mind running through her catalogue of johns, thinking quickly over them. She peeked over at our Mercedes.

Suddenly I felt we shouldn't have come to her home. She was apprehensive, I could see it; she was reluctant. It would've been better to approach her in a public place, maybe. I don't know. Well, I thought, you can't necessarily work out everything in advance. Can't foresee every goddamn thing.

"We're not cops," I said. "You can search us if you want." A small inspiration came to me. "Chino's gonna wait outside. This is just girl talk."

She relaxed a fraction. That was all it took.

"Well, OK," she said, stepping back from the door.

I felt I was taking a risk not wearing sunglasses, just in case she could still see little Lillian in my eyes. But shades are too off-putting to wear in front of someone you're trying to get information from. Duane, we'd agreed, had no choice. Trix had known the postpuberty Duane fairly well, and thus would be much more likely to recognize him, his face as well as his voice.

"Thank you so much."

Duane at this point did a good job. Although I knew he was surprised to be left outside, he didn't try to catch my eye; he just folded his arms, turned his back, and stepped slowly away from the door.

Trix had used a certain amount of creativity in doing up her sex pad. She'd put up twinkle lights and soft lamp shades, laid down one of those shoddy rugs with a Garden of Eden scene woven into it. The furniture was definitely sub–Joshua Doore, more like rent-to-own, more like Mexican ghetto thrift shop. Nothing was clean. The place needed a good vacuuming and some swiping up with disinfectant, to deal with the sex smell.

"Uh, want a drink?" said Trix.

"Sure, thank you. Whatever you're havin'."

She fixed me a whiskey and ginger ale, the whiskey a brand I'd never seen before, Potter's Crown. Handing me the drink, she stepped around the coffee table to take up a lounging posture on the couch. Actually, she stretched herself into an imitation of a lounging posture. Her shoulders were high and tight, and she jiggled one foot so fast it was a blur. She was tweaky all right.

I seated myself in a barrel chair with stinky cushions.

"Let me tell you what I'm about here." I tried to give myself a touch of a New York accent, Brooklynish, not over-the-top. Just a suggestion of dirty bite. "Lemme tell ya what I'm about here."

I took a sip of my highball, and Trix said, "I know it's shitty whiskey."

It certainly was; it was bottom-shelf swill that needed every bit of the sweet ginger ale to ameliorate it.

"Mm, good drink. My first of the day," I laughed. After a pause I said, "I work for a guy on the East Coast. I tried somethin' stupid with him. Maybe after another couple a drinks I tell you the details."

I saw, aside from the despair in Trix's eyes, a kind of greedy passion. It was a type of gullibility, actually. It was that she saw me as a scummy person, and she was eager to believe that I was a scummier person than she was. I watched her look closely at my face.

I went on, "He caught me out. My ass is in I-can't-tell-you how deep of a shitpot. I begged him, 'Let me do something for you. Something to make up for how much of a stupid, selfish cunt I was.' He says 'All right.' So I'm looking for somebody he wants to get in touch with."

"But it's not me," said Trix.

"Right, it ain't you, sweetheart. I got Chino helping me. This guy that I'm looking for, I know him a little. And the bottom line of it is he owes my boss some money. What else, right? It's an old debt. A real old debt. *I* haven't seen the guy in years. A little bug told me you might have some information on him. He's supposed to be here in Vegas."

"Well, who is it?"

"Guy from Miami named Bill Sechrist."

The name visibly punched her in the lungs. Her mouth fell open and she looked away very quickly. Her eyes shifted to the shaded window, to the afternoon sunlight pouring down beyond it.

I waited, sipping my drink. Fortunately she'd poured me a light one. I'd deliberately built up my spiel to give the name maximum punch. And punch it did, oh yeah.

"Bill Sechrist," I repeated. "Goddamn that sonuvabitch. He was smooth, ya know?"

I watched Trix some more. Through whatever semi-stoned fog she was in, she was thinking hard, real hard and fast.

I said, "You know the guy."

Trix suddenly refocused. She scanned the coffee table. There was a pack of Newports on it, which she reached for until she realized she still had an unlit one between her fingers. She leaned forward and picked up a plastic lighter. *Chk!* She inhaled deeply from the cigarette, exhaled in a long stream upward, past the tip of her nose.

"Want one?" she said, gesturing toward the pack.

"No, thank you." Newports are terrible.

Slowly, she said, "I don't know where he is right this second. *But...*"

I waited.

She said, "You said you could maybe help me if I helped you."

I smiled and leaned forward. "Yeah, definitely. Here's the deal. Bill owes my boss $38,000."

"Yeah?" Her eyes got a little sharper.

"An' like I said, it's from a long time ago. Bill thinks the debt's been forgiven because of a job he did one time for my guy. But my boss decided it wasn't. It's still a debt. If I collect it, I'm off the hook, see? I get no cut of that money, so I can't share it around. But I'm willing to give 2,000 to whoever leads me to Bill Sechrist. Because I got two grand, but I don't got thirty-eight grand. And hearing that Bill's supposed to be in Las Vegas, I figured, well, maybe Vegas *is* the place where I can turn two grand into thirty-eight." I sipped my highball. "When I knew Bill Sechrist, and that was, God, a hundred years ago, he was doing all right. This was in Miami."

"You knew him in Miami?"

"Yeah, he bragged that he pulled off all sorts a shit for big money. And he threw it around too."

"He did?" These exclamations popped out of her like gumballs.

"Yeah, oh yeah. I was a stupid kid, didn't know any better than to let him buy me junk jewelry, cheap steak dinners, that kinda shit. I would've been his child bride except for—well, never mind. Yeah, especially he bragged about this arson job he claimed to've done in Chicago, I think he said, this bar that a buddy of his owned, and—"

"It was *Detroit*. Hah! He pulled that off, all right! He pulled that job all the way down the crapper, is where he pulled it." Her voice became throatier. "That son of a bitch couldn't pour piss out of a boot. So he was boffing you in Miami too."

I fought to keep my composure. *I was right. I was fucking right*. Blood rose behind my eyeballs. Oh, how I wanted to know more. *Don't blow it. Be patient. Be patient.*

"Huh," I said, "whaddaya mean he put it in the toilet? Just fucked it up? He kept saying—"

"He never got a dime for that job. Shit! What a mess. All these promises is all *I* got." Her eyes clouded over, and I saw to my grim satisfaction that she was thinking about the innocent lives snuffed out that night. I waited.

"Listen," Trix finally said, "how did you know to come looking for me?"

Earnestly, I said, "I can't tell you that. I mean, I can't tell you because I myself don't know. I got a name and an address."

She digested that. "Who's your boss, then?"

"His name is Steve Goldberg."

"A Jew?"

I nodded. "Big Stevie. I doubt you know the name. Not many people do, and I shouldn'ta told you. But I feel like I can trust you, Trix. I dunno. Somehow I just feel that. Steve's a Miami guy, he's very low-key. He deals a lot with the Cubans."

"Phew," she mused, "I wonder how somebody would've thought—"

"How's business?" I asked suddenly.

She looked at me. "I'd like to get out of it." She stubbed out her Newport and reached for another. She was thinking hard.

"Like," I said with warm sympathy, "you had no choice, huh?"

"Boy, you know it."

"Well, I sure been there. Might find myself there again before long, who knows?" I laughed harshly. "How much do ya charge in this town for a blow job anyway?"

Trix said, "You mean how much do *I* charge? Fifty bucks."

"Well, that ain't too bad."

"Well, I don't know where *you* used to work."

I took a cigarette from her pack and toyed with it in my fingers.

"Hey," she said, "I got somebody coming in soon. I've been thinking. I've got a deal for *you*." She sat upright, swinging her feet to the floor.

I smiled hopefully.

"I can deliver Bill Sechrist to you. But you're out of your mind if you think I'm gonna do it for chump change."

My smile faltered.

Loudly, she said, "What the fuck are you thinking? What the fuck kind of person do you think I am?"

I looked at the floor, as ashamed as a dog that's just clawed the Rembrandt off the wall.

Trix went on, "I'm not gonna sell out another human being for 2,000 fucking bucks!"

I shifted uneasily in my seat and kept my gaze on the floor. "I don't know what to do," I whispered.

She knew she had me. "Well, I'll tellya what you're gonna do! You're gonna get out, and you're gonna come back and give me half of that thirty-eight grand you're gonna get from Bill Sechrist!"

My head snapped up in panic. "Whoa! Whoa, lady! Trix!"

"You're gonna give me that money up front. Yeah, you are."

"I can't! I don't have it!"

"Well, you'll just have to get it, won't you?"

"You want me to give you, what, nineteen grand?" I gripped my head with both hands.

She said, "An even twenty would be better, but I guess I'll take nineteen."

I gazed at her pleadingly. "What if I do get that much money and give it to you, but then Bill don't give up what he owes? Or what if I do, and he *does* pony up, and that's a pretty fuckin' big if! Then I'm still gonna be out half of that money."

"You'll have to tell your guy..."

"Big Stevie."

"Big Stevie that you couldn't get it all. Or," she snickered, "maybe you can double your share right here in Las Vegas, like you said in the first place. Hey, don't cry, look—your boss, he's gonna be over the moon to get *half* of that money. Believe me."

I snuffled, "But what if he wants to know where it went?"

Trix stood up, and I did too. She stepped toward me and put her hand on my shoulder. "Listen to me," she said eagerly, and it was just like when she was helping me with my homework. I glanced at her from under my lashes and felt her whiskey breath on my cheek. "You have to tell him you could only *get* half. Or here's what you do—here it is—you tell Bill you need more, like you tell him you need, lessee, 60,000. Because it's the old debt plus interest. And that's cheap! Your boss told you to insist on that, see."

"Ah, I see."

"Then you're covered."

With a shaky hand I drained my drink. "I gotta think about that. I gotta talk it over with Chino."

"Well, you do that. Think you can come up with it? How 'bout that car out there?"

"I dunno. I dunno."

"It's what I need, and it's only fair. Come to think of it, it's *less* than fair. Honey, you know what? I can tell your ass is in a deeper crack than you tried to make out. He worked you over but good, didn't he?"

I hung my head.

Triumphantly, she whispered into my ear, "And the next time he won't stop there, will he?"

Softly, I said, "No."

"Well, then. I'd say I'm your only hope."

"Yeah," I admitted. "Yeah."

# SIXTEEN

In the car with Duane all I said was, "It's her."

We needed to reconnoiter. The diner we stopped at was the kind that served club sandwiches and decent coffee. The sandwich revived me, and the coffee cleared my head after that awful highball.

Duane was freaking again. Having taken off his cap in the restaurant, a courtesy all too rare these days, he pulled at his lank hair with his fist. "So my dad really—he was involved—he actually—he actually did arson?—I mean that's the way she made it sound—or conspired. At least." His other hand shook as he lifted his coffee mug to his lips.

I said, "Your dad, wherever he is, is an arsonist *and* a murderer."

Duane cried out, "Oh, God!" Other customers looked over.

"Shhh, my friend." He put down his mug and I covered his hand with mine. "You know, whatever happened exactly, it's all over. The dead did all their suffering that night. It's over and done with. Nobody's suffering anymore."

"Except you and me."

"Eat your sandwich. We can get into the self-pity thing, I guess, if we want to. I'm not saying I'm not feeling this. I'm feeling it too. But we've got to compartmentalize here. We've got to manage our feelings. Because we can either fall apart and be ineffective, or we can focus and execute. Eat. Man-size bite  now."

My friend bit into his sandwich. "That's it," I encouraged. They were good sandwiches. Decent food can help ground you when things go freaky.

He chewed, swallowed, and shook his head. "I can't handle this."

"You can. You can, Duane, come on, stick with me here. We've got to go see her again."

I watched him try to pull himself together. I gave him some quiet.

The waitress came with the coffee pot. "Yes, please," I said.

At length Duane said, "Do you want to talk to her again to ask—"

"I really want to find your dad now. I want her to tell me more about that night, about her involvement, and then I want to find your dad. Cut to the chase."

"You think she really knows where he is?"

"No. I think she's scamming us. I mean, I think *she thinks* she's scamming us. My main purpose in coming here was to confirm her existence, which confirms that a crime took place that night. Finding your dad would be a pot of jam. And I want that jam pot. It's obvious there's a lot more she can tell us, but she doesn't know that's what we want to know. She's greedy. You should've seen her eyes light up, all excited and hard, when I said '$38,000.' If we go back there with a bag of mone, she'll loosen up some more. I laid a C-note on the coffee table just before I walked out, and I could see her forcing herself not to snatch it up before I turned away."

"A C-note."

"That's what you're supposed to call them, haven't you watched any movies?"

That got a smile out of him, the first in hours.

"Do you think," he said, "that we could go back there

with, like, a fake bag of cash, and get her to talk more? Maybe she'd do it for the 2,000 anyway. Maybe she knows we're bogus."

"Oh, she doesn't think we're bogus. She knows we're for real, she just doesn't know for real in what way. She's nothing but a low-budget bangtail, and she knows we know it. I'll bet you anything that that hundred bucks is already converted to coke and up her nose. Did you see how scrawny and twitchy she is?"

I took another slug of coffee and went on, "So she needs money, wants it bad. I can't tell yet how much sense she's got left. People coming around offering money for information, that doesn't happen every day. She sees a big opportunity here, a chance for a score, and she wants to make the most of it. We could try to get her to take the two grand, but I don't think she'll do it. I mean, what leverage do we have? A bag of fake money would be stupid. She'd insist on seeing it. What are we gonna do, photocopy a bunch of money?"

"You mean we should just *give* her $19,000?"

"Not necessarily. We need to *have* it. We need for it to be real. Then…maybe we do give it to her. How much is the truth worth to us, after all this time?"

Slowly, Duane said, "I'm not sure I agree with you. Anyway, how're we going to come up with 19,000 bucks?"

"Well, we only need 17,000 more on top of the 2,000 you brought. Seventeen thousand, two hundred to be exact. I sure as hell don't have it. I've got forty-three dollars and eleven cents in my checking account."

He looked at me. "Why did you have to say 38,000 in the first place?"

"It seemed like a believable figure. Big enough to be impressive, not a round number, and yet not too big. Not small-time, not big-time."

"Well, I don't have 17,000 more dollars handy."

"How quick could you get it?"

"Lillian, I'm stretched pretty thin financially."

"Yeah, but you've got equity in your house, right?"

"Look, I only put five percent down on it. No, I don't have that much equity in my house. Even if I did, it'd take time to get it."

"Well—your T-bird?"

"Leased."

"Oh."

"I told you you were naive to assume the trappings of glamour are always paid for."

"Man, Duane, you've been making good money for years, right?"

He nodded.

I said, "And yet your net worth, I mean, is only like—"

"Lillian. Come off it. You know how it is. You get it and you spend it. You do the same thing."

"Yeah, but—" I stopped. He was right. I had to admit that.

He looked me full in the eye. "I don't know about this, Lillian. Be honest now. You don't really know what the hell you're doing, do you?"

"I hate it when people ask me that."

"Well, I'm scared."

"I'm scared too. We're *supposed* to be scared."

"I just don't like it."

"We're not *supposed* to—"

"I want to go back to Detroit!"

"Duane!"

He looked at me helplessly. "What do you want me to do?"

"Lend me your cell phone."

I stepped outside the restaurant into the toxic afternoon heat, consulted my notebook, took a deep breath, and punched

*Lucky Stiff*

in Minerva LeBlanc's number. The sun dropped lower to meet the tips of the mountains to the west.

I was braced for Tillie's voice, but Minerva answered. I started talking. She listened. I talked on. She asked a question here and there, in her deliberate way, but mostly she just listened.

At length I wrapped it up. "So, essentially, all I need right now to keep this thing rolling is $19,000 cash." I tried to sound energetic and unpleading. It was a struggle not to grovel, but I managed it. "What do you say?"

There was a very long pause. I heard her breathing.

At last she spoke. Her voice, in spite of its deliberate pace, was electric with excitement. "Tell Duane to go home if he wants to. Go to the Las Vegas Hilton. Not the Flamingo Hilton on the Strip, the Las Vegas Hilton on Paradise. Wait for me there." Her voice was absolutely alive, dancing in my ear.

*Oh, boy.*


By the time I got there she'd arranged for a room and left a message giving me her arrival time the next day. I was escorted up to something like the 300th floor by a guy in a suit, not a bellman. He insisted on carrying my gym bag. This was an executive type dude. White, fiftyish, moderate paunch, gold wristwatch, manicure. He opened a set of double doors onto a suite of rooms that thank God weren't ridiculously opulent. Windows on the mountains. Fruit bowl.

"I hope you and Ms. LeBlanc enjoy your stay," said CEO dude. "We look forward to serving her again." He handed me his card. "Is there anything you need right now?"

"Uh, no. No, thank you." As he turned to go I said, "Oh, wait a second," and began to dig in my purse.

"Oh, no no no," he said with a wide smile. He looked utterly sincere. "It's my pleasure. Really."

I hung up my change of clothes, put my toilet kit in the bathroom, pulled off the wig, and removed my falsies. I scrubbed my face, fiddled with the thermostat, and flopped down on a comfy couch in a state of relief.

Duane had in fact decided to bail, to my dismay but not to my surprise. He dropped me off at the hotel. Before I got out I handed him back the wad of bills we hadn't used.

"I'm sorry, Lillian. I just can't deal with this now. I'm glad Minerva's coming. But I feel like I'm letting you down."

"No, Duane. Don't waste a minute feeling bad, for God's sake. We got a lot done today, you know?"

"This isn't getting me any closer to finding my mom."

I looked at him. "You really don't think any of this has to do with your mom?"

He didn't answer.

I saw him suffering, struggling, fighting against coming to terms with the facts we'd learned from Trix that day.

I said, "Everything's all right. Tell you what: You go back to Detroit and see what else you can dig up, while I work this end. OK?" I didn't think he'd do a damn thing—he was so spooked—but I wanted to give him a dignified out.

Minerva arrived when she said she would, just after noon the next day. The same CEO dude showed her up, plus a bellman with her stuff on a cart. I'd spent the morning having breakfast, reading the newspapers, and thinking about Trix. And about Minerva. The casino downstairs looked interesting, but too loud and busy for the state of my nerves.

I was holding my breath over the possibility that Tillie might be in attendance, but she wasn't.

Minerva looked fabulous. That serious, intelligent face that meets you with confidence from all those book covers—that beautiful face—the face looked good. It was a face that showed the willingness to be amused. A face that showed, too, the capacity for passion and fury. It's a face that stays with you, believe me.

I jumped up, embraced her briefly, then helped her to a seat on the comfy couch. She was moving lots and lots better than when I'd last seen her. Like her speech, her movements were just a bit hesitant. She appeared to drag her right leg, as if she had to sort of haul it along from her hip. However, the leg appeared to support her well.

Her shape was good, although significantly plumper than when I'd last seen her. I liked her that way. Her breasts were larger, her stomach and hips nice and curvy. Yes, she'd been enjoying the pleasures of the table and had become curvaceous.

Her face revealed only very faint evidence of her ordeal that began with the attack five years ago. It was as if the pain, fear, and elapsed time had melded into a seriousness that added depth to her natural expression but did not weigh it down.

As befits a millionaire literary celebrity, her traveling clothes were expensive and perfectly tailored: sleek little linen blouse, pert jacket and slacks in slubby silk, calfskin slip-ons, and a really good haircut. I hit a bump there, much as I had with Duane: Her rich coffee-brown hair, which she was wearing longer now, was streaked with gray. Not heavily, but it was there. I had to admit, the gray actually looked good. Minerva LeBlanc was an experienced and sexy woman, and she smiled at me in the exact way that had made my heart wobble when I first saw her.

To answer your question, yes, it was wobbling now. Did I let on, though? Huh, no way. All I had to do was picture Tillie the live-in sex queen. That would sober up anybody.

After bringing Minerva a glass of ice water I seated

myself on a chair nearby, at which she smiled. "Oh, come here," she said, patting the couch. I unhurriedly moved over to her.

She curled her fingers and stroked my cheek. I began to long for a kiss sooner than later, but "Oh," she said, startled, "this looks like it hurt." Her fingers moved from my bruised cheek to my lip, which was much less fat than the day before.

I said, "I'm all right."

She appeared to make an internal decision of some kind, a sort of redirection.

She parted her lips and said, "Let's get to work."

Perhaps my face fell.

With a slight but ever so meaningful inflection, she said, "Work first."

"Yes! Absolutely!" I agreed.

We talked out a plan in half an hour. Minerva used the phone to call CEO dude and order a car for us as I began to change into my mob-slut disguise of wig, falsies, infrared lipstick, and tight jeans.

"What would you like?" she said, holding the receiver.

"Didn't you rent a car at the airport?"

"I'm not very steady driving yet."

"Oh. Well, how 'bout a Mercedes?"

She asked for one to be brought to the hotel immediately. She turned from the phone to see me stalk across the room in my Steffi Cordova persona.

"Oh, my," was all she could manage. I took pride in having stunned her into near muteness.

"Pretty good, huh?" I pivoted in front of a mirror.

She paused for rather a long moment, and I realized she was trying not to scream with laughter. She managed to say, "As long as you yourself believe, that's all that matters."

"Is that a line from *Desiderata* or something?"
"Come on."

We went down in the elevator to a special money office. It was a luxury lounge for high rollers to handle their accounts in style. A deferential man with a mile-high forehead and a diamond tie tack gave Minerva a paper to sign.

I noticed at this point that she appeared to have a speck of trouble with her right hand. She signed with her left, but her right failed to hold the paper as steady as she wanted it on the tabletop. It seemed she didn't have as much volition over the hand as she wanted, or perhaps it was just some kind of neurological weakness.

*You'd have been better off never having met me*, I thought. *But here you are, helping me again.*

The man with the forehead took the paper and left, returning a few minutes later with a uniformed guard carrying a small metal cash box.

The man opened the box, which contained four banded stacks of brand-new hundreds. He demonstrated by the serial numbers that there were fifty bills in each stack, for a total of $20,000.

"Thank you, Don," said Minerva. She picked up the money and handed it to me. "Put it in your bag and let's go."

# SEVENTEEN

On my first visit to Trix's crappy tube home I'd noticed a dusty black Mustang, five or seven years old, parked on her slab. The car was there now; a scraped-up Toyota pickup was parked in front.

I rapped authoritatively and listened. I knocked again, this time adding a light bashing of the kick panel with the leather sole edge of my Weejun. Minerva waited at the foot of the steps, holding her sophisticated shoulder bag closely at her side.

Trix pulled back the door a crack and squinted at me hostilely. She was loose-haired and wearing a black slip and bitsy mules with rhinestones.

I said, "I've got the money."

"Oh," she said with a look of sudden awe. She had to believe it, though. "Come on in," she said.

"We can wait out here."

"No, come on in. Who's that?"

"Friend."

"Money friend?"

I gave her a cold stare. My jeans were so tight the key of the rented Mercedes barely fit into my front pocket. The bundles of money jammed my purse fat full.

Trix retreated and held the door open. I ushered Minerva in. She climbed the three steps with a hitch in her gait and a firm grip on my arm.

We were confronted by a shaggy pale fella wearing a towel around his waist.

"What the hell's this?" he demanded.

"Never mind, lover," said Trix. "You gals sit down. Have a drink. Gimme five minutes." Her eyes were hectic, and I guessed she'd recently coked up or, possibly, taken a hit of meth or some other upper.

"Hey," said the customer.

"Come on." Trix took his hand and pulled him into the bedroom. She kicked the door shut. There was a brief silence during which Minerva and I made ourselves more or less comfortable: she in the barrel chair, I at one end of the couch.

Have you ever tried to ignore the hasty and turbulent sounds of sex for hire? It's an automatic reaction, I suppose, to try to award other humans a measure of dignity, but I'm afraid the gamut of sex acts is inherently undignified. Sex, I suppose, is the rawest form of self-expression, and of gratification.

"Lordy," I muttered.

Minerva cocked her head, listening intently. We heard several deep moans, which rose to little shrieky cries.

"Is that him?" I wondered.

"Yeah. That boy's got some coonhound blood in him, if I'm not mistaken."

The shrieks became deeper again, then began to rhythmically rise and fall, like the dive signal in a submarine. Then to our ears came a stage giggle, a laugh so fake it would've even turned the stomach of the most narcissistic stand-up comic. Trix went on giggling for an excruciating length of time.

"Oh, for God's sake," I said. "A razor blade. Give me a razor blade. Anything to put me out of my—"

"They're done," Minerva interrupted.

Trix reappeared, shrugging into a yellow wool cardigan

sweater over the lacy slip. "Hurry up," she yelled over her shoulder.

Her customer came out, clothed, but still jamming a foot into a cowboy boot.

"Oh, baby," he began, "I—"

"That's it, sweetie, see you later."

Trix shut the flyweight trailer door behind him, poured a couple of fingers of Potter's Crown into a highball glass, and tossed it back. I shuddered to watch her, but she didn't flinch. "Want one?" she said, wiping her mouth with the back of her hand. In response to the liquor, she appeared to wind down a smidge.

"No, thank you," Minerva and I said together.

Trix kicked off one spangled mule and tucked her foot beneath her on the other end of the couch from me. She put the other foot up on the coffee table. Her pose looked grotesquely athletic.

I frankly studied her face. There was something ulterior lurking there behind her put-on carelessness. I felt uneasy.

Nevertheless, I said, "All right, let's talk, Trix. This here's Sheila. She knows Big Steve Goldberg from Miami. She'd like to have a conversation with Bill Sechrist too. Like I said, I got the money. You gonna show us where he is?"

"Yeah, um. Yeah."

"Well?"

"Let's see the money."

"Fair enough." I opened my purse and drew out the packs of hundreds. Trix's eyes sharpened, as they had the day before when I talked about money. She licked her lips at the sight of the bills, and for an instant I thought she was about to try to devour them.

I said, "There's 20,000 bucks here." I kept up my vaguely Brooklyn way of talking, not overdoing it. *There's twunny thousand bucks heeur.* Back of the throat.

I laid the banded packets on the coffee table, flicking aside Trix's pack of Newports. "An even twunny."

Trix looked from the money to me. "Half now?"

"No, five now. Five grand now." I tossed one packet into her lap. She gazed down at it as I stuffed the other three packets back into my bag.

She picked up the money and thumbed it. "Yeah," she said. "All right. You get in your car and follow me in my car."

I hesitated.

Minerva spoke up. "No."

Trix leaned forward and picked up the Newports and plastic lighter. She flipped a cigarette into her mouth, then sat staring at the money, flicking the lighter on and off.

I felt my blood pressure rise, simply out of uncertainty.

Minerva said, "We'll do this one of two ways. One, we ride together, either us driving or you driving. Or two, you tell us where to find Sechrist, and I wait here while Lillian goes and—"

She heard me catch my breath, and so did Trix.

"Uh, oh, fuck it," Minerva went on coolly. "What the fuck's your name again?"

I snarled, "I'm Steffi."

"H'h," her tone was equally contemptuous, "Did Big Stevie give you that name? Stevie?-Steffi?"

"Shut up," I said.

Trix kept flicking her lighter on and off.

In a strange voice, Minerva said, "I want to…" She stopped.

"Hmm?" I said, realizing I needed to keep taking cues from her. She didn't respond.

I turned to focus on her, looking for a silent signal.

She was staring weirdly into space, her eyes suddenly glassy. Motionless.

"Sheila?"

Not an eyelid moved.

"Oh, Jesus," I said. "Oh, shit. Sheila! Minerva!" I moved to her, took her hand, and passed my other hand in front of her face. No response. Her skin was as smooth and cool as if she'd turned to stone.

Trix yelled, "She's having a heart attack!"

"No, she's having some kind of—she's gone into some kind of thing. Trix, help me. Call 911, OK? 'Cause if she goes into a major—"

I turned to find Trix in the process of thrusting down her bosom the packet of hundreds I'd tossed to her while stepping into the mule she'd kicked off. She reached down and, with the quickness of a lizard, seized my bag off the couch. She scurried around the coffee table and headed for the door, pausing to plunge her hand into a plastic plant, from which she recovered a small wallet.

As I watched in disbelief, she clattered out the door. This all happened in about five seconds.

"Goddamn you!" I shouted, and turned back to my beloved.

Minerva blinked once, and her eyes snapped into focus. She was back. Her eyes found me, then they scanned the room. "I did it again," she murmured. "What happened?"

We heard the roar of Trix's Mustang backing out.

Minerva said, "What the hell?"

"You blanked out," I said, "and she took off with my purse and the money. Are you—"

"I'm OK!"

"Come on, then!" I hauled her to her feet and propelled her outside. The Mustang shot off in a spray of gravel and dust. Thank God I'd put the Mercedes key in my pocket.

"Good!" cried Minerva when she saw it. She was smiling widely, but that detail barely registered on me right then.

*Lucky Stiff*

We jumped in and I found myself gripping the leather-clad wheel of the Mercedes, standing on the accelerator, rocketing down the trailer court's rutted lane, adrenaline and rage surging in equal amounts through my veins.

Trix's Mustang fishtailed out of the gravel and onto the main road, where the tires got a grip and then that car was *moving*. I took the corner a little faster; the Mercedes slid sideways on the gravel toward a thicket of mailboxes until the rear wheel caught the pavement. We flew along the godforsaken road away from the Strip, out toward the desert floor to the west. The road was narrow, flat, and straight.

But there was traffic. Trix had to hit the brakes behind a bread truck; oncoming cars prevented her passing. She wasn't hopped-up enough to ram the truck, which would probably have spun them both out. We safely passed a handful of side streets, subdivision entrances—Trix's place was on the wrong side of the tracks and a fair distance out from town already. The road was opening up. The bread truck remained an obstacle to Trix.

I stuck on her bumper. She saw me in her mirrors.

"Faster!" said Minerva.

"I'm not going to ram her, for God's sake. Help me watch the road, watch the sides, holler if something's coming from the side."

"Ram her!"

"Goddamn it, I don't want to kill anybody!" I hollered back. "Maybe I should let her go."

The bread truck slowed and signaled a left turn in front of a party store. Trix hauled the Mustang around it *on the left*, just as it was beginning its turn. She made it, but I had to jam the brakes or broadside it. I dropped back and went around the other side.

"Go!" shouted Minerva. "Get her! Get her! Where the hell is she going?" Man, there was blood in her voice.

"She just wants to lose us." I panted. "She didn't expect us to follow, she thought you were falling out."

"Faster!"

"Do you have a death wish?" We must have been going about 90 miles an hour at that point.

The road took us across the open desert now, dry rocks, brush, dust devils, empty sky. The Mustang overtook a camper van and whizzed on. I followed. A reckless convoy of two, we zoomed around a few more cars and small trucks.

"Stay on her!" Minerva fumbled in her purse and I had a sudden horrible thought.

"You didn't bring your gun, did you?"

She didn't answer.

"Oh, shit, Minerva, let's stay calm here. Let's stay calm now."

"Lillian, for God's sake, ram her!"

"What's the matter with you? I ram her, our airbags explode, how'm I gonna keep driving?"

"Shit," Minerva complained. "This was *not* the plan!"

Somehow in the middle of all this I realized she was talking fast and well.

The Mustang's engine is a powerful one, very fast off the blocks compared to the Mercedes. But the Mercedes, and this one was a large sedan, not the sport model, it kept up very nicely on the open road. I glanced at the instruments and saw the speedometer at 115.

*Shit me.*

Without warning the Mustang lurched to the right, a cloud spewing from its rear. Something kicked up and bounced off our windshield. I swerved and braked hard, but the Mustang had slowed so suddenly that we were now ahead of it.

Minerva looked back. "She's had a blowout! She's off the road!"

I checked my mirrors, stayed on the brakes until I got the car down to 15 or so, then let up on them and spun the wheel. I headed back for her, half the car on the right shoulder, half on the road. An SUV blasted headlong past me, swerving and honking.

The Mustang was still moving, picking up speed in spite of the blown tire, and coming straight on.

"Don't ram her!" yelled Minerva.

"Make up your fucking mind! This is chicken now!" Something had snapped inside me. Now I didn't give a flying shit if I slammed into Trix headfirst and took us all to hell.

In spite of the glare of the sun on the Mustang's windshield I saw Trix's eyes, her face crazy and scared behind the wheel, pure terror. The hood of the Mustang loomed bigger. I foresaw in my immediate future a spectacular collision featuring two V-8 engine blocks, two irresistible forces coming together in a deafening festival of destruction. I aimed straight for the goddamned Mustang.

At the last instant Trix swung her steering wheel to her right, and the car blew past us on a trajectory into the rock-strewn desert. A roostertail rose behind the Mustang as Trix forced it to go faster over the dusty earth.

"OK, hold on," I said with calm grimness, and committed my vehicle to the same path, bringing it around to eat up Trix's dust. As soon as I got her in my sights again, I swung out to her flank. Both cars jounced wildly over the jagged ground. Minerva braced herself against the dashboard with both hands. The Mustang dodged a clump of brush that I chose to crash through. The dry bushes gave way easily, blowing into a million fragments.

"Well, she's not going far," commented Minerva over the revving of our engine. "She's knocked out her oil pan."

Sure enough, I perceived a thick trail of black goo drizzling behind the Mustang.

I let up on the gas. "She's not going anywhere now," I agreed. "Might as well just keep her in sight. Then we'll have the advantage of a running car."

"Won't be long. She's likely to shred more tires too, the way she's going."

I steered carefully now around brush and rocks. Trix was punishing the Mustang, forcing the engine to keep going or blow completely.

And in fact, the chase ended in about two more minutes. The Mustang veered sharply again, to avoid a tall boulder, but then caromed hard off another one, the driver's door taking the brunt of the hit. The car lost power and rolled to a stop. Gray smoke poured from beneath the hood.

"That engine's burned out," I noted.

"Yeah, it's on fire," said Minerva. "She's got flames now."

I pulled the Mercedes to a stop a hundred yards away. We were perhaps a mile off the main road. I jumped out.

"Careful now," said Minerva.

I moved quickly around to her door and helped her out. Even in my haste I tried to hold her arm carefully; she seemed so delicate after all. And right now she wasn't quite steady on her feet.

We watched the burning car. Even in the bright daylight I saw orange flames licking out from the grille. The smoke changed from gray to black. Big wide heat shimmers rose from the car and blended into the little quick ones hovering everywhere in the desert that afternoon. Flames engulfed the hood, the very metal now catching fire.

"Why isn't she getting out?" With my hand clasped around her arm, Minerva took a step forward, dragging her leg. "Why isn't she getting out?" she repeated.

"Oh, God."

"She needs to get out of that car. The gas tank."

"Oh, God."

"Lillian!"

I dropped her arm and dashed forward.

# EIGHTEEN

Trix was sitting upright in the driver's seat, clawing at the door latch with both hands. The instant I reached the car, a jet of fire shot up from the hood and blew back toward the passenger compartment. Trix continued to tear at the latch. I saw that the door had been dented inward at the latch point—evidently, when the car glanced off the last boulder. The outside door handle was smashed. The side airbag had deployed and deflated, apparently confusing Trix, whose eyes were locked on me in total panic. She opened her mouth and screamed; her scream barely pierced the roar of the fire. The heat was cataclysmic. Sour smoke stung my nose.

I ran around to the passenger side, pulling off my wig and wrapping it around my hand. Using it as a pot holder, I threw open the door, lunged inside, grabbed Trix by the sweater, and pulled her out. She clattered to the ground like a sack of sticks. The synthetic fibers of the wig bonded to the hot metal door and hung there like a dead thing.

Digging the heels of my Weejuns into the barren desert dirt, I pulled and dragged her by the shoulders, yelling, "Come on! Hurry up!"

She couldn't get up while I was dragging her, but she kicked her feet to help. When I got us away from the huge horrible heat, I dropped her.

Minerva met us. "It's not safe yet!" she yelled. "Come on!"

Somehow we all tottered to the Mercedes.

I looked back at the Mustang, now engulfed in fire from front bumper to rear.

"The gas tank's not blowing," Minerva said.

"Not enough gas in it," Trix coughed, sinking into the dirt. "I've been driving around on empty for a week."

She was shoeless, sweater torn, black slip ripped, her legs bleeding from scratches and scrapes. "Oh, Lord, the money," she moaned.

"You worthless bitch," I said. "Get in the car."

We heard sirens coming from the city, so I drove carefully to the road and continued west into the desert. Minerva produced her pocket revolver and covered Trix as I drove. "You don't need that," Trix told her. "I'm not going anywhere, believe me."

After a few minutes she began to whimper, desperately, in the backseat. "Oh, gawd, you guys are gonna kill me. Just kill me now, OK? Just shoot me once, real good in the head, because I can't stand pain, I really can't. Oh gawd, I lost the mob's money. I lost your money."

"What about the bundle you stuffed down your bra?" I asked.

Trix slapped her chest. "It's gone! It's gone!" she wailed. "It must have fallen out!"

Minerva said, "To hell with the money. Keep driving."

"Trix," I said, "you're gonna talk to us."

"But I don't know where Bill Sechrist is! Oh, gawd, I don't know where the son of a cocksucker is! I haven't seen him in twenty years! Thirty years! Oh, gawd."

"I knew it," I said. "Shut up. Calm down. Trix, we're all in the same boat now. Don't be afraid."

We came to the piedmont, such as it is, of the Spring

Mountains, and there I pulled over in the shade of a weird little oasis. There was a gas station and a mini-mart, a shitass motel, and a bar.

"We're gonna go in that bar," I told Trix, "and you're gonna clean up, and we're gonna sit down and talk. And we're gonna figure out what to do next."

Trix said quietly, "OK."

"It's happy hour," Minerva observed.

"Huh?" I said.

"Their happy hour starts at 2 P.M., the sign says."

"Oh, goody," I said. "Well, nobody gets a drink until we do some talking."

Minerva returned her weapon to its quick-draw pocket in her purse and we went into the Palace of Palms Bar.

It was a cavelike, stale place: typical and crummy, and to me, comfortable. Yes, speaking for Trix and myself, we fit the demographic just fine. A pair of slutty, disheveled tavern rats. Minerva might pass for our accountant, I supposed.

The few heads in the bar turned when we walked in, but soon enough went back to their afternoon draft beers. What I mean to say is, this was the kind of bar where a barefoot woman in a torn slip attracts men's gazes but doesn't necessarily raise their eyebrows. A couple of guys were playing pool, and we heard the clack of the balls.

Minerva seated herself at a table in a corner while I accompanied Trix to the ladies' toilet. I washed up and combed water through my hair with my fingers while she used the toilet, then I peed fast while she cleaned up at the sink. We didn't speak.

We joined Minerva, who was surrounded by six glasses of beer.

Sweetly, she explained, "The bartender came over, and the

vibe wasn't right for me to just order water or something."

Patiently, I asked, "But why *six* beers?"

"Happy hour!" I hadn't known of this naughty side of hers.

Trix and I pulled up chairs. Our eyes adapted to the darkness. We all reached for a beer. I took a slug, and it sure tasted good down my hot throat. The wooden tabletop was sticky. Trix's hand trembled.

I put down my glass and drilled my eyes into Trix's. I said, "You know me, Trix Hawley."

Trix stared at me slow and hard. Her eyes filled and her lip trembled. "Oh. Dear Jesus gawd. Oh, dear Jesus *gawd*." She blotted her eyes on the sleeve of her sweater.

"Lillian Byrd," she snuffled. Her breath came hard. "Dear Jesus gawd. Oh, you poor kid."

Minerva watched us.

I said, "I'm not a poor kid. Pull yourself together. I'm not with the mob. I met up with Bill Sechrist's boy about a week ago and we got to talking. Duane. Remember Duane?"

"Oh gawd. I'm in it now, I'm in it all the way up to my orchid now."

I'd never heard that expression. "Look. Trix. One night the Polka Dot burned down. I was there. My mom and dad died screaming. Duane's mom disappeared. A burned-up body wearing your wedding ring was found in the bar. That much I know. When Duane and I talked, I realized that body wasn't you."

Trix opened her mouth.

"Wait," I said. "Trix, I want you to understand something. I want to talk to you. I want you to talk to me. That's all I want here. I don't think I can make you go to jail, though I know you were involved. The police have other things to do." I spoke deliberately, so that through her mounting hysteria she could easily understand me. "I don't know how much involved you were. For my whole adult life I thought the fire was an accident. You might think I want vengeance on you. But I don't. All I want from you is the truth. All I want is to know why it happened, and how."

Trix shook her head and gulped her beer. She said, "My nerves are shot."

Minerva let out a startled laugh. "*Your* nerves."

I said, "Trix, not that you have a whole fuckload of choice here, but you owe me an explanation. You owe it to me to willingly tell me what you know."

She adjusted her butt in her chair, settling in. Weakly, she said, "All right."

"Good."

"How'd you know I was alive?"

"Duane reminisced about his stepmother, the woman Bill Sechrist met in Florida after he uprooted Duane from the neighborhood in Detroit. He spoke of you rather fondly." She nodded, flattered.

I went on, "All it took was for him to recall how you talked. What did it was *I didn't know whether to shit green or go blind.*"

"Are you shitting me? You're not shitting me."

"Have you ever in your life heard anyone else say that?"

Trix thought. "Well, my Aunt Flora said it."

"Then when Duane said you told his dad *You couldn't pour piss out of a boot,* that more or less nailed it. When he told me you dyed your hair dull brown and had red roots—"

"There ya go," she said thoughtfully. "Then how in the hellja find me?"

"I paid a call on Robert Hawley, your surviving spouse."

"You mean he—"

"No. His wife showed me your letters. With return addresses

in case he decided to send you any money. She intercepted them, you know, after the first one."

"I thought she might've done that." She studied me. "My gawd, you were just a kid. I didn't think I'd ever..." She stared off into the dim room.

"Kids grow up," I said. "Listen, you want a cigarette?"

Gratefully, she said, "Yeah."

Minerva offered, "I'll get them."

"Newports," said Trix. "The machine's down the hall."

"And some Camel Filters while you're at it, please," I requested. This appeared to amuse Minerva, who moved off to ask the bartender for change.

"Matches!" called Trix. "And how 'bout a few more beers?"

I said, "It was her money that just got burned up in your car."

Sadly, she said, "All that money."

"Do you know who she is?"

"No."

"She's Minerva LeBlanc."

"Really? Minerva LeBlanc that writes books? Butter my muffin! Really?"

"Really."

"She's my favorite! I love her books. I didn't recognize her."

"You read?"

"Yes, I read!"

"Well, we'll have to get her to give you an autograph."

"Yeah!"

Minerva returned with the smokes and two books of matches.

"My God, she *is* Minerva LeBlanc!"

Unappreciatively, Minerva said, "Lillian."

"Wow," said Trix. "Wow. Hey, I've got some stories to tell you. I could tell you these stories and then you could write them, and then—" she broke off. "Didn't, like, something happen to you?"

Minerva said, "Have you realized yet that Lillian saved your life by pulling you out of that car?"

Trix reached for her pack of Newports. "Yeah. For whatever it's worth." She looked at me, and a new clarity came over her. "You must hate my guts."

# NINETEEN

"I don't hate your guts," I said, unwrapping the Camel Filters. "I want to talk." We lit up simultaneously. Minerva abstained. I said, "Let's keep talking about our particular story, OK?"

Trix took in a deep mentholated lungful, savored it, exhaled, and began.

"First of all, speaking of saving lives, did you know that Bill Sechrist saved your dad's life? In the navy?"

"Yeah, I knew that."

"So Martin Byrd owed Bill Sechrist big time."

"Yeah."

"And that was Bill's way into the whole thing. See? He and I got friendly. That wife of his, unhhh…"

"She was a piece of work," I agreed encouragingly.

"Yeah. Well, eventually Bill and me got serious, real serious, and he figured out a way to make all of our troubles go away. He was crazy about me, he really was. No man was ever crazier about me." The combination of cigarettes and beer settled Trix's nerves satisfactorily. She stopped to take another gulp. She raised the cold-beaded glass to her forehead and nuzzled her temple into it. The gesture reminded me of the way Adele Hawley had rolled her beer bottle across her forehead. She said, "You know, for a long time…for forever…I've wanted to tell somebody about this. And I thought someday I *would* tell it all to somebody. But I never thought it'd be you."

I nodded.

She went on, "See, Bill and I wanted to elope. I'd never eloped before, and I thought it'd be fun. Plus, I was so sick of Robert. You said you met Robert."

"I did."

"Well then."

"Yeah. Why," I asked, "not just run away, then?"

"That's what I said. Bill said, *That's not my style. Bill Sechrist doesn't run away from trouble.* He thought his wife would be better off dead. He felt, deep down, that he had, like, an obligation to...get rid of her. She was making his life a hell on earth. And so he had an obligation to end all that pain and everything. He had a hold on me, I tell you. I never met his wife. To me she wasn't real, really. It was like a TV show. Oh, I loved that man. He was a rock-hard military man. A fighting man. I used to play with his dog tags, that always got him excited. The thing was, Bill Sechrist was the only man who ever valued me for myself. For what was inside me."

"Yeah?"

"He gave me things."

"Things that proved his love?" I suggested.

"Yeah. To me they did. And he did things for me."

"Like what?"

"Like he'd burn himself with cigarettes. He'd hold a cigarette to his arm or he'd pull up his pants leg and hold the cigarette to his leg and he'd say, *This is for you.* He'd pull bits of skin off himself with a pliers, saying the same thing." Trix gave a short laugh. "Isn't that unusual?"

Minerva and I exchanged glances.

Trix was warming up. "But it showed me something," she said, "you know? Anyhow, I went along with him. He told me every step of it. He went to your dad and said he was in trouble and needed money. He said he'd done a bad thing and gambled away some money he didn't have. Some union boss's money—you know—that he'd offered to deliver somewhere. He took it to the track, thinking he'd make something for himself on the sly, but he lost it. That was his story, and your dad believed it. Bill was big in the union over at Dodge Main.

"A pile of money, 50,000. Your dad didn't have it to give him, he knew that. He went to work on your dad. He reminded him how he'd saved his life. He said, *They're gonna come after my wife and the boy. They told me that, Marty.* And he brought up the idea of burning down the Polka Dot for the insurance money. Your dad was careful, he had insurance. Bill told your dad, 'Look, me *and* my family's gonna be dead if I don't come up with that money. I'll pay you back, honest Injun! I'll take care of everything, I'll do it right, the bar goes, you all go to live with…' uh, Marty's brother…"

"Uncle Guff."

"Yeah. And he says, 'You give me the insurance money when you get it, and then in a few months I pay you the money back. I swear I will. You find a nicer bar, nicer home for your family—you *happy* about your little girl growing up in a place like this? Maybe you wanta get out of the tavern business anyway. Open a garage. Or a grocery store.'"

Trix lit another cigarette off the butt of the first. "Your dad, he wanted to help his friend. I think he tried to think of another way to do it, but finally he agreed."

"He agreed," I said.

The three of us sat thinking about that.

Bill Sechrist had floundered through the ship's flooding galley, reached underwater, and grabbed my dad by the belt and hauled him out. My dad was struggling there in the water, thinking, *This is it. This is it.* And then Sechrist's determination and brute strength changed the world. Sechrist gave my dad a gift beyond price.

In wartime men do hideous things and they do saintly things. That was about as much as I knew about war.

You might not think that the life of a tavern keeper is inherently honorable. My dad served beverages that gave comfort, but they also unleashed demons. He liked it when people drank. But I must insist on this point: Martin Byrd was an honorable man. I never knew him to show fear of anything, and he had never given me occasion to be ashamed of him. This is why I say he was honorable.

I wondered, "Why didn't he sell the bar and give the money to Sechrist? Why scheme to defraud the insurance company?"

"Kid," said Trix, "he did try to sell it. I remember that. Your mom thought it was a good idea. I guess no one wanted to buy it *right now*, though. Bill put the pressure on him. *I need that money, buddy.* What could he do?"

Minerva suggested, "He probably decided to let Sechrist do the arson, then somehow he'd pay the insurance company back."

I shook my head. "That'd be a stretch." But something was starting to resonate.

"Lillian," said Minerva, "your father—"

"My father was an honorable man." It mattered to me to tell Trix and Minerva that, here in this cruddy tavern. "As an adult, I look back and feel that maybe his sense of honor had a...utilitarian side. I think he understood that things—principles— aren't always crystal-clear. Morally speaking." Trix and Minerva listened. "I guess I'm realizing that sometimes in order to fulfill an obligation...you have to take on a new one."

"You said it," said Trix.

Minerva said nothing but looked at me with softness in her eyes.

"Go on," I said to Trix.

"Well, then I went and talked to Robert. I said, *I've got an interesting opportunity for us.* Bob was working like a dog for dogshit pay, driving a dump truck. We had a dream. Get rich, go to live someplace nice like Las Vegas. I thought Las Vegas was the cat's ass."

"I remember."

"Yeah. And I thought I was lucky, I thought I could work my luck so that I'd have it good someday, have it easy. So I told Robert…" She lowered her eyes.

I waited.

"I told him to take out a life insurance policy on me. Then I die, but I don't die, and we get the money, we blow this donkey-butt town, we have a ball in Vegas. Double that bankroll! That's what I thought. I actually thought we could walk into a casino and double that money in an hour. Break the bank if we stayed all night." She laughed nastily at herself. "Somebody told me it takes money to make money. I thought that's all there was to it. You know, I wasn't that much older than you, Lillian."

"I know it."

"You were a smart kid. You've prob'ly done well in life. Haven't you? Prob'ly a good job, or a good husband. A husband who isn't a drunk, or a fucked-up gorilla. Nice house, I bet. Kids? You got kids?"

"No, Trix."

"Hmp. Well anyhow, I sell Robert on going along with it. I mean, he never knew Bill. He never knew anybody in this… Not your dad, nobody. All he knew was, the bar where I was working was gonna be burned for insurance, and I was gonna pretend to be burned up in it, and we'd take *our* insurance money and take off. All's I'd have to do'd be hide out for a while until the insurance company paid off."

"I see," I said. "Bill didn't know Robert, and Robert didn't know Bill."

"Bill knew I was married. But I was fed up with Robert."

"So…I'm not following."

"So *my* plan was, as soon as Robert got the insurance money on my life, I'd get *my* hands on it, and beat it to Florida with Bill. What could Robert do at that point? Tell the police? He was in on it too, right with me. Bill helped me with that part too.

"So Robert took out a policy on me. Fifty thou. Same as your dad had on the Dot. I was surprised the Dot was worth that much, actually."

I put in, "Well, it was the whole building."

"Yeah, that's right. So Bill—boy, he planned it. He got rid of the kid, took him to camp."

"Why didn't he murder Duane too?" I asked grimly.

"That's a good question. I think Bill had hopes for the kid. I dunno. Then, that night, he drove back home with the wife. He got her plastered—fed her her medicine, you know, only more of it. And booze. He knew how to do it. He'd practiced on her. She never knew it. He was a good thinker, Bill was. He could hold so many different facts in his mind at one time, it would amaze you. He thought it all through, how she'd need to breathe smoke in order to die right, how she'd need to be burned almost totally up in order to be me. He thought of all that in advance. 'N' then the fryer was my idea. I said I'll break the thing so it catches on fire. I knew how it worked. When the guy came to install it he told me what would happen if this or that broke. Those things are dangerous, you know, they're really dangerous. You know that? I told Bill, 'Then you help things along, you give it a boost with some lighter fluid maybe, then flash your Zippo at it, and you get the hell outta there.' I gave him my wedding ring."

"Were you at all afraid?" I asked.

She paused. "Can't say that I was. It was—it was like a prank or something. It was exciting. So that night I busted the fryer, all I did was take a fork and jimmy a little pipe on it, and that made it heat too high. And I made sure to leave it on while me and Marty were cleaning up. 'You go on up, I'll let myself out,' I told him. So I let myself out, then an hour later I sneak back in. I seen a light in the upstairs—I thought, *Marty thought of everything*. I assumed everybody was gone. I leave the door unlocked and I beat it again. As soon as I'm gone Bill brings in the wife—holding her up like she's drunk, see, which she basically was—"

"Juanita."

"Huh?"

"Her name was Juanita."

"Oh."

"Where did you go?"

"To a motel in Sterling Heights. I just picked one. Robert gave me some cash. And Bill did it. He pulled it off." Trix gazed at her second glass of beer, then at me. "It went just fine. Except for one thing."

I said, "He did it on the wrong night."

"It was the wrong night, oh gawd, it was the wrong night! Gawd help me. Gawd have mercy. I don't know what happened. Bill told me which night to be ready. I told Robert which night to be ready...ready for the police to come and tell him.

"Marty—your dad—he was supposed to take the family out for the night, you and your mom were supposed to be gone. Gone, gone somewhere, over to you uncle's or someplace. I had no idea you and your mom were upstairs the whole time."

"We were playing cribbage and drinking pop." I heard my voice tremble.

Trix wiped her mouth with the back of her hand. "Oh Lord, oh gawd. I don't know, I never knew what went wrong. Bill carried out the plan like he thought they'd agreed to. He positioned the body. He did it all just so, and he lit the hot fat, and he left. He had no idea until the next day that…that—"

"That he'd killed my mom and dad." I felt Minerva's hand come to me under the table. She placed it on my thigh and I covered it with mine. I felt steadier.

Trix murmured, "He had no idea."

"I think he did."

"What?"

"I looked at the news pictures. His car was parked down the alley at least as long as it took a newspaperman to get there to take pictures of the burning building. Then a little later the car was gone."

"Well, I don't know."

"He could have raised an alarm when he heard my mom and dad screaming."

"Well, I don't know. He sure didn't want your dad to die. Your dad was gonna give him that insurance money. No Marty Byrd, no insurance money. He was gonna skip out on your dad, I mean, that goes without saying. He had no intention of paying him that money back. But he wasn't gonna kill him. Didn't wanta kill him, for gawd's sake."

"What happened afterward?"

"Well, I stick around this motel in Sterling Heights. I change my hair and how I look. I go shopping. I eat at a restaurant. Watch TV in the room. Robert came to see me a couple of times. Bill came to see me quite often. I got nervous they'd run into each other. This was while the kid was at camp."

"Duane, that would be Duane."

"Yeah."

*Lucky Stiff*

"The boy whose mother you helped murder."

"No, no, I wasn't even there when she died."

Sudden rage blurred my vision. "You stupid puke! You helped kill her and then you helped cover it up!"

I felt Minerva's hand tighten in mine. I wanted to smash Trix's face in. But I got ahold of myself because, more than that, I wanted her to keep talking to me. In a calmer way, I said, "You were, in fact, an accessory before *and* after the murder of Juanita Sechrist."

Trix considered that. "I guess so. I guess I feel like I had something to do with it, even if I wasn't right there."

Minerva's grip grew even firmer.

I said, "The only thing that kept me from dying too was luck. And the Detroit Fire Department."

"I'd say it was mostly luck," Trix reflected. "It usually is in these types of things. If you really think about it, Lillian, you're an extremely lucky stiff. Luckier than me."

Ignoring that and keeping control, I said, "And then Robert double-crossed you."

"Yeah. He got the money in his name. Who else's, right? The insurance company was suspicious, but they couldn't find any evidence of anything. They gave him the money, and he put it in an account right away. When I got in touch with him, he said he'd decided to keep the money all to himself. I thought it was a joke. I can still hear him laughing at me."

"He double-crossed you before you could double-cross him."

Minerva exclaimed, "A triple cross!"

"Yeah, that was a good joke," I said. "There would've been no way for you to get the money. Same exact problem he would've had. Couldn't cry foul and run to the police."

"No, no way. I trusted that bastard to play fair with me. That's what comes from being too trusting."

181

I'd have laughed myself sick if we'd been talking about a crime other than homicide. I said, "So neither you nor Bill Sechrist got anything off those two $50,000 insurance policies."

"That's right. What a couple a chumps, huh?"

"I would use a different word."

"Well, we got away with it, at least." A touch of pride came into her tone. "You can say that much for us." She sighed wistfully. "Your uncle got the fire insurance money for you, and I guess there was life insurance too."

"Yeah."

"You didn't hurt for anything growing up, then."

*Control. Control.* I said, "I always had clothes and enough to eat."

"Yeah. Well."

"What happened in Florida then?"

"Another fiasco. Bill'd always wanted to go to Florida. So that's where we met up. The kid was an inconvenience."

"Duane."

"A real inconvenience. That period of time in Florida was tough. You know, we fucked up big-time. But I was willing to stick with Bill Sechrist. I don't know what happened. I thought we'd do Florida for a while, maybe figure out something else to do to recoup that money we never got. There's a lot of money around Miami, you know? Then too, I thought we'd maybe give Vegas a try. But we never did get to Vegas together."

"What happened to Bill?"

Slowly, Trix said, "Well, I don't know. That's a mystery to me, I think prob'ly the biggest mystery of my life. What happened to Bill? One day he said he had to go see a man about some work. Some man told him he could earn a bucket of money doing practically nothing. It was dirty work he wanted done. That's what it sounded like, anyhow, when Bill told me about it. He was excited. *Ten grand for one night's work,* he kept saying. *I think my luck's finally turning.* He went out at midnight to meet this guy. Wouldn't tell me where he was going. He never came back. I never saw him again."

I found that a very interesting story.

Trix said, "The kid was already out of control. When a swishy kid like that hits the streets and starts to turn tricks, you're gonna have trouble. And then when Bill disappeared, it was like...well. Looking back on it, I'd have to admit that kid had a pretty tough time of it."

"No shit."

"No shit. Well, the kid took off, God knows where. And then, *finally...*" She paused and scanned the barroom.

A scrim of smoke hung in the air. A chair scraped. The bartender laughed at a joke. The desert sun beat in through the slits around the shades.

Trix inhaled, long and deep. "And then," she said, "I finally made my dream of being in Las Vegas come true."

# TWENTY

I had heard of high rollers at Las Vegas hotels, people who get free suites and gourmet dinners and obsequious personal attention, who in exchange drop hundreds of thousands, if not millions, of dollars per year at the tables in pursuit of the thrill of chance. The people at the Las Vegas Hilton treated Minerva LeBlanc as such a VIP, but I hadn't known she was a gambling woman.

"You didn't know that?" Minerva said. "But I gamble every day of my life."

I appreciated that.

The room service steward had just closed the door noiselessly behind himself, and I turned to Minerva with a smile.

"Know what I mean?" she said.

"I think so. Will you go down to play in the casino on this trip?"

"Probably not. They're glad to see me, and they know I'll be back soon."

"What's your game?"

"Craps. I love to throw those bones." She rubbed her hands over the feast the steward had laid out on the suite's dining table for us. There was a mound of caviar the size of a meat loaf, a platter of frighteningly tiny roasted birds lined up in a row, seared vegetables in a fragrant sauce, raw ones that smelled of rain and sun, a silver bin of toast points, along with butters and things caramelized, reduced, rouladed, truffled, and gilded.

"That's some snack," I remarked. "Are you really that hungry?"

"Famished." She lifted a lid and inhaled. "Mm, this, I believe, would be the conch chowder. Come on, let's eat." She lowered herself into one of the smoothly upholstered dining chairs.

"Conch chowder? That soup they serve in Key West?"

"Mm."

It seemed obscene to me to fly saltwater mollusks 2,000-plus miles from the Atlantic Ocean to the desert so that a chef could spend half a day with them in order to make a customer say "Mm." On the other hand, the stuff sure smelled good. I had to smile again.

"Have some. There's champagne, too. See?"

"Actually, I'm in the mood for a cup of coffee and some of this fish roe." I helped myself generously.

"Ugh. Caviar and coffee."

We sat at the table together. She was genuinely hungry; I watched as she worked her way through ninety percent of the food. The steward had opened the wine and poured a glass for her, and she sipped it.

I wanted to know if she knew what had happened to her when she blanked out in Trix's trailer.

"Oh, yes," she said unhappily. "Since my accident I've had seizures." Her accident, she called it. "Stress or thrills can bring them on. I had them a lot, for a while. Not the big ones with convulsions and tongue-biting, just moments when something goes funny in my head. I started on medication for them right away, and the stuff worked. I was seizure-free for a couple of months. I'm disappointed."

"So that one came out of nowhere, sort of?"

"Yeah. I felt it coming but couldn't stop it. I regret that."

Maybe it was my imagination, or maybe I was getting more and more used to her, but it seemed she was speaking totally normally.

I said, "Dear God, Minerva, what you've been through."

She paused. "I know you might not accept this, Lillian, but it's all right. Everything is really all right." She smiled at me in a way that made me believe it. And wonder. We went back to eating.

I enjoyed the caviar, which I applied thickly to buttered toast points, and ate slowly. The glistening black spheres made small, succulent explosions on my tongue, tasting of the sea, of dark depths and secrecy. I thought the coffee went perfectly well. The combination would make a luxurious breakfast.

Far from making her logy, the food and sips of champagne energized Minerva. I saw her revive, the light in her eyes strengthening. We had taken (separate) showers and I'd washed out my dusty clothes and hung them to dry. I felt revived too.

I poured coffee for Minerva as she rang for the empty dishes to be taken away, which shortly they were.

"Oh, that was good," she sighed. "I'm comfortable with you, Lillian. You know?"

"Yes. I feel the same way."

Then we talked about our remarkable day. I was experiencing a strong, bottled-up, sorrowful feeling. A whole raft of feelings, to tell you the truth.

We had driven Trix back to her slut hut. Minerva counted a thousand dollars out of her wallet and handed it to her.

"This'll help," said Trix as she got out. She ducked her head back in and addressed me. "I want to tell you something."

I waited.

She looked very tired. But her eyes smiled faintly as they

met mine, and she reached to touch my hand. "You know, I always got a boot out of you, kid. You had a funny way about you."

I made no reply.

Softly, painfully, she said, "Kid, I'm sorry."

Now, as Minerva and I talked, I felt sadness creeping over me, stronger and stronger. The shock I'd felt since talking with Duane and finding out the things I did at his kitchen table in Indian Village had ebbed. To let the sadness flow in, I supposed. I was much less confused than I'd been. Yet I didn't feel any more peaceful.

Minerva and I moved over to the wide couch with our cups and saucers.

She said, "I wondered earlier today if you'd feel a sense of finality about things after talking with Trix. Do you?"

"I was hoping I would."

"But you don't."

"Not really."

"How do you feel about her now?"

"Oh...ambivalent. At best. It's just so strange. She was rather a significant figure for me. We really got to know each other."

"Or so you thought."

"Yes, I feel betrayed."

"I would expect that." Minerva drank some coffee with a tiny slurp. She liked hers with cream.

"Grown-ups," I said, "keep things from kids, of course. But I thought—I just didn't think these particular people could be so careless. And in the case of Trix, so...casually malevolent."

"When you're a grown-up you sort of *expect* betrayal, or at least you know to watch out for it."

"That's right. The thing that bewilders me is—her little apology to me aside—how she's still *Trix*, she's still got this kooky, half-assed approach to life. I'd expected her to have achieved a more mature outlook by now."

"Lillian, she's a drug-addicted hooker."

"I know! I know! I'm *still* hoping she gets it together someday!"

We laughed at that, marveling at the relentless absurdity of life. Man, I enjoyed that laugh.

Serious again, I said, "Minerva, I…"

"Hmm?"

"I must formally apologize to you for losing that money. I'm very sorry. I'll…" I swallowed. "I'd like to pay it back."

She made a dismissive sound.

"Yes, but," I said, "that money didn't just fall out of the sky on you. You worked for that money. I'm making no mistake here: Just because you have a lot of it doesn't mean you don't care if a whole big wad of it goes up in smoke."

"Lillian. I don't care if a whole big wad of it goes up in smoke."

"You're just trying to make me feel better."

"Dear heart, it was money well spent."

"Mph."

"Listen, I've lost more than that in a night in the casino downstairs. In an hour, once or twice, to be honest."

"My God!"

She looked at me mirthfully. "There's something still so innocent about you, do you know that? Something very little-girl-like about you."

I didn't want to be little-girl-like.

"I'm making you uncomfortable," said Minerva gently. "Never mind. Now, what do you want to do next?"

*Lucky Stiff*

"Find that son of a bitch Bill Sechrist."

I poured some more of the perfectly brewed coffee and we sipped. The cups and saucers were paper-thin china. Bone china, I guessed it was. The cup rim felt almost *crisp* against my lips. Minerva said, "Don't you want to talk to the police?"

"I don't give a shit about the police. Minerva, come on. I mean—yeah, OK, I could talk to the Detroit cops and maybe find one who'd really listen. Ciesla could help me, I guess he knows most of them. I could try to get Duane to stay involved on it. But," I paused to view the jagged mountains beyond the windows, "all I want now is to find Bill Sechrist. Did you think I'd be satisfied after hearing what Trix had to say?"

"I honestly didn't know."

"I'm glad as hell to have found her. I guess it was lucky it played out like it did. She was gonna trick us and split with that money somehow, or try to."

"Yes. What do you want from Bill Sechrist?"

I looked at her intently. "Please understand something important. I don't want a goddamn thing from him. I want to talk to him. I want him to hear what I have to say."

Quietly, Minerva asked, "What do you want to say to him?"

I put down my coffee. "I want to tell Bill Sechrist that my father was forty-four years old and he had a strong back and arms and he liked to play horseshoes, he was a very good horseshoe player on those hot Sundays when we would go to Belle Isle for a picnic, and he would organize horseshoe tournaments with every other family in the picnic area. I want to tell Bill Sechrist that my father could run fast and he knew how to whistle incredibly loud between his fingers and he knew how to get a sliver out and what to do if a poisonous snake comes around; that he had a tattoo of Betty Boop on his left biceps and a pair of bluebirds on his chest; that he could jump up and kick the top of a door frame with the flat of his shoe, and nobody else I've ever met in my life could do that. I want to tell Bill Sechrist that my dad bought a microscope from a wino who'd probably stolen it and he liked to look at things under it and show me things; that he liked to drink beer and tell jokes and beat his hands on the bar tremendously fast in time to the polkas on the jukebox; that he let guys win dime bets off him on whether that fly would land on the rim of Hiram's glass before the end of 'Soldier Boy Polka.'"

Minerva listened.

"I want to tell Bill Sechrist that on the last day of my mother's life she worked on the seed pearl bodice of a wedding gown for one of the Kaminsky girls, the transmission shop heiresses, and when a pearl fell off she gave it to me and I put it in my treasure box; that she wore a size eight dress and her favorite flowers were lilacs and she liked to take me to Sanders' for a hot fudge sundae for no reason once in a while; that she hated Cream of Wheat and never made me eat it either; that she liked Johnny Carson and Rosemary Clooney and Harry Belafonte and Adlai Stevenson; that she wished she'd taken up an instrument and she insisted on midnight Mass on Christmas eve and thought that John Steinbeck walked on water. I want to tell Bill Sechrist that my mom didn't get mushy about the Kennedys or little kids who got cancer, and she liked to play cards; that a few hours before she died she showed me how to balk the crib, why you don't want to get stuck at the 120th hole, and why it's funny to say you have a nineteen when you have a crappy hand.

"I want Bill Sechrist to know that neither my dad nor my mom laughed at me when I expressed a serious interest in growing up to be a garbageman. Riding on the back of the truck looked exhilarating. They understood that."

*Lucky Stiff*

I stopped and breathed. "That, more or less, is what I want Bill Sechrist to know."

Minerva had moved closer to me, listening, watching. Now she drew me into her arms. And the anguish that I'd carefully managed in the days and years following the fire came coursing out, unstoppable. I laid my head on her shoulder and gave in to it. For a long time, she patted me and murmured and waited and was there for me.

Afterward, I felt sleepy, and almost napped on her shoulder. Maybe I did for a minute or two, because when I lifted my head I felt clear and OK.

No, the truth was I felt more than OK. From our perch on the couch we watched the mountains as the pink glow of twilight intensified to an impossibly pure hippie purple. The air in the whole suite tasted cool and fresh; I'd opened the glass door to the small patio out there, hanging so high over the desert. We sat in silence like that for a long time. I went to the bathroom and washed my face. The bathroom, too, featured excessively huge windows and a view out to the mountains. I watched them some more as they settled into deep blackness.

I returned to Minerva, who was nibbling on a finger cake, a plate of which, along with a fresh pot of fragrant coffee and a bottle of cognac, had mysteriously materialized on the low table next to the couch.

She stretched herself, plump and inviting, on the cushions. Lifting an eyebrow, she offered, "Dessert?"

I believe I forgot to mention that neither of us was wearing clothes. That is, after our showers we'd slipped into the sophisticated, crest-pocketed bathrobes supplied by the hotel and had lounged through dinner barefooted and refreshed.

The V of Minerva's bathrobe plunged effortlessly down the

slope of her smooth neck, across the plump plateau of her upper chest, then down the intriguing ravine between her breasts, where my gaze lingered openly and long.

I knelt on the lush rug between the couch and the treat-laden coffee table, more or less facing this lovely, wise creature who regarded me without pity, who looked at me with gentle naughtiness and, I thought, a certain amount of desire.

"Just a minute," I said. "Do you take me for a masochist? A glutton for punishment?"

She lifted herself on an elbow. "What are you talking about?"

"I'm talking about Tillie, what the hell else?"

"Ohhh," she sighed, her lips curling into a conscience-stricken smile.

I continued, "I was good for a one-nighter once for you, but don't think that merely by flying across the country, drawing out $20,000 of your own cash, letting it get burned to cinders, not uttering a peep about it, and helping me get to the bottom of a terrible crime that resulted in the deaths of my own parents, that I'm just gonna jump in the sack with you for tonight's fling, when you've got your little hot nurse babe at home keeping the waterbed nice and—"

"Lillian!"

I stopped, panting with ardor. Oh, how I wanted to caress those curving hips, how I wanted to test the nervous system underlying it all—how I wanted to kiss that hesitant hand, that reluctant foot, perhaps finding a way, some magical way, to bring full function back to them.

Minerva sat up, drawing her legs in, hugging her knees. "Did you really think," she said, "that all I wanted was that one night?" She set her chin on her knees and gave me a *You're not going to get away with anything* kind of look.

"I don't know," I admitted.

"That's all we got. But that wasn't all I wanted."
I blinked. "Really?"
"Lillian, do you think you're unlovable?"
I realized that I couldn't say.
She touched my hand. "You're so...*appealing*. I don't know how you did it, but somehow you've got a grip on my heart. When you move, when you talk, I feel..." Seeing my face, she stopped. "All right. Let me tell you about Tillie."
She drew herself a bit more erect.
I gnawed my lips.
"As I believe I mentioned," she began, "I met Tillie in rehabilitation. She helped me. She was very good. We became friends. When I began having seizures I realized it would be a good thing if I had someone at home with me. Living alone with frequent seizures is no fun. Won't you have a shot of cognac?"
Indifferently, I poured myself a small quantity of the aromatic liquor and sipped it. She reached for my glass, and I shared.
"Should you be drinking hard liquor at all?" I wondered.
"Damn it, I like a drink now and then. Listen. I offered Tillie a good salary to move into my apartment—*into her own quarters*—and coordinate the last stages of my rehab and recovery. And look after me when I had a seizure. With the new medication, the seizures tapered off. In fact, I thought they were all over. I was about to tell Tillie—"
"So Tillie is—"
"Tillie is a paid employee. As I said, I do consider her a friend as well, but not the kind you...suspected. She's a divorced grandmother and she was happy to have a cushy break from the grind of the rehab facility. When I no longer need her help, she's going to take a vacation and then, she told me, look into teaching."

There wasn't much I could say except, "Oh."

"Now, don't you feel ashamed of yourself?"

"No, goddamn it. I don't feel ashamed of my feelings for you. They're strong and proprietary and I want to kiss you right now and go on kissing you for days on end, until we get evicted from this ho—"

"So do it."

And so to her smiling lips flew mine. Oh, my lips were happy then. The level of happiness in the rest of me was somewhere between the Hubble satellite and edge of Mars.

After an agreeably long time on the couch, I helped Minerva to one of the suite's two super king-size Las Vegas bedrooms and its super king-size Las Vegas bed. We shed our bath wraps and there began the lengthy, meticulous process of rediscovering each other.

Now and then we burst into joyful laughter.

Her body was as marvelous as I'd remembered but different too. Her newfound appetite for food had given her the physical voluptuousness I've already described, and because of that, her body looked and smelled and felt enriched, more robust. To my surprise, the word *healthy* came to mind. Yes, Minerva LeBlanc appeared, except for the slight weakness on her right side, healthier than she'd been when I first met her.

My lips explored her face, my hands explored her head, where, beneath her shining distinguished hair, I felt evidence of the attack on that astonishing skull. There were bumps and hollows from the injury and the surgery, a deep seam that ran in an irregular shape, something like the outline of South America. A steel plate, I knew, kept her wondrous brains together in there.

"Do you still have pain?" I murmured.

"No, not at all."

I caressed her head, then moved to the other main compass points and most of the ones in between. I elicited delicate moans and soft pleadings: No music could have moved me more.

She was amazingly energetic. Her hands, hungry and knowing, made the whole of my skin—just everywhere—register a deep ache that only more touching transformed into pleasure.

The night, there in the desert beyond the windows, flowed in on us and engulfed us in nourishing darkness.

# TWENTY-ONE

In the morning Minerva and I decided to fly to Detroit, where I would inform Duane of what I'd learned from Trix, collect Todd from Billie, and figure out what to do next. Minerva made the arrangements.

"But don't you want to go back to New York?" I asked.

So far neither of us had uttered the L word. *Love.* I felt as good as I'd ever felt in my life. Something akin to a small nuclear reactor had been implanted just beneath my sternum and was generating constant superefficient energy to all the cells in my body.

Minerva moved about the suite in smiling serenity. I'd tried heroically to cure her of her lingering afflictions last night, but had to satisfy myself with the glad tranquillity I seemed to have produced.

"New York," she answered, "can wait. I want to be with you for now. I want to see you through to the end of this…this quest you've undertaken." She paused. "Um, would you like that?"

"Yes."

We avoided discussing the future beyond that. And that was all right with me. I felt alive enough just then without getting myself all worked up about what was next with Minerva. And my drive to find Bill Sechrist was growing stronger and stronger, filling me with a feeling I'd never known before. The feeling was cold and hot at the same time, like the strongest of cravings. Was it justice I yearned for? No, nothing that explicable. Maybe I wanted vengeance. Did I? The hot-cold feeling of vigor dominated me, that was all I knew.

As we packed our things I said, "Do you mind if we leave for the airport a little early? I'd like to make a quick stop on the way."

"All right."

Minerva wasn't surprised when I pointed the Mercedes in the direction of Trix's mobile-home court.

"There's something I have to ask her," I explained. "It'll just take a minute."

However, an incident had occurred at Trix's place. Two cop cars and a medical examiner's wagon were parked out front.

"Uh-oh," said Minerva.

A motley assortment of neighbors hung around pretending to have gone out for a walk and merely happened upon this interesting scene.

I don't know why, but I felt neither surprise nor anxiety. I looked for the ringmaster neighbor, but she wasn't around. Minerva went up to a lady cop and handed her a card. "Hey, lieutenant," said the cop, handing over the card to a plainclothes detective who'd just stepped from the trailer.

The lieutenant looked from the card to Minerva and broke into a smile. "Welcome back to the land of the living," he said. "Or, as the case may be..." He let that hang.

"Thanks," said Minerva, extending her hand. "Ramirez, isn't it?"

"Good memory. What are you doing here?" Lt. Ramirez's tone indicated that he ranked the importance of the present situation as somewhat below an incipient hangnail.

"My friend here wants to talk to the occupant."

"No can do."

"What happened?"

"Overdose, it looks like. Maybe deliberate."

Minerva's eyes flicked to mine.

"May we go in?" she asked.

To my utter shock, the plainclothesman skipped up the steps and opened the door for us.

"I know the routine," said Minerva. To me she murmured, "Don't touch anything."

I don't remember what the lieutenant or Minerva said to the police staff inside the trailer. All I remember is walking slowly through Trix's tacky living room to her bedroom and standing at the door, looking in.

Trix lay faceup on the bed, crosswise on it, one arm flung out as if in surprise, the other clutched to her chest. Her wasted body was naked; there were no marks of violence on her that I could see. Her lips were drawn back in a grimace, her eyes wide and empty.

Minerva said quietly, "A crack or meth OD could result in cardiac arrest. Sudden and painful, at least painful at first."

On second look I saw a trace of emotion in Trix's face: It was resignation. Her body had been seized in a wracking grip, then as death neared, she met it knowingly, somehow. That was the impression I got.

One of the cops said, "She started out with enough shit to get this whole neighborhood high. She made the rounds last night, bought a thousand bucks' worth of stuff."

Another cop asked, "Who told you that?"

"Neighbor who knows the dealers here. He said she had a fistful of cash and went on a spree. I'd say the street value of what's left here is about 200 bucks."

I sat, chin in hand, watching the planes taxiing, barely aware of the clang of the slot machines in the concourse. Minerva handed me a paper cup of water. "What was it," she said, "that you wanted to ask her?"

A taxiing Aloha jet stopped to make way for a Southwest jet hurrying to deliver more passengers to the town of Trix's dreams.

"One time," I said, "I got into a fight with a bully girl in the neighborhood. This was a real mini-bitch. She liked to pick on me, trying to get me to fight her. She'd walk behind me on the way home from school, shoving me in the back. One day I turned around, even though I knew I was about to get the crap beat out of me. She slapped me and I kicked her. She was bigger. She knocked me down and got on top of me and spit out her bubble gum into my hair and mashed it in. I went home to the bar, torn jacket, bloody knees, the gum in my hair. My dad was totally oblivious. 'Hi, sweetie,' he says. Trix took me into the toilet and helped me wash up before I went upstairs. She snipped the gum out of my hair and said, *Yeah, kid, she's scared a you now.*"

I watched the planes some more. "I wondered if she remembered that."

Minerva had paid for first class, her usual. We settled into our deluxe seats, and she got out a notebook and started to write. The plane took off into the magnificence of the desert sky.

My mind was going too fast, and I found myself getting more and more nervous. The hot-cold feeling surged through my chest. I gazed out the window at the western slopes of the Rocky Mountains, their crags flattened by the noon sun, every gully exposed. Those mighty mountains appeared tame in that flat light. Tame but somehow not benign.

I turned back to the interior of the cabin. My mind needed rest. It needed escape. It needed...

I rooted in my gym bag, found my copy of *The Ransom of Angeline Carey* where I'd thrown it in the bottom, and opened it. Right away, the story occupied my mind and settled my nerves.

Calico Jones was a marvelous heroine. Oh, the competence of her trigger finger; oh, the lustiness of her grin. I took up where Calico bursts in on the bad guys—you remember Calico's mission in this one: This sexy young beef jerky heiress has been kidnapped by a PETA-like organization. The organization does not demand a cash ransom; they want nothing less than the immediate destruction of all beef jerky processing machinery in the western hemisphere, starting with the state of California.

As a person who enjoys a chaw of jerky now and then, I really got involved in the ethics of the story. I myself began to question the motives of the beef jerky industry.

Well, these thugs who are really committed idealists, they got hold of Angeline Carey and spirited her to this very secret location, which is the place Calico Jones needs to figure out and get to, before it's too late. The Carey family is bossed by this crusty old patriarch who wishes like hell the animal rights people would take money. He totally refuses to bargain with them in terms of destroying the beef jerky processing machinery. Beef jerky sales, you may or may not know, run to the millions and millions of dollars per year, a tremendously significant share of the snack food market. The author of these Calico Jones books—I forget her name—boy, she really does her homework. Anyway, this patriarch has hired Calico Jones to rescue his precious niece, but he keeps telling Calico what to do and how to do it, and he keeps dicking around, getting in the way of her investigation, all the while yelling at her to do it faster. *So* annoying. I kept wishing Calico Jones would just blow the bastard away so she could really flex her muscles and get the job done.

The amazing thing is that Calico Jones is a vegetarian, yet still she took on this case. Well, that's because she's a professional. She doesn't let principles get in the way of business.

So the bad guys—I should say "bad" guys, because in their eyes they're the good guys—they've got Angeline Carey, and they've lost patience with the Carey patriarch, who still thinks he can buy them off. They're about to do away with her in a particularly grisly fashion when Calico Jones, wearing her trusty .45-caliber semiautomatic, finally breaches the security of their hideout. I hate to ruin it for you, but get this: Having invaded the compound and neutralized the guards outside, she threads her way through the air shafts and *drops down from the ceiling* right onto this depraved scene of bondage and menace. Single-handedly, she rescues the helpless, gorgeous, innocent yet sexually competent heiress just as the "bad" guys are about to begin their chopping procedures, and she drills only two of them (out of a total abduction team of five) only after they pull their illegally modified 9mm Uzis on her.

At this point Angeline Carey's pure violet eyes are bottomless pools of gratitude, and I was betting that Calico Jones would receive quite a special and intimate reward for her tremendous achievement, as of the very next chapter, when I became aware of Minerva reading over my shoulder.

"My God, that's awful writing," she commented.

"What?" My jaw dropped. "What?"

"Well—Lillian. Just look at it. Is every sentence in the whole book hackneyed, or is it just that page? I mean, the vocabulary is fourth-grade level, the clichés are so abundant they're practically—"

"Whoa," I said. "Wait just a minute. Are you *kidding*? Do you know how *popular* this writer is? Are you telling me that her millions and millions of fans must be *dimwits* or something? Take me, for instance, I have a college degree. Don't you think I can tell the difference between a good story and a pile of—"

Minerva backed off fast. "Lillian, Lillian…" She patted my arm comfortingly. "No, I certainly am not saying that. It's just that—"

"I know a good story when I see one!"

"Yes… Yes, absolutely."

"I think the Calico Jones series is *great*."

"I think they're about to give us lunch."

I knew in my heart Minerva was right, but I couldn't admit it out loud. I just love those books and that's all there is to it. My soap bubble of fantasy is tenuous enough as it is, without somebody coming along trying to mangle it.

I helped Minerva settle in at the Ritz-Carlton in Dearborn, her favorite local hotel, helped her hang up her elegant sophisticated clothes, then got ready to go pick up Todd and look up Duane.

"Lillian, wait a minute," said Minerva. "I want to talk to you."

"Yeah?"

"Sit down."

I did so.

She sat beside me on a beautiful upholstered thing that I somehow knew was called a divan, not a couch. It's hard to say why. This hotel was tremendously classy; I'd first met Minerva in its flower-bower lobby. The lack of a clanging casino made the place calmer than the Hilton in Las Vegas—quieter, certainly—but also somewhat boring by contrast. The view from Minerva's upper-floor suite could hardly compare to Las Vegas: instead of sere mountains and desert—or the dazzling Strip,

*Lucky Stiff*

depending which way you faced—the windows here in Dearborn overlooked the Southfield Expressway, the Ford Glass House, sundry office parks, and the monotonously level, albeit treed, glacier-scraped land. But it was a familiar landscape to me. I was back in Michigan. Back home.

"I have something to ask you," Minerva began. She took my hand. Her eyes were solemn. "I want to write your story."

"Uh...what? I mean... You what?"

"I'm ready to write a book again," she said eagerly. "My next book. I'm well enough to write again. And I want to write about this. This incredible story you're living right now, this amazing story you're discovering, this puzzle you're solving."

Had she whacked me between the eyes with a kielbasa, I couldn't have been more surprised.

"How do you feel about that?" she asked.

"Uh," I said, "you mean a book about—"

"About the fire at the Polka Dot Bar so long ago, and about why the embers there are still hot."

"Uh," I said.

"What do you think?"

"Uh... I guess I should have realized...uh. I don't know if I can answer you right now."

"Well," she said, looking at me closely, "please think it over today, OK?"

"OK. I—I will."

I walked out of the hotel into a taxi for home. I expected to drop my bag in my flat and turn right around again and take the Caprice out, to pick up Todd at Billie's. My car was all right in my spot at the curb, but as soon as I walked into the vestibule, the McVitties' door swung open and my landlord, Mr. McVittie, motioned me urgently to come in.

Their place never changed, except that the footpaths in the shag carpet got deeper and smoother over time. Ever deeper and smoother. That's shag for you.

To my astonishment, I beheld Duane Sechrist lying limply on their living room couch. His clothes were filthy, as if he'd been digging a trench. Mrs. McVittie was in the act of applying a damp washrag to his forehead.

"Duane!"

He was barely able to speak. "Li—Lillian?"

He tried to sit up, but Mrs. McVittie murmured, "There now, there now."

"What the hell are you doing here?"

"He got arrested," Mr. McVittie explained briskly, "and we bailed him out. Five hundred dollars it cost. Come in, lemme shut the door, I got the air conditioning running."

"*What?*"

Clutching his damp cloth, Duane struggled to a sitting position. "It's true," he said. "When I got back from Vegas I—I sort of lost it. You said to see what I could dig up. So I did."

For the second or third time that day, my mouth fell open. "Duane. You didn't."

"I tried to, last night. I didn't get all the way down before morning, though. So I got caught."

"Oh, my God."

"I couldn't stand it anymore! I had to know!"

"Were you—by yourself? Or—"

"Yeah. That money—that $2,000—that was the last of my ready cash. I used it to buy a shovel and an axe—for when I—got there, and to bribe the night watchman. He was only too glad to—"

"And then you started digging up the grave of Patricia Lynn Hawley."

"That's right."

Addressing me, Mrs. McVittie said, "I baked some gingerbread, dear, would you like some?"

"No, thank you, Mrs. McVittie."

"Duane's already had some, haven't you, Duane?"

"Yes, ma'am."

"I'll have some," said Mr. McVittie.

"Something to go with?"

"Glass of milk."

"All right, coming up." Mrs. McVittie made her unsteady way to the kitchen. The both of them were getting up there agewise. Mrs. McVittie's tremor had become more pronounced in the last year or so. And she had to inject herself with insulin every day, not to mention forego the heavenly gingerbread that was her specialty.

Duane repeated, "I had to know. Something inside me… When I got off that plane I felt like a complete failure. Then something just went *bang!* inside me, and I went and did it. You'd mentioned Mt. Olivet, so I knew where to go."

I said, "But how were you going to—"

"I knew what was…there… I knew I wasn't going to be able to recognize…a person, OK? I knew that. I had a plastic bag. I was going to get a piece of…something that would…have DNA in it. They can tell, if you give them a sample from a body, and blood from you, they can tell if you're related."

I sank into an armchair. "But morning came before you got done."

"Yeah!" he said passionately. "The day crew showed up and found me asleep on the grass. I was exhausted!" His voice rose to a wail. "Just look at my hands!"

They were torn up all right, raw and blistered. Mrs. McVittie returned bearing gingerbread and milk for her husband. Mr.

McVittie set the milk on the coffee table, then balanced the plate on his knee and dug in. There was something so effortlessly matter-of-fact about the McVitties.

Duane went on, "So I got arrested for desecrating a grave. I knew you were still in Las Vegas. Like I said, my cash was gone."

"Why did you call the McVitties?"

He touched his sore fingertips to his muddy hair. "Lillian, I didn't want my friends to…to know about this."

"But you'd never met these people."

"I remembered their name. I remembered you speaking well of them."

I turned to Mrs. McVittie, who was watching Mr. McVittie chomp his gingerbread. "And you two just…you just…"

Mrs. McVittie said, "He explained that he was a friend of yours. That was good enough for us. He has no family, you know. So we got the money together and went on down."

I turned to Mr. McVittie, who nodded grudgingly.

I was about to say something about the bail money when I sensed Duane gazing at me intensely. I turned my attention back to him. There was fear in his face, dread in his eyes, yet I also perceived a question. Yes, there was a question, the question he wanted to ask, the final horror. He wanted to know.

I gave him a steady look, just to make sure. His expression didn't change. He was ready.

I said, "It's her in there. You almost reached her. Your mother's body is down there in Trix Hawley's grave. Trix told me how they worked it—very close to the scenario that had occurred to me. Your dad got your mom plastered on booze and her meds. While she was passed out, he brought her into the bar, put Trix's ring on her finger, and started the fire. And that was the end."

His eyes spilled over and a moan came out of him, from deep in his gut.

I said, "You know it's true. I'm sorry, Duane."

Sinking back into the cushions, my friend sobbed and sobbed and sobbed.

# TWENTY-TWO

I went upstairs, dropped my gym bag, and phoned up Billie. It was Monday, her day off.

"How's Mr. Todd?" I asked.

"Fine, but he misses you."

"Really?"

"Yeah, he's been kind of listless."

"Well, I'm coming right over."

In her living room I picked up my good, calm, intelligent furry friend and looked him over.

"He does look a bit peaked," I said, feeling his body through his thick silky fur.

"How the hell does a rabbit look peaked?"

"Well, like this. See him? I think he's losing weight."

"He didn't eat much, at that. How old is he?"

"Eight and a half."

"Mm, Lillian, you know, they don't live all that long."

"Yeah, I know. I think I'll get the vet to look him over."

While Todd didn't look quite exactly right, he had the same effect on me as he always did: tranquilizing, reassuring. I fancied he was glad to see me.

Billie reminded me that I'd promised to explain to her what the hell I was up to these days.

"Oh, Billie, it's a long one."

She folded her arms and stood stolidly on her career-waitress legs, ropy with varicose veins. "Why don't you sit down and tell me?" she said.

*Lucky Stiff*

"I can't, I gotta go. You know, this—investigation I'm doing isn't over, so whatever I tell you wouldn't even make any sense yet."

"Don't you trust me?"

"I trust the hell out of you, Billie!" I did, too. "It's—this is a family matter."

"About Uncle Guff?"

"No, he's not involved at all. This is from a long time ago."

"Your mom and dad?"

"Yeah."

"I wondered. Other than the bruises you had the other night, there was something I'd never seen in you before. You were somewhere else. Like there was something...about *mortality* in your face. Look. I love you."

"I love you too, Billie."

"I don't have to know the details, but...just...can you just tell me if you're really all right?"

"Yeah. Yeah, I am."

"Is there anything I can do?"

"You're doing it."

"All right. Go on now. I'll call you. We need to eat together. Soon."

"Yeah. Let's break some bread."

"Soon!"

"OK."

I loaded Todd into the Caprice's passenger seat and we began the drive home, twenty minutes from Billie's house in Warren.

"Gonna get you an appointment with Dr. Gatz," I told him. "Gonna get you checked out, buddy, OK?"

I flipped on the news radio station and we listened along.

Part of being home in Detroit is hearing the familiar voices on the radio, the announcers with their well-worn nasality or chestiness, the intimately annoying advertisements, the excruciating jingles, the traffic reports on the notorious expressways with their potholes and bottlenecks. It's a year-round challenge to drive in Detroit. In winter the ice and snow make treacherous the smallest trip, and in summer half the expressways are under repair from the ravages of winter. The expressways all have names, and each calls up a different feeling and image. The Lodge with its sheer concrete canyons, the soaring skyway of the Fisher, the dismal grittiness of the old Davison.

The radio reminds you of the reality of Detroit. It's a hard-luck town, what with the struggles of the automobile industry in the last few decades. But perhaps because of that, it is, thankfully, a totally unpretentious town. You don't pay extra for jicama garnish. There is no jicama garnish. You get a ham sandwich and you pay for a ham sandwich. Ham sandwich is on the menu. Your UAW windbreaker coordinates with jeans or a skirt. A six-pack of Stroh's is a nice companion for a Red Wings game on TV or while you give out candy on Halloween night. Adventure travel means riding the Gratiot bus line. You've got an uncle in the furniture business.

It was 5 in the afternoon; drive time was heating up. I listened to the national report at the top of the hour: a slow news day. Congress couldn't make up its mind about a bill affecting agriculture policy, the Federal Reserve wasn't about to lower interest rates after all, a Third World government had been found to be more corrupt than most. On the local front, a coalition of downtown businesses was raising money to pay for extra street cleaning, a suburban drug bust had nailed ten rich kids, and then there was another item.

"A Novi woman turned herself in to police this morning

in connection with the murder of her husband. Robert N. Hawley, 61, was found dead yesterday in the bedroom of his home in Novi. WWJ reported that a family friend discovered Hawley, who had been stabbed repeatedly. According to Novi police, at 8:30 this morning the victim's wife, Adele C. Hawley, walked into the police station and confessed to the murder."

I pulled into a Farmer Jack parking lot and listened.

The station cut to a reporter at the Hawleys' home, where news of the arrest had brought out the neighbors. The reporter put his microphone to one of them.

"She *told* me she did it!" the man said excitedly. "She came out yesterday morning to get the paper? I was walking the dog and we spoke? *I finally killed the SOB*, she says. And I'm like, 'What'? An' she says *Robert*, that's her husband, she says, *It was just a matter of time*. An' I go, 'Adele, are you all right?' She says, *Never better*. I thought it was a joke, so I just kept walking. I had no idea. He was a nice guy, a real nice guy. I never knew what a monster *she* was, though. You never know about people."

The reporter asked, "Why do you think she did it?"

"I don't know. I always thought she was a nice lady. All the neighbors here, we're all stunned, just stunned."

I sat listening, panting. "Holy hell," I whispered. "Holy everloving hell."

The reporter said, "Novi police are investigating, and a statement is expected from the Oakland County prosecutor's office later today."

*She killed the bastard. Oh, my God, she did it.* She said she was going to do it, and she did it. I remembered sitting with Adele Hawley at her kitchen table, I remembered her face with its flattened nose and the look of shame in her eyes. I'd watched that shame turn to rage, those eyes shooting needles of fury as I talked with her about her husband, and as the light of realization came to her. Well, Robert Hawley was a piece of dung, a hateful batterer. And that was the end of him. I switched off the radio, swallowed, and got back on the road.

My guess was that Robert slapped her around pretty bad after I fled with the letters from Trix. Adele had been mad then, that day, but had she found strength in her anger right then? Maybe. But most likely Robert got the best of that match. Perhaps, though, it was for the last time. Perhaps that very night Adele began laying her plan, began honing that carving knife; began, already, the process of giving up her freedom. Of course, she had traded away the freedom of her soul long ago, having remained married to a batterer. Now, having committed murder, she was merely exchanging one kind of incarceration for another. I wondered what she had done in the twenty-four hours or more between the murder and her trip to the police station. Why didn't she flee? Why didn't she feel she deserved freedom, albeit with a bastard's blood on her hands? There was a terrible honesty to what Adele Hawley had done. She had overcome her fear, had gathered her guts to attack and kill, most likely in cold blood. She had gathered herself to plunge a knife into human flesh, pull it out, plunge it in again and again, hear the sounds he would have made—certainly she would have attacked as he slept. Did he wake and struggle, did he fight for his life, or did he sink in shock to oblivion without knowing what was happening and why?

At home I released Todd into our flat, where, as always, his careful habits entitled him to the run of the place. It was stuffy,

*Lucky Stiff*

so I opened all the windows wide, letting in a nice warm breeze. Then I went down and brought Duane upstairs. The McVitties stood together in their doorway.

"Thank you," I said fervently.

"Thank you for your love," Duane added.

Upstairs, he drew back when he saw Todd. "Does he bite?"

"No, don't be afraid of Todd. He's my closest male friend—since you, anyway."

"I bet he sheds."

Todd bumped up and sniffed Duane's muddy shoes.

I said, "I keep the place clean. Why don't you take those shoes off?"

"Are people allergic to rabbits?"

"I don't know. I guess some might be."

"I've never been tested."

"I wouldn't worry about it."

"Otherwise, this is a nice place."

"Why, thank you, Duane."

"Kind of ghetto chic," he mused. "No, not ghetto—which is not an insult, by the way, but...more like military base dumpster aesthetic."

"Yeah, I guess it's pretty utilitarian."

"Books warm up a room, though. Even if they're just stacked up against the wall like that."

"Yeah. Look, why don't you take over the bathroom for a while? Strip off those clothes and get in the shower? I bet you'd fit into a pair of my jeans and a T-shirt. You'll feel better. Or would you like me to draw a bath for you?"

"OK. Not too hot."

I set Duane up in the tub with a glass of ice water handy, then called the animal clinic and made an appointment for Todd for next Thursday. I'd left his food and water dishes clean and had only to fill them. He nibbled up some bunny chow and drank readily enough. "You're OK, Toddy boy. I'll get you some raspberry leaves in a little while. I'm glad to see you. Hang in there with me, OK?" I needed all the friendship I could get. I was so ashamed of how I had failed him in the parking garage. I couldn't imagine going on without him. I sat with him and patted him and let him hop around. We played Follow the Finger, one of our quieter games.

I thought about Bill Sechrist. I got out my notebook and wrote down everything I could think of. My brain was starting to really take hold of this one.

When Duane emerged from the bathroom in a pair of my blue jeans and my black Zildjian Cymbals T-shirt he looked like a new man. A shaky man, a troubled man, to be sure, but renewed nonetheless.

"Hey, cutie," I said. "Feeling better?"

"Yes, lots. I feel so butch in this T-shirt."

"Yeah, well, I want it back. Listen, you want to stay here for a while? You need a friend, you know."

He smiled sadly. "Oh, Lillian, thank you. You're the best. And I would stay, except that it's just so *hot* up here. Look, I'm sweating already." He blotted his upper lip with the back of his hand. "I have central air in my place."

"Well, OK."

"Could you run me over to the cemetery to pick up my car? It's still there. I mean, I hope it is, I parked outside the gates." He stood expectantly.

"Sure. What about a lawyer? Do you have a court date?"

"Yeah, I guess I'd better talk to a lawyer. Do you know a good one?"

"Well…no. Not really. But I can ask around."

"I'm pretty broke right now."

*Lucky Stiff*

"That's two of us. But you're going to pay back the 500 dollars to the McVitties, right?"

"They'll get it back. I mean, I'm gonna show up in court."

"All right. What about work? You've got a job, right? In some architect firm? Like, do you have a steady paycheck from that place, or do you get paid on some kind of..." I stopped because he wasn't listening to me.

"Lillian, I feel... I feel that my life has changed. And is about to change more."

"Yeah?" I waited for him to explain. He gazed into the middle distance. I said, "You mean because of all...this?"

"Yeah. Lillian, I need some time and space to deal with it."

"OK, but I was hoping I could get you to help me find your dad. Because I'm sorry, but I'm going to hunt down that son of a bitch if it's the last thing I do. And I mean that, I really mean that."

Duane sighed miserably. "You want him to pay for what he did?"

"In one way or another."

"What's that supposed to mean?"

"To tell you the truth, right this minute I don't know what that means. All I know is, I'm not through with this. I have not yet come to the end."

"Well...I think maybe I have."

"You don't want to find your dad?"

"I'm...I...my dad..."

"I want to make him acknowledge what he did, if only once."

Duane's lean jaw worked side to side. It looked painful. At length he said, "The last person in the world I want to see is my dad. Lillian, he'll never give you what you want. I know him."

I saw how empty Duane felt.

Maybe he was right. Maybe I would never get a feeling of

finality about it all. Maybe I was delusional. But I sure as hell had made a tremendous amount of progress. I'd gone from point zero to knowing what had happened that night and why it happened.

My friend spoke again. "Lillian, are you after vengeance?"

"No!" It came out automatically. But in fact, I wasn't sure. Was the hot-cold feeling pure hatred? I was sorrowful and obsessed, that much was true. Did I want to take Bill Sechrist's life? Actually kill the bastard? I couldn't be sure, right then.

# TWENTY-THREE

That night found me back at the Ritz having a room service dinner with Minerva. Dishes of seriously prepared food surrounded us. "You know, you could stay with me," I offered. "Save a lot of money. I could fix you a steak like this. Honest."

"You're the dearest person," Minerva smiled. "I feel so secure when I'm with you."

"Really?"

"Yes. But I want to stay here at the hotel because of the space, and the staff. I've asked them to set me up a private fax line here in the room; I've already got two phone lines, and they're bringing me a PC tomorrow. They can simply produce whatever I need."

"Wow."

"You can get a lot done fast if you're willing to pay for it. And you know money isn't an issue for me."

"Yeah."

"Besides," she said, "I love room service, don't you?" We were sitting in springily upholstered chairs the waiter had pulled up to the dining cart. The suite, four rooms plus two baths, was larger than the one we enjoyed in Las Vegas. The furniture was a bit heavy, but there were some fantastic pictures on the walls, an assortment of vintage and contemporary art I admired and envied. They actually had a Lewis D. Lewis in that suite, a small exquisite landscape done in fine pencil. It made me feel good just to look at it.

"Oh, yes," I agreed, inhaling the pleasant aromas. "This beef is awesome. And the side dishes. I've never seen such side dishes. Minerva, I—"

"You make me smile, Lillian, you make me feel so good. Your energy. Your purposefulness. You make me feel *whole*."

She was relaxed, and I saw that she was continuing her journey toward better and better health. This made me so happy. She was preparing to fling herself into work again. And this too should have made me happy.

"Minerva, I've got something to bring up. And I'm just going to, uh… I'm kind of worried. Uh, OK. You know I want to find Bill Sechrist. You know I want you to help me find him. We've talked about that. You've got resources like I never could hope to have. I've blatantly and shamelessly asked for them. I've asked for your time and effort and however much money it takes."

She listened with a bemused smile.

I said, "But I'm not sure I want you to write about it afterward."

"Well," she began carefully.

"Wait. Please wait. We need to have an agreement before we go any further. Do you really want to help me?"

"Yes, Lillian."

"Will you help me even if I—" I stopped. "I just realized you have the right to write about any of this whether I want you to or not, with or without my permission, or even my cooperation."

"Lillian."

"I'm not saying you would. I'm just realizing you could."

She swirled the wine in her glass. Her hand was graceful, holding that crystal bulb, her face thoughtful.

"What," she said, "is your objection to my writing your story?"

"I'm just not sure I want the world reading it. I don't want people to know... I mean, ideally I want Bill Sechrist brought to justice. Of course, I don't know whether that's possible. I want him to at least be brought to *my* justice. The justice of Lillian Byrd! You know I want to confront him. I feel if I can do that, I'll be able to put the whole horror behind me. I want to look into his eyes and see what's there. I don't feel the need for the world to know the whole goddamn story."

I paused, and Minerva waited. "And I—I care for you, Minerva LeBlanc. You feel that I'm good for you. Well, you're good for me. You're good as hell for me, I'll tell you. But frankly, I'm so...well, so obsessed, I know I am, and I can feel it growing. It's like I want to work Sechrist out of my system, find my way to the end of this nightmare first. And then...there's you. I don't want my passion for resolving this thing to get mixed up with my passion for you. You're an amazing woman, but I don't know that I'm an equal for you."

With a direct look, she said, "Are you trying to say you want to back off from having sex with me?"

"I don't *want* that. But I feel it might be the right thing to do, temporarily. What do you think?"

"I want you. And you want me. I delight in you. Why didn't you bring your mandolin tonight?"

That took me aback. "Do you remember me playing for you that night?" I asked. The night she was attacked.

"Yes, I do." Her face just opened up, right at that perfect moment. "I want to hear your music again."

She circled the top of her wine glass with her middle finger. The gesture hypnotized me.

"Lillian. Listen to me now." Her voice was low and steady. "You know I want to tell this story. I don't need money, but I need work. I need work to feel alive. This is the work I do, I write crime. I write the real thing. You just don't know, you don't understand how much I could do with this story." Plainly, her feeling for what she was saying was intense, yet I also thought she was making an effort not to frighten me with it.

"Lillian, you would be a heroine in this book. You *are* a heroine. My God, you set out to solve a crime that's more than thirty years old. You were a kid growing up in a rundown bar—"

"It wasn't rundown, it was blue-collar."

"Well, in a blue-collar bar where there were probably *rats*, and you almost lose your life in a hellish conflagration, and you become an orphan, and you overcome *that*, and one day a chance encounter prompts you to relive the whole tragic thing, and you set out to solve this mystery you never even knew existed! You dig around, you get your face bashed up, you fly to Las Vegas, you impersonate a mob babe, you get involved in a high-speed auto chase, you rescue this drug-addicted hooker with your bare hands from a burning car, you uncover the kind of betrayals that would absolutely destroy a weaker person, you persist in the face of danger and hopelessness, and yet you sit there as if you're just some…*average person*, drifting through life!"

She paused to catch her breath. I had to catch mine, too, after all that.

I said, "How did you know about the rats?"

"Damn it, Lillian, I wasn't trying to be funny! I was trying to make you understand!"

"I'm sorry."

"Don't apologize!" I thought she was going to throw something. But I waited, and she calmed down. She sighed, and flipping her hair out of her eyes, said, "Look, we don't have to decide anything right away. Anything about what I will or won't write."

I said, "Do you think I'll owe something to you if you help me?"

"Absolutely not."

I could see pressing the issue would do no good. I still felt uncomfortable. "Minerva, I just don't know."

Quietly, she said, "What's really bothering you about this?"

I took a long breath and came out with it. "I don't want you exploiting my pain in a book."

She was insulted into blankness. She opened her mouth but nothing came out.

I said, "I—I'm sorry. That's just the way I feel. I'm glad we're having this conversation now."

She composed herself with visible effort. "Lillian, we should give this issue a rest. Let me simply tell you two things. One, I promise that I'll give you all the help I can, all the resources I can muster, to help you find Sechrist. Ask anybody in law enforcement who knows me, and they'll tell you that's a lot. And two, I guarantee I won't let the issue of my writing come between us."

"That relieves me," I said. "But how?"

She smiled patiently. "You can't control everything, you know. Just leave this part to me. All right?"

"Well...OK." I was baffled, but Minerva's smile was so kind and loving that my fears slipped away.

"Now, my brave ideal, tell me what you're thinking regarding Sechrist. You said you organized some ideas. What do you say we start with those?"

Instantly I warmed to our mission. "OK," I said, sitting forward. "We ought to start in Florida, in Miami. I figure public records would be one way to go. He doesn't have any need—that we know of—to use an alias, so the public records are a reasonable bet. Do you have any sources in the military bureaucracy? I mean, I guess some military records are public, but not all, right? Since Sechrist was in the navy, if he got an honorable discharge, he'd be eligible for certain veterans benefits. Loans, maybe health care. And if he filed for something, if he filled out forms, those forms would have his address and maybe much more information, right?"

"Right." Minerva just smiled away.

"Then," I went on, "aside from the navy, there's other public records. Like if he got arrested for something, even something minor, there'd be a record of that."

"That's right."

"I'm so glad you're on my side, because you've got access to—well, you're like a private investigator. You've got access to all these specialized, consolidated computer databases they have these days, don't you? Where you put in somebody's name and all kinds of shit comes up—real estate transactions, bankruptcies, that kind of stuff." I looked at her. "How'm I doing?"

"Superbly."

I really liked how her lips formed that word. "Well, you know, I've read all your books. Plus, I've read Calico Jones. I know what you think of those, but that author knows all about that stuff too—she endows Calico Jones with this supercomputer where she can find out all these incredibly arcane bits of information, with just the click of a mouse."

"Relax, Lillian, I know better than to sneer at Calico Jones."

Now she was making me laugh. "So, in the morning, you'll get going on all that? You've got investigators you can call on to do those database searches, right?"

"I do and I will. But…"

"Yeah?"

She picked up a stalk of asparagus and paused with it. "I have a funny feeling about Bill Sechrist."

"Yeah," I agreed. "Trix's recollection of him just disappearing into the night. That was somewhat disconcerting, wasn't it?"

"Exactly."

"Well, let's see what we can turn up." I began to feel like a real investigator. "Duane's not going to be of any help right now," I went on. I told her about his getting busted for trying to dig up his mother's corpse beneath Trix's grave marker. "I wouldn't have thought he had it in him."

Minerva was impressed. She closed her eyes and nodded slightly, as if viewing a movie behind her lids.

"Now," I went on, "that kind of crazed boldness is valuable to our cause. But I can't count on Duane's stability yet. Tomorrow, I'm going to see Uncle Guff. I called him today and set up a fishing date with him. I want to get him out on the river, where it's quiet and we can talk, and I'm going to tell him what I've found out so far. I owe him that much, anyway. Before, when I brought up the subject of the fire that night, he didn't want to talk about it. But he has no idea what really went on between the people who were involved, he has no idea about that deal between Bill Sechrist and my dad about the insurance money. He has no honest information as to what led to the events of that night. He has a right to know. I want him to know. I don't want to be the only one in the family with this knowledge."

Minerva remarked, "It will be painful for him too."

"Yeah, but he's a tough bird. I've never known anything to faze him. My goal is to get him to be our ally here. Once he sees how much I've found out, he'll be willing to…get on board with us. If your people pull up something on Sechrist, Uncle Guff could maybe help us get to him. Maybe set a trap for him. Or surveillance! Let's say we find out where Sechrist works or hangs out, we'll go down to Florida—Guff and Rosalie can drive their motor home and we can use that as headquarters." The possibilities excited me. "It'll be our clubhouse, and we'll get Aunt Rosalie to fix us hamburgers and these home fries she makes, they're really good."

Minerva suppressed a smile at that, but I didn't hold it against her. I thought some more. "Sechrist was always hot for easy money, a big score," I went on. "Maybe we could approach him with some kind of moneymaking scheme. Something he'd lick his chops over and say *Yeahhh*."

"Lillian."

"Yes?"

"Those are all really good ideas. OK?"

I looked at her.

She said, "But I think your mind is getting just a bit fevered here. Maybe we shouldn't jump so far ahead."

I reined myself in. "OK."

"How about first things first. Let me get the database searches going, let me look into the military records, let me talk to my South Florida sources."

"Right."

"Have you given any more thought to that bastard Robert Hawley? Because now that Trix's dead, he might—"

"Oh, God." I'd already forgotten about Robert Hawley. Isn't that amazing? But once he was no longer an element in my quest, my mind just dropped him. I said, "As I believe a Las Vegas cop once put it, no can do."

Her eyebrows quirked up.

I told her about the radio report. "We can probably get a little more from the papers tomorrow. But it looks like that avenue is shut to us forever."

Minerva just sat there, gazing off in astonishment. For a minute I thought she was having another seizure. But no. She was merely absorbing things, her mind churning. As I had when I first saw her, walking through the lobby of the Ritz those years ago, I watched her mind in motion: thinking, evaluating, categorizing. She was intensely happy. She appeared to be awed, gladly overwhelmed. She murmured something very softly.

I leaned to her. "What was that?"

She shook her head and smiled at me helplessly. "This is a hell of a story. Lillian, this is a world-class story. A staggering story. My God. What I could do with this story."

"Minerva, now—"

"There's got to be some way I can convince you to—"

"No!"

"All right, all right, let's not get—relax. Lillian, please don't worry. It's just that I get fired up. I understand you. Here. Come here. I want to kiss you."

"Yeah, but I just want to make sure you—"

She startled me by ripping open her blouse and presenting her breasts and belly to me. So smooth and creamy, what a sight. Oh, praise the creator. God the parfait maker. God the pastry chef. God, she looked luscious. I made an incredulous sound. Minerva smiled a smile of pure mischief. I was speechless. Speech, I realized in the next moment, was beside the point.

Her lips widened and curled deliciously, the tips of her ears pinkened, and her eyes told me I would not get away from her that night. The sight of her set my body to throbbing, and I allowed myself to be drawn into her arms as a skier drops over a blind cornice and commits to the open space below, trusting that the powder on the downslope will be deep enough and forgiving enough to afford an unforgettable run.

# TWENTY-FOUR

Uncle Guff throttled back the motor, then cut it. On one knee in the bow, I hefted the anchor and dropped it overboard. He had built the pancake-shaped anchor by melting scrap lead into a shallow mold and adding a steel bar with an eye for the line to go through. The braided line raced through my hands, following the anchor to the bottom. I fastened the line to a cleat on the gunwale.

Then comes that distinctive moment when the current sets the boat against the resistance of the anchor, and you feel one tug through the skin of the boat as your momentum stops. Then come the tiny movements of the boat at anchor, if you care to notice them: up and down in response to the small wavelets driven by the breeze; side to side when the wake of another vessel, degrading on its way to you from the channel, reaches your boat and slips beneath.

Late afternoon is never a great time for catching fish on the Detroit River, but if you're willing to stay as dusk comes on, you might have some luck.

Uncle Guff had had to run errands in the morning, then there was Aunt Rosalie's hair appointment, so the sun was well on its way to the west when he and I shoved off from the marina. I'd brought some salami sandwiches I'd made, plus two Cokes apiece in my LunchMate cooler. We had plenty of worms, packed in a paper tub that I placed in the shade beneath my seat.

The afternoon was clear and hot, so Uncle Guff wore his pith helmet—an old, old thing, God knew where he got it. It was a real one, carved from that corklike stuff and sewn over with white cloth. The leather chin strap was slung daringly behind the crown. Most people would look ridiculous in such a hat, but Uncle Guff wore it with dignity. It served a precise purpose: to protect his bald spot from the sun. Beneath the thick brim his seamed face regarded the river attentively. His blue eyes behind their bifocals scanned the water, judging our position relative to the tip of Celeron Island, south of Grosse Ile. He seemed satisfied. It was a place we'd fished many times before.

We rooted in our tackle boxes and set up our perch rigs. I passed the worm container to him, he helped himself, and passed it back. The nightcrawlers writhed healthily in their cushion of black dirt. We baited up and cast our lines to the lee side of the boat. I settled on my seat with my back to the dropping sun; I felt its warmth through my short-sleeved blouse. My Vietnam hat kept the worst of it off my head. As usual, there was a faint but steady breeze from the west. Gulls skirled overhead, checking us out for possible garbage.

My uncle hadn't spoken since we left the dock except to say "Thank you" when I passed him the worms.

There was something so meditative about him this day, and something so lulling about the water, lightly slapping the sides of our open boat, and something so simple about our lines angling from the tips of our rods down to the khaki-colored water that I almost hated to speak.

But I did.

"I've been kind of busy," I said. "I know you didn't want me to poke around. You told me there was no mystery to Daddy and Mom's deaths." I watched Uncle Guff swallow. "But it seems you were wrong on that. I've come across some pretty interesting evidence."

At that word, *evidence*, he coughed ferociously, cupping his hand over his mouth. He adjusted the drag on his reel, pulling out some line to test it. Then he reeled up the slack. He placed his eyes on his rod tip and kept them there.

I said, "Here goes, Uncle Guff. I met up with Trix. The barmaid. Remember I was telling you about my friend Duane Sechrist, and how Trix showed up as his new mom after the fire? She didn't die in the fire after all. I met her. I spoke with her. I got her to talk to me. The fire was an arson job. Bill Sechrist, Daddy's friend, was the reason it all happened. Daddy made a deal with him to let him burn the bar and give him, or lend him, the insurance money. Sechrist wanted to kill his wife and run off with Trix. Daddy didn't know that. He just knew that he owed a big favor to Sechrist for having saved his life in the war."

If I hadn't known my uncle so well, I'd have wondered if he was hearing me. But, the same as how the river's current yields small clues if you pay attention, Uncle Guff gave me to understand that he was listening. Just the way he held his head, that told me.

When fishing, your senses get sharper, and your mind unclutters as you focus on what might or might not be going on in the underwater world. People have written books about it. But just as you can't make someone understand exactly what swimming feels like until they do it, you can't make someone who's never held a fishing pole know that weird clarity that comes to you when you fish.

I was feeling such clarity, and from it I sensed that Uncle Guff's and my relationship would be transformed before the day was over. Transformed how? That I didn't know.

I opened Cokes for us and narrated everything, from my interview with Adele Hawley to my midnight encounter with her husband, through my Las Vegas investigation, to Duane and his arrest. I told Uncle Guff that Minerva LeBlanc had joined me on my quest for the truth. He knew very well who she was. I left out the sexy parts.

I talked it all through methodically because, number one, my uncle had a right to know, detail by detail; and two, because I felt that the weight of the many facts I had gathered and the the circumstances of their gathering would convince him of my commitment.

All of it took so long that the sun began to touch the treeline of the western riverbank. Nothing was biting. I stopped talking and got out our sandwiches. We ate them, watching the day fade. I'd learned Uncle Guff was a patient man with a very long attention span. I felt it best to pause and let what I'd said soak in.

Uncle Guff said, "Do you need to go ashore?"

"Yeah." We pulled up our rigs, discarding the puffy, water-logged worms. "Sorry, guys," I murmured to them. I pulled up the anchor and we motored to the shore of the little scrub-covered island. The mosquitoes were coming out. I helped Uncle Guff haul the boat out and we went separate ways into the bushes.

We met up at the boat, slapping mosquitoes, and jumped in. Uncle Guff started the mighty Johnson outboard and steered us to a different place, southeast of Sugar Island, where I dropped the anchor. The mosquitoes thinned out away from shore, and to keep us even more comfortable a light breeze came up. It riffled the water. We put fresh worms on, cast out our rigs, and almost immediately began catching fish. The perch population of that part of the river really turned out for dinner right then. We reeled in fish, tossed them into our bucket, pinched worms in two, threaded them onto our hooks, and cast out again.

Something heavy grabbed one of my hooks, and before I knew it my whole rig was gone, the line snapped. An adult carp, maybe.

They can do that if they get ornery enough. I hastily tied on another rig and threw it out again. In an hour we'd caught a bucketful of perch, mostly, plus a few walleye. We released a couple of bullheads, a sucker, and some perch that were too small.

There was still enough light to see by. The fish stopped biting. We'd hit that magical hour. Just to be sure, though, we put our lines back in. The fish may have been through biting, but we weren't finished talking.

There wasn't any point in asking Uncle Guff how he felt about what I'd told him. He had made no sound as I talked. No shock. No anger. No dismay. I realized I wasn't afraid of what he might say or how he might feel. This last week had changed me. I thought about how Uncle Guff differed from my father in the greater measure of fierceness in his approach to life. Well, I now had that fierceness in me. That was what that hot-cold feeling was. I had uncovered a reservoir I never knew existed. It wasn't something I would need all the time. But when I did, it would be there. Blind Lonnie was right: I had more than I needed.

The air took on its mossy evening smell. A cabin cruiser probably on its way to a dockside restaurant churned past us, politely keeping its wake low. A woman's laugh carried over the water. I was just able to tell that the skipper had put his running lights on.

I said, "I need to find Bill Sechrist. I'm going to find him. I imagine, after hearing what I've told you, you'll want the bastard found as much as I do. Minerva LeBlanc is going to help me. I invite you to join in. If we got together and pooled our resources, I bet we could find him and get…and get…resolution. I have some very specific ideas on how to do it."

My uncle said nothing.

I went on, "Of course I could let this thing go. It's been so long. But something's happened to me, Uncle Guff. I guess I

*Lucky Stiff*

don't know if… The thing is, I'm no longer worried about what will become of me in life. I don't have very much concern for my own comfort anymore. There are lots of ways to get at truth, I see this now more than ever. You know?"

"Mm-hmm." His eyes moved along his line as it left his rod and descended into the water.

"Anyway, I know Sechrist is out there. I feel I owe that much to Daddy and Mom."

He shifted on the bench seat of our little boat. Watching his posture, I saw I'd gotten through to him. His back was straight, his head, crowned by the white dome of his helmet, was erect. Yet he wasn't stiff. His expression was steady, and I saw something else too. There was a look of relief about him. As if he'd just come to a decision.

He cleared his throat. "Lillian."

"Yes, Uncle Guff." The sun had set, and the last of the day's light was blue and soft.

"You won't find that man."

The water darkened.

"*What?*" I said.

"He won't be found."

Suddenly I felt disoriented. The breeze shifted. I searched the nearest shoreline—which island was it? But the world was receding into darkness. The red and white lights of the channel buoys emerged from the gloom, as the buoys themselves disappeared. Houses on either riverbank became pricks of light floating above the black water. The summer sky sent its deep blueness down onto everything, and everything was shadows.

I said, "Tell me."

His shoes scraped the bottom of the boat as he aligned his body squarely toward mine.

His tone was neutral, his cadence deliberate. "Your dad

came to me saying he needed money. He wouldn't tell me why he needed it. I had some I could've lent him, but I didn't do it. I thought he'd gotten into trouble, and I didn't want any part of it. When the…bar burned—I knew it was…"

He couldn't bring himself to say Sechrist's name. So I said, "Sechrist?"

"Yeah. I knew it was him."

"How?"

"It's one of those things you know. I saw him sitting and talking with Marty—with your dad—the week before it happened. The way he talked. The way he moved his hands. I took Marty aside and told him I'd lend him the money after all, but he said no, he didn't need it now, he had it all worked out. He was mad that I didn't give it to him right away." My uncle took a long breath. "Wish I had. Well, when that man left town with the boy, I knew it for sure."

"Did you talk to the police?"

"They said they looked into it. They said there was no evidence. Until tonight, Lillian, I knew he'd done it, but I didn't know the rest."

We held our fishing poles firmly, as if the fact of them, the realness of them, created safety for us.

I felt a fish tug at my bait. A small perch, it felt like, the way it went tug-nibble-tug so fast. I let it eat, not setting the hook. The tip of my rod quivered. I saw Uncle Guff glance at it. I could barely see his face, but I thought he smiled very slightly.

He went on, "I tried to put it out of my mind. I tried to accept… I prayed. But…" He paused. "It was no use."

I waited, breathing the damp river air, feeling the fish below working at its dinner. Stars were coming out.

My uncle said, "You know you resemble your father?" His voice was strong but not rough.

I said, "I always hoped to grow up looking pretty like Mom."

"I'm not talking about that. I'm talking about how you...trust people."

I thought about that.

"You and your dad were the same. Neither him nor you could ever understand how people really are. You never wanted to see it."

My heart began to race.

Uncle Guff said, "I couldn't let it go. Three years it was, then. I figured the boy would be almost grown up."

"Oh, my God."

"I found that man."

"Oh, God, Uncle Guff."

"It wasn't hard. He wasn't hiding. I went to Florida and I got him to meet me. He didn't know who I was until it was too late."

I could only see the outline of my uncle, as the night overtook us completely.

He said, "I tried to tell myself I didn't mean to do it. But Lillian, I did. I took care of it. For all of them. And for you."

I said, "You killed Bill Sechrist."

"I killed him."

"And you got away with it."

Very clearly, my uncle's voice came to me out of the darkness, "He's a John Doe in a public cemetery in Florida. I guess nobody ever reported him missing. I rented a room for cash in a flophouse in Miami. He met me there."

"Did you guys talk?"

"Not much."

"What did he say?"

"Enough for me to know." He stopped with a tight sound in his throat.

I knew I must ask now or never. "How did you do it?"

Expressionlessly, he said, "With a piece of iron."

I couldn't speak.

"I took his wallet," Uncle Guff continued, "and threw it away later. I kept one thing to prove to you I'd done it. I thought you'd find it in my things, you know, when the time came. You might not know what it was. I brought it along today, thinking we might have this talk."

He reached into his back pocket and pulled out something that jingled. He handed it over to me.

It was a chain with a pair of metal dog tags on it. I couldn't read the stamped letters in the dark, but I didn't have to.

# TWENTY-FIVE

Blind Lonnie was kicking off one of his specialties, an indigo version of "Younger Than Springtime," when I walked up. I waited until he finished, then set down my mandolin case on the sidewalk and clapped.

"Lillian!" At the gladness in his voice I almost burst into tears. Listeners dropped money into his case and moved on.

I held my voice steady. "How are you, Lonnie?"

"*Fine*. So very fine this evening." His fingers wandered over his guitar, chording and plucking lightly. He tilted his broad, pleasant face toward me. "I just been warming up." His stout archtop Guild rested easy on his thigh.

It was Friday night and Greektown was coming alive. I breathed it in: the food and spices, the toasty brown coffee, the cigarette smoke and the cologne and the aftershave.

Lonnie's playing, and those familiar smells, cut through my numbness.

"By the sound of you," he said, "you've had a long week."

"Let's just play," I said.

"Name one."

"Ah, how about 'You're the Top'?" It was the first cheerful tune that came to me.

"All right."

We tuned, and Lonnie let me plink an intro. Then he threw down a rhythm and played some lead, ran the melody just once, then gave it the throttle, so to speak. He played it hard, with a driving beat, and people stopped to listen. He lifted his thigh and clomped his heavy shoe on the pavement. The people on the street were arrested by the joy pouring out of him, held there by the curious beauty of a familiar song moving from major to minor and back again. He handed it to me once in the middle, and I decided to drop the tempo and unleash some Mediterranean tremolo. That got him laughing. I boosted the tempo and gave it back to him. Lonnie's music challenged any indifference a passerby might be feeling that night.

When we finished the song we sighed in unison.

Next we played "Minor Swing," "It's Magic," and the goofy "Cleopatterer," a throwaway Jerome Kern song resuscitated on a recording by Joan Morris and William Bolcomb in Lonnie's collection. I sang a couple of verses, trying to mimic Morris's agile mezzo-soprano. But as had happened the last time I played with Lonnie, my music felt awkward. I felt a barrier between me and the kind of free improvisation I longed to master. Still, it was so pleasant being with Lonnie and listening to his sure playing.

"Oh, Lonnie, I needed some fun," I said, feeling so much better.

A quartet of middle-aged suburbanites on a double date passed by; Royal Oak, I judged, or Huntington Woods. Good clothes, but hairstyles that were just a bit too self-conscious. One stooped and dropped some change into Lonnie's case even though we were on break.

"Thank you!" Lonnie called. "Next time, for you, it'll be free!"

He played softly, moving around in G minor. "Your friend was by here," he said.

"My friend?"

"Your friend named Duane."

"Oh, yeah?"

Lonnie drummed his fingertips on the glossy top of his guitar in a scat rhythm. "Last week you told Lonnie you were going to Las Vegas."

"Yeah, I did."

"Well, did you win or lose?"

I considered the question. I said, "Every loser is a winner in Las Vegas."

Lonnie liked that.

I said, "Well, the state of my life tonight is that I did what I intended to do in Las Vegas, and I found out what I wanted to know. Then I came home and found out the rest."

"The answer was right at home?" Lonnie asked.

"Essentially, yes. And like Dorothy, I had to leave home first to find it. Unlike Dorothy, my answer is a secret. A secret that I didn't know better than to pursue."

Lonnie said, "Well, maybe that secret is not such a bad one. Think of the alternatives."

We played more songs, and I gazed at the passing cars, and up to the black sky. I couldn't meet the eyes of any listeners who stopped.

I played chords and thought about my parents. They had lived and they had died. They had gotten me off to a reasonably good start in life before it was over for them. What difference might Uncle Guff's vengeance have made to them? Where they out there somewhere? I didn't think so, had never believed they'd hung around in the ozone to look after me. I'd always had the feeling they'd moved on that night, moved firmly on without looking back. I was the one who'd needed to look back. Now that was over. *Farewell, beloved parents. Someday I too hope to rest in peace.*

Lonnie and I continued to play, and my thoughts turned to Uncle Guff.

As he and I stowed our rods and tackle that night, I asked, "Does Aunt Rosalie know?"

"No," he grunted as he swung our bucket of fish onto the dock.

He never would have told her. Aunt Rosalie's constitution, while not as delicate as she liked to think, could never withstand the possession of such knowledge.

Now Uncle Guff and I had a secret from the whole world.

I had avoided Duane in the last few days. How could he not guess it, seeing my face? How could this secret not be seen in me by everyone? Looking in the mirror, I could see it myself, there in the lines around my eyes, that terrible secret.

Uncle Guff's hands were bloody.

It was not innocent blood. Is that what he had protected me from, when he did what he did? My whole body went icy when I thought of that. I pictured myself, with my newfound fierceness, confronting an aging, stupid, selfish Bill Sechrist. What would I have done? How much was I capable of? Could I have tempted myself to pick up an iron bar? What excuses might I have made? Uncle Guff had spared me learning the answers.

Sechrist hadn't intended for my parents to die. If my father hadn't agreed to give him the insurance money, my father and mother wouldn't have died. What, exactly, went wrong? That, I'd never know.

Juanita Sechrist was marked for death days, weeks, months before that night. What of Duane? What was he marked for?

What was I supposed to do now?

I had taken Todd to the veterinarian on Thursday. He looked him over, checked his blood, and did an X-ray.

"Todd here is all right," said the doctor at last. "He's just getting old." Todd looked from the doctor to me with his black shining eyes.

I cried all the way home.

Later that day Minerva summoned me to the Ritz. Of course

she told me that her associates were coming up empty on Bill Sechrist. I felt terribly uncomfortable. She wanted in on me.

"What's the matter?" she said.

"I feel—I feel tired."

She encircled me with her arms. "Of course you do. What a strain all this is for you. I should get Tillie to come and look after you. She gives marvelous back rubs."

I made no response. *Shall I resign myself to her wants?*

"Well, how about a nice lunch?" she urged. "I'll order us something. Or we could go out somewhere. Me, I'm feeling better and better."

She was catering to me. She wanted to appease and charm me, so that I would cooperate with her on the story she was determined to write. She tried to hide her determination from me, but the more she tried, the more I saw it.

I couldn't prevent her from writing, from working. She was catching up with her life, for God's sake. She'd suffered so much—a year in a coma! Lingering disabilities!—all because of me. How could I begrudge her what she wanted from me?

*When Uncle Guff dies, I'll have to keep the secret all by myself.*

It occurred to me that I could cooperate with Minerva, up to that particular boundary. It was a boundary she need never discover. Maybe I could do that.

I played simple two-note chords and single-note rhythms behind Lonnie. I focused my attention on the music but continued to feel disappointed with my playing. My sound remained constricted somehow, as if my hands had stiffened as I stood there, thinking and playing and trying. Lonnie kicked off "Steeplechase," and I made an effort to concentrate, breathe, relax. It was a struggle.

A startlingly familiar figure appeared before me in the small crowd of listeners that had gathered, as if someone had suddenly held a crazy mirror up to me.

It was Duane, dressed in the jeans and T-shirt I'd lent him days ago. Could he possibly be as haunted as I was? But he smiled at me. He stood there lounging vertically, as it were, smoking one of his Marlboros. He looked tougher and happier than I'd ever seen him.

Lonnie stepped on the tempo and I followed. People began to clap along, Duane too. His smile grew broader. Lonnie and I pounded out our ending, Lonnie's last sharp chord ringing in the city night air.

Duane came over to me, took my arm, and said to Lonnie, "Can I borrow her for a minute?"

Lonnie ignored him.

I said, "Sure, Duane."

We walked together down the sidewalk and stopped in front of the glass window of New Hellas. People inside were eating their dinners. A waiter poured wine. He must have told a joke as he did it, because the people laughed.

Duane said, "I thought I'd find you here. Lillian, I have something to tell you. I quit my job."

"You did? How come? Gimme a cigarette."

"Here." He cupped his hands around a match, and I touched his warm hand as I took the light. He said, "Last night I had a very dark night. A dark night of the soul, Saint John style."

The both of us had read far too much hagiography growing up. Fortunately, we interspersed it with forbidden texts like *Valley of the Dolls* and *Mad* magazine.

"I was home," he went on, "alone, trying to be honest with myself, for a change."

I smiled nervously and took a hit from the Marlboro. Its cutting smoke punished my lungs.

Duane said, "I realized that I've been adrift without knowing it. Lillian, I finally came to terms with it. I said to myself, *Yes, Duane, your mother is dead. Lillian told you the truth. She's at rest. Mama is at rest.*"

I put my hand on his shoulder. He grasped for my hand and brought it down in both of his. "And Lillian, I know… Something told me that now it's time to move to the next step." He looked up at me suspensefully, from beneath his floppy hair.

I said, "Yeah? What step is that?"

"I need to find my dad."

I let out a chuffing, desperate stream of smoke.

Duane said, "I want to tell you, my good friend, that I'm on board with your…with your obsession. It's the right thing to do. We'll both find peace, I know, if we can find my dad. And Lillian—are you all right?"

"Yeah. Fine." I summoned all my strength to look at him with a clear and even expression.

"Lillian, I want to talk to you about forgiveness. I…last night I forgave my dad. Can you believe it? And now, I want nothing more than to tell him that."

"Oh, Duane."

"It must come as a shock to you, I know. Well, you've got your own feelings about it. I wish you could somehow get to the place in your heart where you can forgive him too."

"Dear Jesus Christ."

Do I need to tell you? I didn't know whether to shit green or go blind.

"Lillian, I'm going to devote myself full-time to this quest. I'm going to sell my house, maybe I'll get twenty or thirty thousand profit out of it. That'll hold me for a little while. It'll hold *us* for a little while. We'll start in Florida just like you said. Minerva LeBlanc's working on it, right? Well, how can we fail?"

I concentrated on not fainting. Inside the restaurant the waiter approached the table with a sizzling serving of saganaki. Holding the plate aloft, he flashed a butane lighter over the alcohol fumes hovering there. "*Opa!*" Oily yellow flames leaped up to the blackened ceiling. The waiter quenched them with a fist of lemon, and the diners, having made their wish, fell to eating.

Duane said, "I rejected all that Catholic stuff when we were growing up. I rejected it all for a long time. We both did."

I nodded.

His eyes brimmed with gentle feeling. "Forgiveness was the hardest part for me. But you know how I feel right now? Free, Lillian. I feel incredibly free."

"I'm glad, Duane. I'm very glad."

"Well, you look kind of shook up. You probably need to let this sink in. You probably were ready to write me off." He laughed joyfully. "But now the new Duane!"

*What the hell am I going to do now?* I could not let my friend wear himself to tatters trying to find the unfindable. *I'll think of something. I'll make something up.* It would have to be convincing. It would have to sound genuine.

"Tell you what," I said. "I'll call you in a couple of days, OK?"

Lonnie kicked off "Me and My Shadow" in the deep bass register, and I joined in, plucking a sixteenth-note line over the top.

The notes flew out and upward from our instruments, in an arc of sound toward the people on the street. We played a string of variations. My hands began to loosen.

A woman threaded her way through the dozen people who had stopped to listen. An alert, intelligent woman, quietly sexy, whose very slightly uneven footsteps suggested a life lived not in safety. Yes, it was plainly a woman who accepted a measure of risk as a matter of course. Minerva LeBlanc, smiling,

*Lucky Stiff*

dropped a piece of folded money into Blind Lonnie's case and stepped to the edge of the crowd.

"Thank you, lovely lady," said Lonnie, thumping out his bass notes. Lonnie was right about everything.

Minerva settled her weight evenly on her feet, folded her arms, and listened. She watched my hands as I played.

And just then, on that street corner, my improvisation skills took a sudden leap. A barrier was gone. I found myself able to invent, embellish, juggle, and modify as never before. Blind Lonnie smiled, he poured it on, he shouted with happiness. "Go, Lily!" He handed me the melody.

I dove into it, bending the tune, drawing newness from it, hiding the melody, revealing it, hiding it again. The notes I'd played in the past were not completely gone—my mistakes and my little successes—and I understood then that each note *determined* the past the instant it was played. The future was nothing but notes waiting to be released. I stood on the night-time city street and played on and on, better and better, pleased to find it now all so effortless.